LOST SON

by

MARCUS ABSHIRE

Marcus Abshire   LOST SON

Marcus Abshire **LOST SON**

All rights reserved. No part of this book may be used or reproduced in any form without permission, except as provided

by the U.S. Copyright Law. Printed and bound in the United States of America.

This is a work of fiction. Names, characters, places, and incidents are either the product of the author's imagination or are used fictitiously. Any resemblance to actual events, places, organizations, or persons, living or dead, is entirely coincidental.

Scanning, uploading and/or distributing this book via the Internet or any other means without the permission of the

publisher is illegal, and punishable by law. Please purchase only authorized

electronic editions, and do not participate in or encourage the electronic piracy of copyrighted materials. Your support of the author's rights is appreciated.

Books by Marcus Abshire

The Alliance Series
Redemption
Retaliation-coming soon!

Gauntlet Rite of Ascension

The Demon Hunter Series
Hard Skip
Pale Rain

Santa vs Zombie Apocalypse

Available at

https://mabshire1406.wixsite.com/marcusabshire

Chapter One

Caves were dark places, perfect for hiding. They provided a place to rest during the day, somewhere consistent in temperature and normally free from predators.

This cave was no different. Almost no light penetrated the cavern's shadowy depths and the thick air hung heavy with stale moisture from the lack of a breeze. However, unlike most caves, this one had predators lurking within the darkness.

Normally, I would rather be anywhere else than sneaking around in a cave, hunting things that were far more dangerous than bats, but I was looking for someone, someone who was running out of time and needed my help, help I intended on giving.

"I can't see a damn thing in here," I complained. I sent my thoughts to Neal, the only one who could hear them.

We are in a cave, a place that is defined by its location underground, somewhere that is normally without the light of the sun, Neal answered in my head.

Neal is my partner, adviser, and teacher. He is an Atlantean SENTINEL, created specifically for me with a mixture of technology and magic. He is extremely smart and has a number of cool tricks, all packaged in the body of a large black Labrador.

I ducked low, squeezing through a tight spot. Neal's dark body led the way, his black coat allowing him to blend in with the cave's deep shadows.

Marcus Abshire   LOST SON

"Are we really in a cave? I had no idea, really, I thought you might have forgotten to pay the electric bill," I sent sarcastically.

I am unsure of what you mean by that. Are you attempting to inject humor into this situation?

"Wow, you really suck, you know that?" I entered a larger space slightly illuminated by a battery-powered lantern. Its LED bulbs used a minimal amount of energy yet provided enough light with which to see.

I took a quick look around, seeing the one whom I had come here for in the far corner of the space. I hurried over to the small figure huddled in a tight ball, reaching out slowly to get his attention while I spoke in a calm and reassuring manner.

"Harry. Harry, it's okay. Hey, I'm going to take you out of this place, get you home to your dad, okay?"

The boy turned to look at me when I mentioned his dad, and his expression broke my heart. Dried mud matted his hair, and the clothes he wore were torn and filthy. Bruises marred his face and gave him a sickly look. His eyes flickered at me with trepidation as if fear paralyzed him from looking directly at me.

"Harry, my name's Jack. This is my dog Neal, and we're going to get you home." Neal came over and inched close to the boy.

He seemed a little startled by Neal's appearance, but quickly recovered. Dogs are amazingly effective in calming young children. Harry reached over slowly and patted Neal's head before remembering where he was and curling back in on himself.

"You have to go. They'll be back, they'll be back," Harry moaned in defeat. His pain broke my heart and at the same time made me furious. The bastards who did this were going to pay.

I reached down and grabbed the metal that encircled his ankle. The restraint was attached to a small chain bolted to the rock. With a grunt of effort, I broke the cuff, tossing the twisted metal aside as Harry looked at me with awe.

I do not like this. Werewolves do not need the light to see, Neal thought.

"*You don't sense anything do you?*" I asked.

No, I cannot detect anyone near but us, however, the rocks may be interfering with my scanners.

"*Okay, well we can't help that, just stay alert, let me know if anything changes.*"

Of course, my lord.

"You should have listened to the kid."

I spun around and saw a man standing on the far side of the wall. With long black hair, a beard in need of shaving, and a robust athletic frame, he looked like a very fit hippie.

He stood in front of the only exit, blocking our way.

"You know if you wanted a friend, this is the wrong way of going about getting one. You should try poker or maybe a game of basketball; kidnapping doesn't really scream socially acceptable behavior," I taunted.

I took a few steps back, putting space between us and the boy.

"I have no need for friends; the boy is to be a prelude to the full moon's hunt -- you and that mongrel will only add to the bounty," he growled, and his eyes flashed yellow, blazing in the darkness.

"Seriously, why is everyone so literal? Has no one heard of humor?"

He took a few steps forward. "Wait a second," he stopped out of reflex. "The kid said 'they,' they'll come back," I thought out loud.

A large wolfish grin spread across his face, his white teeth reflecting off the lantern's light. The effect freaked me out.

"Yes, he did," I heard a woman say from a few feet away right before she launched herself at me, having stayed undetected by hiding within a small crevice, deep within shadow.

I hadn't expected two of them. Their numbers made this whole rescue operation twice as difficult. Her shoulder-length blond hair framed a hard face. She wore a black tank top and tight pants. Her eyes flashed a deep yellow.

"*Protect the boy!*" I thought furiously, diving away from the woman and rolling onto my feet, pulling my sword from the sheath on my back in a quick motion.

I looked left then right, seeing a werewolf on either side. Their yellow eyes blazed with a feral intensity at what they saw as easy prey. It was going to be fun to help them realize their mistake.

By some unspoken consent, they both leaped for me at the same time. I couldn't let them grab me; werewolves were unnaturally strong and fast, but, then again, so was I.

I could easily beat one by himself, but two of them, working together, may be more than I could handle.

I dropped and sprang toward the woman, spinning so my back was to the ground and thrust my sword up, feeling as she passed overhead and the sharp metal sank into her thigh, slicing a deep gash that drew blood. Its bright red color stood out in stark contrast to her tan skin.

She howled in pain and crashed into her partner. They quickly regained their feet and faced me. I saw as Neal tried to get Harry moving, circling around the wall, towards the exit.

Tank Top's leg quickly stopped oozing blood, her body knitting itself up from the wound, a tribute to her werewolf nature.

I watched as their canines grew to dangerous lengths and their nails elongated into deadly claws. They narrowed their eyes and raced towards me together, no longer underestimating my abilities. They worked in concert, each one taking an angle and furiously attacking; thankfully I was skilled in fighting -- far more skilled than they.

I brought my sword up, using the blade to keep Hippie from ripping my throat out, while lashing out with my foot and kicking Tank Top in the gut, causing her to double over. I thrust forward, forcing Hippie back and then, before Tank Top could raise back up, I turned and chopped down, sending her head to the floor as her body slowly followed.

"NOOO!" Hippie yelled and redoubled his attack.

His anger and fury gave him a renewed energy as he ignored the lethality of my sword and managed to punch me in the face before I could recover. The blow left me dazed, his fury giving him a strength that astounded me.

I backpedaled away, trying to regroup as Hippie pressed his advantage. Somehow, I managed to keep him from killing me as I got my bearings back. His rage over seeing his partner decapitated drove him to a fury, and unable to control himself, he attacked with a wonton abandon, slashing, punching and biting, forcing me to reel from the sheer ferocity of the attack.

I dodged a wild slash and spun, kicking him in the side of his face, stunning him for a second. That second was all I needed.

Using the momentum from my kick, I followed with my sword, removing his arm. Hippie bellowed in pain, instantly trying to protect himself, and I stabbed forward, thrusting through his throat and neck, with a twist and a spin I finished what I had started and sent his head to rest with Tank Top's, away from their still bodies.

I wiped at my mouth with the back of my hand, and saw it come away red with my blood. I looked around and saw no one else in the cave. Neal had been able to get Harry out -- hopefully before he saw what happened in here. I'm sure he had already been through enough; I didn't need to add watching me kill his captors in such a brutal fashion to the list.

I hurried outside, following the path that led us here, and exited into the open air of a bright Alaskan day. I took a deep breath, the rich fragrant air from the surrounding forest helped clear the last vestiges of the dank, stale environment inside the cave, I felt like I had exited from another world, one that consisted of pain and darkness.

"*Neal?*" I knew he would have kept Harry moving, to get him as far from here as possible.

We are near the river; the child will not stop, now that he has begun moving, Neal answered.

"*Good, I'll be there in a few minutes*," I responded.

This time we had succeeded; we had saved an innocent from the clutches of monsters. I knew there would be ramifications from killing two pack members, but right now I didn't care. We managed to get Harry out safe; he was going home. That was good enough for me.

Chapter Two

The freezing cold water did wonders for clearing the mind. I swam through the frigid bay, veering around large slabs of ice, the last remnants of the blistering winter of western Alaska. My skin suit allowed me to move through the salty water like a shark, which, with a few strong thrusts of its tail, easily catches fast-moving prey. The suit had been a gift from my ancestors. Atlanteans were masters of the ocean's depths, having adapted to the harsh environment at the bottom of the sea, they used their advanced technology to survive.

It fit me like a second skin, adhering to my body easily. It protected me from the harsh extremes of the water and was tough enough to stop a bullet. All Atlantean children were given one at birth; they grew with the child and never came off. The suits were a marvel of technology, invisible when not in use and gave the wearer the same sensations as real skin. They only showed when activated. The suit's glossy silver sheen was probably the reason the local fishermen decided I looked like a fish in need of a harpoon.

The impact knocked me from my wandering thoughts of my mom singing to me at night in a soft voice that carried a heavy sadness. She would always end by moving my dark hair from my forehead with a loving gesture.

"Raiphaim," she would say quietly, before leaving me alone in the dark to wonder at her words.

Swimming always seemed to allow me to do that easily -- think, that is. I found the soothing waters of the freezing Alaskan sea to be quite therapeutic. Being an Atlantean did have its perks -- having the ability to tolerate the most extreme water conditions was just one. Being extremely strong was another, as well as having an accelerated healing system -- which came in handy after going toe to toe with a couple of werewolves.

Right now, I needed to disappear before another local decided I resembled dinner and tried to catch me in his net. I'm sure I could have gotten out after they brought me on board, but then I'd have to try and explain why I was swimming in below freezing waters with nothing on but a thin skin suit. There would be questions and most likely the authorities would be notified, which could lead to me becoming a visible dot on the Atlantean warlord's radar.

No thanks, I wasn't ready to climb that mountain just yet. My best option to avoid scrutiny was to become a story the fishermen would tell their friends tonight over some cold beers and a warm bowl of soup.

I took a deep breath and quickly dove under the surface of the water, my skin suit swiftly flowed up over my throat and chin, covering my nose and mouth. The suit easily drew oxygen from the surrounding water like gills, transferring it to my face, allowing me to breathe.

I didn't really need to take a deep breath before submerging, but it always felt like the right thing to do. My feet looked like I wore flippers, but they were just adaptations my skinsuit provided when I was in the water, with a few powerful kicks, I sluiced through the green-tinted water and headed under one of the large ice chunks still fighting the oncoming summer. I moved far faster than any human could, my enhanced strength and skin suit allowed me to propel myself through the water as fast as any seal, and almost as nimble.

Once under the ice, I peeked out to see the dark silhouette of the fishing boat above me. The vessel floated like a large piece of driftwood left to go wherever the tide demanded.

The fishermen were no doubt wondering what they had targeted, what type of creature I was -- one that had taken a harpoon and shrugged the projectile off only to dive beneath the depths and disappear.

A small smile stretched over my face, and I took off towards the shore. I'm not sure how I knew, but I had no doubt that if I kept swimming I would eventually surface exactly where I wanted.

A few minutes later the color of the water changed and became shallower as I reached my destination. I came up to the surface and turned back towards the boat, slowly raising my head above the water.

The boat appeared as a small dot on the horizon; bobbing up and down in the water, moving at the will of the ocean. Confident I wouldn't be spotted, I turned toward the rock wall that served as my ladder to land. I easily scaled the wet rocks, climbing them with ease. I reached the top and soon stood on a flat expanse of old road. A few feet away sat my motorcycle, waiting for me like a faithful lover, knowing I would return and willing to wait forever for me if need be.

Marcus Abshire   LOST SON

I loved her; she was a Harley Davidson Sportster Iron 883. She had a dull black paint job with a few chrome accents, with Coker 5.10 by16 inch tires. They were beefy and gave the bike a seriously tough look. I earned her after saving a Japanese businessman's daughter from an underground sex slave racket. Every time I fired her up, she growled and shook my bones in a way I completely loved. She was the only thing, other than Neal, and my own life, that I valued.

On the other side of the road, the woods rose like a towering wall of trees, shutting off the land with mysterious grandeur and hiding its secrets in shadow. From the treeline a huge black Labrador trotted towards me, his tongue hanging out of his mouth. He was larger than a normal lab. Weighing in at 110 pounds, he carried no excess fat. His flanks rippled with muscle as his dark, almost obsidian coat shone in the meager sunlight. His eyes held a deep intelligence and, if you looked hard enough, you could see a faint golden glow coming from their depths. Deep at night, when the stars and moon were all the light provided, his eyes gave off a slight luminescence that gave him a devilish look.

"Why the hell didn't you warn me?" I asked aloud.

He came even with my bike and sat down calmly. I heard his voice inside my head; we had an intimate link and could communicate without talking but sometimes you just needed to raise your voice.

You were in no danger. I assessed their threat level and it was not high enough to warrant telling you.

Neal sat there looking at me, still as a statue. I had the impression he could sit there for eons if needed. In fact, he could, Neal, short for SENTINEL, was an ancient and wonderful piece of sorcery and technology. A remnant of Atlantean science and magic, he was a guardian created for nobility, designed to serve, protect, and teach members of Atlantis's royal bloodline -- a bloodline that died off millennia ago.

He came to me on my fifteenth birthday and had been my companion for almost ten years now. He has many wonderful gifts, one of them being able to communicate with me telepathically; the other having the duty to assess any threat and to counsel me on the best course of action, one that preferably would result in me *not* dying.

"Yeah, well, a heads up would have been nice," I said angrily.

I knew my ire would have no effect on Neal, he wasn't created to feel emotions, but *I* still had them, and I was kind of pissed he didn't warn me. Even though my suit could stop bullets and apparently harpoons, that didn't mean I wasn't going to be sore for a while.

I assure you, had there been sufficient threat presented by the operators of that vessel; you would have had ample warning. Part of my existence is to prepare you for what lies ahead, in that you need to be able to adapt to ever-changing situations. This seemed like a good scenario for you to gain valuable experience.

What lies ahead, you might ask? Don't bother, I've been asking him for ten years and he won't tell me jack.

"Whatever, did you at least inform the client I will be by to pick up the rest of my fee?"

Yes, my lord. I sent an e-mail to his web address, letting him know you will be at the meeting place in two hours to receive full payment.

"Don't call me 'lord,'" I said, for the billionth time.

Yes, my lord.

I don't know why I even bother sometimes. I went over to my bike and pulled out a tee-shirt, jeans, and boots from the saddlebags. I checked to make sure my pistol was still hidden, and my sword was securely in its scabbard. I took my homemade cloaking pin, created with the patient and limitless knowledge provided by Neal, and transferred the device from my motorcycle to the scabbard I had strapped to my back. Now anyone who walked by would be able to see my bike, but not the sword handle sticking up behind my back.

Just then, Neal stood at rapt attention and stared off into the woods. His change in posture told me something was approaching, and I probably wasn't going to like it. I calmed my thoughts and focused on the world around me, trying to discern what had Neal's interest.

"What is it?" I asked.

I detect a large presence of werewolves in the vicinity. Only one has a threat level high enough to be wary of, but all of them together would be formidable. I suggest you get on your bike and ride. They will be here in twenty seconds; you have ten to retreat.

"Retreat, where's the fun in that? Besides, wasn't it you who told me that I needed different situations in order to prepare me for what lies ahead?" I sent to him.

If you choose to stay, I believe I can keep most of them busy enough for you to survive, should violence erupt.

Remember, you always have the ocean behind you. None of them are your equal in the water, my lord.

"Yeah, but do any of them know how to waltz?" I asked. "And don't call me 'lord,'" I added, just for fun.

Are you referencing a form of dancing as a synonym for fighting?

"Nothing gets past you, does it, Neal?" I thought.

From the dark shadows of the woods stepped a large-framed man. He wore a ragged flannel shirt that looked like it had barely survived being burnt, stabbed, and rinsed in mud, along with a matching pair of jeans. He had no shoes on and his feet looked dirty, but he moved with no reaction to the hard, cold, uneven terrain. His eyes shone from a dark scowl; they had hints of yellow within them and a wildness that bespoke of power and animal strength. He stood with the air of a leader, someone who gave orders and expected them to be obeyed. His obvious physical strength matched his aura of command.

"I'm afraid I cannot let you leave," he said. His voice sounded rough and had a wild quality.

"Listen, I know what it's like to have to say goodbye, but your pain will get better with time. I'll write," I said, hoping my sarcastic indifference would keep him off balance.

I'd been expecting him to find me, in fact, I was surprised he had taken this long. When you enter a pack's territory and kill two members without permission from the pack leader, well, they tend to be angry with you. Normally, I would have visited him first, but time was of the essence and I was more interested in saving a young man's life than following rigid pack protocol.

Neal sat quietly by my side, for all appearances he seemed to be just a loving, albeit larger than normal, black lab. I reached out and rubbed his head in an offhanded motion, the action looked like nothing more than an owner petting his dog. However, I used Neal to infuse my hand with a powerful electric charge. My dog channeled electricity from the air and ground and funneled the energy into a small stable field around my hand, the field was not permanent and if I didn't discharge the electricity soon the charge would dissipate on its own, but it was a neat little trick that allowed me a first punch with a kick.

The pack leader scowled at me even harder, if that was possible, and growled at me in a very deep and quiet voice, "You have invaded my boundaries and brought violence upon my kin, which is an affront I cannot let go unanswered."

Upon? Seriously who talks like that? No one born in the last hundred years.

Werewolves could be very long-lived if they were smart and strong enough to survive the violent and volatile pack lifestyle. If this guy was old *and* pack leader, that meant he was not only very smart, but powerful as well. I ratcheted up my own sense of caution.

I smiled calmly, not wanting to set him off until I was ready. Sometimes talking can gain you more valuable information than fighting.

"You've got a good thing going on here. Plenty of land to run freely during the full moon and game to hunt.

Having pack members kidnapping children to hunt and eat is not conducive to keeping the humans from snooping. Seems like you wouldn't approve of their actions. I actually did you a favor, if you think about it," I said, trying to see if this was something the pack tolerated. If they accepted the practice, I would have to come back and kill them for hunting humans, all of them.

He narrowed his eyes at me and took a step forward.

"I run a tight pack. The two pups would have been properly dealt with for their transgressions. You have no right to interfere. Pack issues are pack issues," he snarled.

I had the sinking suspicion this wasn't the first time they had snatched up an innocent for their sport. This pack had grown too strong up here in the wild, with no oppressive human society to keep them from getting too brazen. Perhaps they needed to be taught a lesson.

I narrowed my own eyes, "Maybe your control is slipping. If you can't handle two foolish pups, how can you control the rest of your pack?"

It was a good thing the moon was in a waning cycle. If I had to fight him closer to a full moon, the task would have been a lot harder. At this stage of the moon's cycle werewolves were weaker, unable to shift into their more violent and vicious beast form. That didn't mean they weren't still very dangerous, with superhuman speed and strength, razor-sharp claws, and a healing ability allowing them to survive almost any trauma, they were a force to be reckoned with.

The pack leader launched at me the second I finished asking my question. He moved with a speed I wasn't prepared for and raked a clawed hand at my face. I turned to the side and pulled back, trying to dodge his claws. I felt a stinging pain as he connected with my cheek and left two deep gashes that bled freely. As he passed in front of me, I punched him in the back of the head, unleashing the stored electricity.

I hit him at the base of his skull, where his brain stem became his spinal cord and all his nerves united in a tight bundle. Shooting 20,000 volts of electricity into his body's electrical highway really screwed him up. He hit the ground face first, flopping like a fish, unable to control his limbs.

I knew his paralysis was only temporary and reached back to pull my sword from its sheath. The blade wasn't silver, that shit only works in the movies, but I could still kill him if I moved fast enough. I heard movement and saw in my peripheral vision as a large number of werewolves emerged from the shadows of the woods.

You'd better be fast; they will be on us in a few seconds, Neal said telepathically.

My sword's blade shone blue as its metallic sheen reflected the sun's rays. The weapon had been forged from Atlantean steel. It had taken me years to gather the raw materials I needed and even longer to perfect the skills required to forge such a magnificent weapon. Atlantean steel would never rust or dull and was stronger than any known metal.

I thrust downwards and felt a satisfying impact as the sharp metal easily sliced through the pack leader's neck. His nearly headless body flopped erratically, and I was unable to sever his neck completely, though. A small amount of muscle and tendon kept his head from rolling away. A loud explosion ripped through the air as Neal emitted a sonic assault on the pack hurtling towards us, intent on taking their revenge.

The offensive maneuver overwhelmed werewolves. Their sensitive hearing made the sonic blast devastating -- but the effects were only temporary. I considered trying to finish the job, but the pack leader had somehow scrambled a few feet away and the rest of the pack had started to recover from Neal's audial assault. I figured leaving might be a smart move; I could finish the job some other time.

I jumped on my bike and sheathed my sword in a quick motion. Hitting the ignition, the motorcycle rumbled to life. I had no time to savor the deep, throaty growl as I kicked her into first gear, released the clutch, and gassed the throttle. The motorcycle roared in answer, the back-wheel spinning for a second before gripping the road, shooting me forward like a rocket. I yelled in excitement as I felt a couple of bounces from running over the pack leader's legs.

The wind whipped through my hair and the fresh scent of the ocean and forest overwhelmed me as I sped away from a crippled pack leader and a pissed-off bunch of werewolves.

I looked down to see Neal's familiar shadow running alongside me. My speedometer showed sixty-five miles an hour – a speed at which he easily kept pace. I reached up and wiped at the dried blood on my cheek knowing the gashes would already be healing.

You did well, but you underestimated his speed. He should not have been able to make you bleed. If you insist on disregarding my advice, I suggest you make sure to perform to the best of your abilities. Neal said.

"*Sometimes things do not go as your programs say they will,*" I thought back.

Yes, my lord, but you were faster than him. If you are to be ready for what comes you must be as good as my programs say, so be faster.

I didn't have anything to say to that. He was right. I *am* faster than that and I slipped; I let him get to me. If my enemy had been a sea witch, whose fingernails hold powerful poison, I would be dead by now. Or at least very sick -- sick enough to be unable to defend myself.

"*Don't call me lord,*" I sent, trying to salvage some of my pride.

Chapter Three

I drove away from the ocean and towards the coffee shop where I was supposed to meet my client. I had an hour to kill before our scheduled meeting and figured I could spend the time sipping coffee and reading the news. I liked to keep abreast of current events and looked for anything that might warn me of the approach of the Atlantean warlord who was hunting me. I didn't think he would sit down for an interview, but you never knew what you can learn from the paper.

I pulled up to the curb, parking off the main street in an angled parking space. The town was still small and quaint enough to have parking right in front of the shops. I liked how I could see my ride from inside. Cups O' Brew was a locally-owned shop; the bigger chains had a couple of stores in the larger cities but hadn't encroached on this small town...yet.

Neal came around the corner in a trot, showing no signs of his exertions. It must be nice to be a super-advanced, magically enhanced Atlantean guardian.

"You know the deal, sit here and be a good little boy. I'll be out in a bit."

I don't think he liked being called that, but I didn't care. He wouldn't stop calling me my lord, so turnabout's fair game.

Yes, my lord, I could have sworn he said that with a sarcastic air.

I went inside and nodded to the cashier, a middle-aged man with balding hair. He was ringing up a customer and nodded back absently. Places like this often bought a few copies of the morning paper and let the customers look through them, hoping to get bigger tips. I found a table near the front window and sat down, picking up the front page, I smiled at the headline.

"Missing Boy Found Alive -- Authorities Still Looking for Suspects."

"Finally, something in the news you can be happy about," I heard my waitress say as she came over to my table.

Her face glowed with the flawlessness of youth. With ample breasts and hips, she would never be a supermodel -- but who wants a skinny waif anyway? Her eyes looked at me with gentle reproach. They were dark brown and accentuated her wavy hair that she tried to keep under a ponytail with an errant strand falling over her forehead anyway. She had a pencil stuck behind her ear and she pulled it out along with a notepad from her apron to take my order. She smiled at me, eliciting a responding smile of my own.

"It does seem as though there's only bad things in the news. It's nice to see something else for a change," I said.

"The boy is a good kid. His dad was wrecked when the police said they had no leads," she looked at me closely for a few seconds, "People are saying you were hired by the boy's father -- that you found the kid."

I folded the paper and set it down. I didn't want to be mean, but I didn't like people knowing about me or asking too many questions. The less someone could tell others, the better. You never knew who might be asking those questions.

"I'm just passing through," I said non-committedly.

She watched me for a moment, gauging my answer. Finally, she let out a quick breath; I could tell she didn't believe a word.

"Modest, too. You gonna be here later tonight? I get off at eight," she said. Her posture had shifted to one of open invitation.

I'm sure if I wanted to, I could have a nice and enjoyable evening with her. I couldn't risk it, though. Being close to me would put her at too much risk.

"I would love to. Unfortunately, I have to leave in an hour. It's a long ride home," I answered.

She showed disappointment that then turned to acceptance, "It's always the good ones that are unavailable. Too bad, I think we could've had a lot of fun. Is there something else I can get you?"

"Yeah, I'd love a coffee -- black if you don't mind."

"Sure thing, coming right up," she said, turning away but keeping eye contact for a second.

I was soon on my third cup. The coffee wasn't bad, and I loved to watch the normal comings and goings of the customers -- people living ordinary lives, doing ordinary things. Their simple, everyday routines always fascinated me.

Here comes Mr. Stavinaugh. He's ten minutes early, Neal's voice came to me clearly, startling me out of my thoughts.

I held my cup in both hands, elbows leaning on the table when Mr. Stavinaugh came in. His large frame filled the doorway, heavy in the belly and chin, but his eyes shone with a calm thankfulness. His love for his son gave his demeanor a robust life that was infectious. He carried a small paper bag.

He came to my table and sat down, smiling at me.

"Jack, you're an angel. I can't thank you again for all you've done."

"How's the boy doing?" I asked.

A traumatic experience such as the kid had gone through can be hard to overcome. A loving family and support system is extremely important. I had the feeling he was in good hands.

"He's doing wonderful; glad to be home. His recovery will take some time but that doesn't matter, as long as he's home, everything will all work out," he beamed.

"Here, the rest of your fee as promised," he brought the bag up and handed the crumpled sack to me. I took the payment and put it in my jacket without counting the money.

"I'm glad I could help," I said, rising to my feet.

Mr. Stavinaugh grabbed my arm, not letting me go. His face flashed a shadow of pain and memory for a second, "Jack, my son keeps talking about monsters and wolves. His therapist says it might be good to figure out what he means in order to help him. Do you know what he is talking about?"

I slowly pulled away from his grip, turning towards the door.

"Men can be monsters. There's nothing more complicated to it than that," I said. The bell above the door rang as I went outside.

Marcus Abshire   LOST SON

Neal rose from where he sat next to my bike. I got on and started her up, the sound loud in the calm small town's main street.

Home?

"*Home*, I agreed."

I pulled out onto the street and headed south, knowing the temperature wouldn't warm up until I got closer to where I lived. Most people wouldn't consider Oklahoma City to be the kind of place for an Atlantean to call home, seeing as how the state was landlocked -- but that was kind of the idea. Oklahoma City was right in the middle of America, a wonderful place to live when you had to travel a lot. The city was as good a place as any, although I desperately wanted to be somewhere near the ocean. That's why when given the chance I would swim anywhere, even a frigid Alaskan bay.

After a week on my motorcycle, pulling up to my home/business was a welcome sight. I lived on the second floor of an old building in the historic part of Oklahoma City. The place had a wonderful vibe. It was mostly in holding with the old-style brick construction yet placed in a part of town that tried to capture that big city feel. I pulled around to the back. I parked my bike and sat still for a minute, letting Neal do his thing.

He came trotting up to me a few seconds later, his intelligent eyes shone in a way that screamed for me to play catch with him.

Initial scans show the building has not been tampered with -- though that doesn't mean someone cannot be watching you, just that no one has entered while we were away.

"God, I need a shower and some food," I said as I walked to the door. I unlocked it and then went inside.

I had every intention of sitting down and watching some of the football games I had recorded. I went inside and flipped on the light switch next to the door. The fluorescent lights hummed to life and I held the door open, letting Neal in. Yeah, he was an ancient Atlantean guardian, but he couldn't open doors. Go figure.

My business consisted of two rooms, one main one in the front that housed a desk, a computer, and a phone. The back consisted of a small storage room and a bathroom I kept clean in case a client needed to use it.

I sat down at my desk and checked the phone for messages. There was nothing. Then I powered up my computer and checked for any emails but only found a bunch of spam. Neal said the computer was unnecessary, but I felt having one was important. My desk faced the front door, but I had a small wall built that separated my workspace from the rest of the office, I had the wall reinforced with steel plates just in case someone came at me and tried to shoot me while I worked. That left a small area right inside the front door that had a couple of comfortable chairs and a small table.

I turned the computer off and was about to go upstairs for a hot shower and watch football when my phone rang. I picked the receiver up on the second ring and said, "Jack Industries, this is Jack speaking. How can I help you?"

"Oh, thank God you're there, I wasn't sure if I should call, I didn't want to talk to an answering machine. Wait, this *is* the place that helps find missing persons, right?" The woman on the other end of the line sounded excited, desperate, and slightly insane all at the same time. It was a common reaction when someone you love mysteriously disappears without a trace.

"Yes, this is the right place. How can I help you?" I said calmly, not wanting to spook her. She sounded frazzled enough already.

"How does this work? Do I come in? Should we meet somewhere?" she asked frantically.

"Well, that depends; do you need to find someone?" I asked.

"It's just, the cops said it hasn't been more than twenty-four hours, but I know something's wrong. Jessica wouldn't run off, not my Jessica," she said in between sobs, she struggled hard to contain herself.

I hated these calls; most times a kid goes missing because they've run away. They get mad at their parents or they fall in love and split town. The parents usually know this, but they're in denial and think something other than their bad relationship drove their kids away. Sometimes, however, their kidnapping is real; the kid is missing because someone took them. That's where I come in.

"Do you know where 4515 Easton Street is?" I asked.

"Yeah, yes, that's downtown, isn't it? I'm actually not far from there. Do you want me to meet you there?"

"If you can. If not, I can meet you someplace else," I offered.

Clients liked to feel they are doing something proactive when in this situation; coming to the office makes them feel this way.

"No, no it's fine. I'll be there in ten minutes," she said. Her desperation almost spilled through the phone and onto the floor. I heard the line go dead and I hung up.

"Well?" I asked aloud.

The phone call originated not far from here, in a residential neighborhood approximately eight minutes away if you obey the posted speed limits. The house is shown to have been recently purchased after the property had been on the market for six months. That is all I can find.

Like I said, we really didn't need a computer.

"Keep an ear to the ground, let me know when she gets close, I'm gonna grab us something to eat," I said as I headed towards the front door.

My lord? Neal said.

I stopped with my hand on the knob. I knew what he was going to ask. He knew I knew, but I still wanted him to ask.

Will you pick me up something to eat as well?

Even Neal had to eat.

"Sure, what do you want?" I smiled at him.

Cat food, please, he said. I could see him staring at me, if he could feel anger, I know he would be seething.

"Okay," I left, it's the little things, ya know?

I walked down the street for about a block, coming to a nice burger joint on the corner. I went inside and placed my order and then I left to get Neal his food. I hurried over to a small market and picked up a couple of cans of his favorite cat food and hurried back to pick up my burger. I had just returned to my office, set Neal's food down in a bowl in front of him, and settled down to eat my cheeseburger when my door opened.

She's here, Neal said. He sounded almost smug; I might add.

"*Thanks*," I answered, getting up to meet my guest.

I entered the small seating area at the front of my office and knew I was about to get a job. In the detective books, there's always some leggy beauty that saunters in to hire the out of work P.I. Her story as flimsy as her brassiere, but the P.I. takes the job anyway because he just can't say no to a pretty face. The woman who walked through my door wasn't a long-legged damsel-in-distress. She looked more like a soccer mom barely holding on to her composure. She looked to be middle-aged with a few hints of grey in her hair -- hair that hadn't been brushed in days. Or maybe she had run her hand through it so many times it looked disheveled. She was overweight but not obese; she just carried with her a few extra pounds that showed she spent more time behind the kitchen counter than in the gym. She had a soft face and gentle blue eyes that were rimmed with red, puffy skin. She clutched a handbag for dear life -- as if she expected someone to jump out of the shadows and try and take the small purse from her. She was a caring mother, racked with worry over her missing daughter, and I knew at that moment if she said aliens had taken her daughter, I would search the heavens to find her.

"Hello, Mr. ... Jack?" she asked.

"You can just call me Jack. Please, sit down," I motioned to one of the seats and I took the one across from her.

"Caroline, Caroline Bennett," she reached over and shook my hand.

"So, what do you think I can do for you, Caroline?"

She looked scared, afraid to start but more terrified of leaving and doing nothing.

"It's okay. You can tell me," I said.

"Well, it's my daughter, Jessica. She hasn't come home. She wasn't on the bus and I know something bad has happened. I just know it," she started crying, her whole body shaking. She pulled out a tissue from her bag and began wiping her tears away. "I'm so sorry. I don't know what to do. I called the cops, but they said they couldn't do anything and I'm afraid if I wait too long, it will be too late. I know there are people out there who take children and do horrible things... I can't let that happen, I just can't," her worry and fear threatened to consume her, but she held herself together, barely.

"Why don't we start with when you realized she was missing," I said.

"Okay, okay," she looked at me with hope, "I went to pick her up at the corner, where her school bus always lets her off. I watched all the children come off, but she never did. I thought maybe she was playing a game, hiding on the bus, so I went on and looked, but I couldn't find her. I asked the driver about her and he said he hadn't seen her get on -- neither had any of the other kids," she paused to blow her nose before continuing.

"I went back home and called the school, but they said she wasn't there; not in the nurse's office or with her teacher. I drove to the school to look around, to see if maybe she had stayed with her friends to play, I don't know. A million things were running through my mind. I went to the playground near the school and found her backpack on the ground near the swings. I knew something had happened. I immediately called the cops, but they said they would have to wait, that she was old enough to have run away. They asked if I was divorced and suggested my ex had taken her," I saw anger flare-up in her then; a deep hatred only a mother has when something happens to her children.

"The bastards didn't care. I knew I only had a few hours before her trail went cold, at least that's what all the shows say. I got online and saw your company and called," she finished with a rush as if telling me had helped her somehow.

"Is there anyone who she knows that might have taken her? Her dad or other family members?" I asked.

"No, her father moved away five years ago and has never been the sort to take her. He's too self-absorbed. There is no other family. Our parents are all gone."

"Do you have a picture of her? Maybe something that belonged to her?"

"I have a picture right here," she began to reach into her purse when she stopped, absorbing my second question.

"Wait, you're not going to try and track her by her aura or use something of hers to follow her psychic trail? Because I'll walk right now. I don't have time for nonsense," she said with absolute certainty.

I smiled slightly, "No, if we can go somewhere she might have been, my dog has a wonderful sense of smell. He may be able to track her scent." On cue, Neal came over and sat down next to me. I scratched him behind his shoulders.

She looked at me and then at him. Her body relaxed a little. Following an aura was silly, but somehow my dog being able to follow a scent hours old from an old trinket was believable. That's exactly what he was going to do, but it didn't count. He wasn't a normal dog.

"Okay, here's her picture. I have her backpack in the car. I'll be right back," she handed me a small photo and then stood up and left. I looked at the picture and my heart turned over in my chest. She looked to be about twelve, her black hair held back in a ponytail and she sat on a swing. She wore a simple tee shirt and shorts, an easy smile lit up her face. She looked so familiar, something about her tugged at me but I couldn't figure out what.

Caroline came back in carrying a pink backpack with a popular cartoon character on the front.

"This is all I found," she said as she held the pack out to me.

I reached over and took the bag, looking inside. There were a few library books, a folder filled with worksheets, and a permission slip for a field trip to the zoo.

"So how does this work? Do I pay you now?" She never mentioned the amount, but I knew she would give me everything she had if I asked.

"I charge two hundred a day, plus any extra expenses incurred while on the job. Payment is due after your child is returned. If I am unable to find your daughter, then all payment is forfeit. If you don't get what you want, neither do I," I said.

"You mean if you can't find her you won't charge me for your time?" She seemed shocked.

"That's exactly right. Rest assured, however, I have every intention of finding her. Now if that seems agreeable to you, I just need a number or email address where I can reach you. In the meantime, please try and stay patient," I handed her a blank piece of paper and a pen.

"What was the name of the park where you found her bag?" I asked.

She looked at me for a second, deciding if she could trust me. Irrational fear and worry rushed over her as she quickly scribbled down a phone number.

"Chandler Park across from Johnson Elementary," she said in a rush.

"I know the place," I responded, I had no idea where the park was, but I knew Neal would.

"Thank you, thank you so much." Tears threatened to come again.

"Don't thank me yet, just get home and wait by the phone, there's a possibility your daughter may come home on her own and you should be there to greet her if she does."

"Yes, yes, of course. Thank you so much," she repeated as I ushered her out of the office. I didn't want to be rude, but for me to get started, she needed to be gone. I closed the door gently behind her and looked over to see Neal already sniffing the bag, his nose almost touching the fabric. I gave him a few moments, letting him get the needed information.

If there is a viable trail at the park, I should be able to track the scent so long as she has not boarded an airplane or boat.

"Right then, let's get started," I walked past my uneaten burger, my stomach growling in hunger. I reached out to grab my meal and wrap the burger up, intent on eating my food at the park when Neal's thoughts came to me.

There are four werewolves approaching, two from the front and two from the back. All four of them are carrying pistols, individual threat levels minimal. Taken together, I would advise caution.

I had about two seconds to absorb that information when my front door exploded in a hail of gunfire and I felt three rounds hit me in the abdomen.

I grunted from the impact. One of my ribs felt like it cracked from the force of the rounds. I ignored the pain and hurried into the back of the office, heading towards the stairway that led up to my apartment. I snatched my sword from the weapon's hiding space by the stairwell. The cloaking pin kept the blade invisible from everyone but me, and hurried upstairs, hoping the bastards hadn't done anything to my bike.

Neal followed me and as I entered my apartment, I heard one of the werewolves yell, "Your insult to the pack will not go unanswered! Come die like a man!"

Yeah, that's not something I was willing to do.

Your pistol is still in your saddlebag. There is nowhere to go from up here.

"I know. That's why we're going to jump out of the window," I answered.

Sounds like a reasonable plan, my lord.

I know he wasn't supposed to be capable of sarcasm but, at that moment, I couldn't be sure about that. I reached the window that opened to the back alley and peeked out. Two werewolves were standing, waiting for me to try and run out the back so they could shoot me dead. I didn't bother with opening the windows; they would hear that and know I was up here. I only had a few seconds. There was a chance, if they were good enough, for them to hear me anyway but I figured that the gunshots had deafened them for a few seconds.

"Don't call me 'lord,'," I said and jumped out of my perfectly good window with Neal right behind me.

The sound drew the attention of both werewolves and they spun towards us almost instantly. Neal released another sonic blast and they both cringed at the noise, causing them to miss as they began shooting. I unsheathed my sword on the way down and landed right next to one of them. One quick slash later, I watched as his head rolled off his shoulders.

Neal landed on top of his target and his bulk drove them both to the ground. He bit down on the werewolf's wrist, severing the tendons that allowed him to grip his gun. His weapon clattered to the ground. Neal released his grip and went for his throat, but his opponent managed to get his other arm up and hit Neal with a devastating backhand sending him into the side of the building.

I rushed over and, with a quick series of slices, took off his good arm at the shoulder and watched as he tried to keep his intestines from falling onto the ground. I spun and landed a powerful roundhouse to the side of his head and he fell in a heap.

Neal had recovered and came over to me.

We must hurry; the other two are coming through your office.

"I'm getting tired of running," I said, getting on my motorcycle anyway.

Thankfully, they had not hurt her. That would really have pissed me off. I hit the throttle and rushed down the alley away from my home.

I understand, but if we killed them all we would have to clean up the mess. This way they will take care of their own, saving us the burden and making sure the authorities do not find their bodies.

No one wanted the cops called. Humans had a way of being far more powerful in mobs armed with pitchforks and torches than the most dangerous vampire.

"I know. Why do you think I left?"

Because I counseled you to.

I couldn't help it; I let out a hearty laugh. I know he didn't mean to be funny, but that just made me laugh even harder.

Chapter Four

The park sat directly across from Jessica's school, just as Caroline said. What I saw was a normal-looking play area. There was a multicolored plastic playground set that had a straight slide on one end and a tunnel slide that twisted like a corkscrew on the other end. On one flank was a climbing area and on the other a swing set.

The sun had almost set, and dark storm clouds had begun gathering. A stiff cold wind whipped my hair around. Due to the time of day and incoming weather, the park was empty of children.

Neal stood by the swings, trying to locate Jessica's trail. I stood nearby, patiently waiting.

There are many different scents in this area. Locating just one out of the many is difficult.

"Are you saying you can't do it?"

That I did not say. I believe I have found a positive match; the trail is faint and leaving fast. I fear if the rain falls, the water will wash away any vestiges of her. We must hurry.

Neal raised his head and pointed north. For a second he looked exactly like a pointer dog who had found his target. Then he shot off like a rocket, keeping his head level, following Jessica's trail.

I hurried to my motorcycle and fired her up, rushing to follow. We didn't talk much when Neal locked on a scent, concentrating required a lot of his attention. I remained silent so as not to distract him.

He kept to the shadows and alleys while I used the main roads. He had to stop and wait a few times while I caught up to him after getting stuck in traffic, but thankfully the weather held, and we made our way farther north -- where the residential and downtown areas made way for the industrial district. We passed a bunch of warehouses whose windows had been broken. The smell of chemicals and oil permeated the whole area. The workday ended an hour ago so there wasn't much activity right now, but occasionally a big truck transporting some harsh liquid or processed metal would pass us.

Eventually, Neal stopped in front of a rundown old building. There were no markings on the front, making it hard to determine what it had been used for. It could have been a storage area or used to house large pieces of equipment involved in everything from making signs to processing, housing, and transporting volatile chemicals. The smell of dust and grease lay thick in the air near the building. A few birds that had taken up residence on the building's eave made some noise as they were disturbed by my motorcycle's engine. I turned it off and the silence hung heavy in the air.

I waited while Neal made a quick circle of the building. People would be suspicious of a *person* snooping but never thought twice about a *dog* looking around.

There is a white van parked in the back and my sensors indicate three distinct heartbeats within the facility. Two are deeper and less frequent; the third is far more rapid and would indicate that of a child, one that is in a heightened state of emotional excitement.

"Good, she's still alive. Okay here's what we're going to do. I want you to go to the side, by that door over there and start barking. See if you can't get them to check out what the noise is. Once they are distracted by you, I'm going to sneak in, neutralize them, and get Jessica."

The plan is simple, yet sound.

"Gee, thanks."

Neal padded off towards the side door, probably used for employees needing to get out and take a smoke break. I quickly got into position and stood below an open window ten feet off the ground.

"Okay, I'm ready."

Neal began barking. At first, the sound was like any other dog bark, but he kept getting louder and soon the noise grew to deafening levels.

I crouched and then leaped, easily reaching the bottom of the window. I grabbed the ledge and pulled myself up high enough to get a view of inside. A large empty space opened before me. There were old pieces of mechanical equipment scattered haphazardly around the dirty floor. Off to the side, near the back of the building, I saw two men sitting on a couple of chairs. They looked like the metal fold-up kind used during company functions. It was hard to discern any of the men's features, but they both just sat there, not moving at all. At first, I thought they may be asleep, but then one of them blinked and turned his head towards the sound of Neal's barking.

Jessica sat in a large dog cage behind them. She was curled up to fit in the small space and had her knees bent so they were below her chin. She hugged her shins and rocked back and forth slightly. Her hair hung down almost to her waist and was a deep black that seemed to shine in the dingy light.

Finally, the one who moved first stood up and walked slowly towards the side door. He moved with distracted motions, like a robot being controlled by someone else -- only moving the parts of his body necessary for locomotion. His partner sat still and unmoving. I decided it was either now or never; hopefully, whatever made him so sluggish would also make sure he didn't see me climbing through the window.

I pulled myself up further and swung inside the building hanging with my feet about four feet from the ground. I looked down; making sure the floor was clear and let go, landing in a silent crouch. I began sneaking over towards where Jessica was being held, quickly moving from shadow to shadow, making no sound.

Neal's barking kept ringing in the hollow warehouse.

We are going to have to deal with the werewolves you now have hunting you.

"*Seriously, you want to talk about this now?*" I kept moving slowly closer to my target.

No one can hear us. Besides you need the experience of handling two things at once. You are more than capable of discussing this while advancing.

"*I'm glad to see you have so much faith in me.*"

Faith has nothing to do with my confidence in your abilities.

"*Yeah, yeah, I know,*" I was almost halfway there.

"I know I'm going to have to deal with the werewolves eventually, but right now all I care about is getting Jessica away from here."

You do realize by not killing the pack leader you have just angered him and ensured his attention until one of you is dead?

"Have you thought about how they were able to find me so quickly?"

Yes. Have you?

Another one of Neal's "learning experiences."

"Well, I figured they've been using my blood, I so carelessly gave them."

That does seem the most plausible scenario. This is why there is great importance on you being the best, to perform to your abilities and to listen to my council, my lord.

"Even a broken clock is right twice a day."

I was only ten feet away from my target. The man sat still, unmoving, staring off into space. His behavior struck me as being weird. I crept up behind him, the cage housing Jessica to my right. She saw me and whipped her head towards me. I raised my hand up, putting one finger on my lips, hoping she would keep quiet. She didn't make a sound, just sat there with the small kindle of hope growing in her eyes.

I thought about unsheathing my blade, but I knew killing humans was only a last resort. I had to let the local authorities deal with them.

Two feet away, he finally sensed something was wrong and started to turn towards me. I landed a hard punch to the side of his head, careful not to crush his skull, and he fell off his chair, unconscious.

The other one is coming back, Neal said.

I spun left and crouched behind Jessica's cage, waiting. A few seconds later I heard the second guy approaching, his feet making scraping sounds as she shuffled them. He stopped, seeing his partner on the ground, and looked around, slowly. He looked as though he was only going through the motions. Like he wasn't really seeing anything.

I stood up and came at him faster than he could react. He just stood there, watching me. At the last second, I saw him begin to reach over towards a metal pipe that was leaning up against a railing, but he was far too late. I knocked him out with a right cross to the chin and he, too, fell to the floor. I waited a second to see if he was going to get up, but he was out cold.

"That was almost too easy."

I dropped next to the cage, eye level with Jessica.

"Don't be afraid, I'm here to help you. Your mother sent me and I'm going to get you out of here," I said while I reached out and broke the meager lock with my hand.

"My mother?" She asked, confused.

"Yeah, kid, your mom hired me to get you. Just keep quiet and we'll be out of here in a few seconds."

She tenderly climbed out of her prison and stood up with obvious soreness. I was again struck by her familiarity. I don't know why but she struck a chord within me and I couldn't stop looking at her. I wanted to make sure she was safe. Like a big brother, I was instantly protective of her, more so than normal.

I reached out and gently guided her away from the warehouse and out into the open air. Neal kept watch over our kidnappers while the cops came; he had already called them. I kept Jessica warm with a blanket from my saddlebag and waited with her until the police arrived. I pulled out a cell phone from my pocket and called her mother as well. She seemed overjoyed and said she was going to be here in a second.

Twenty minutes later and the cops still hadn't arrived, our kidnappers had regained consciousness, but I had zip-tied their hands together and Neal sat by them, making sure they didn't try to get away. They just sat there, like earlier, with an absent look on their faces.

A vehicle is approaching. The car matches the one Caroline used earlier.

"That's great, but where are the cops? You called them earlier didn't you?"

Of course, their average response time in this area is around ten minutes. They should have been here approximately eight minutes ago. I will wait two more minutes and call them again.

Caroline pulled into the drive where we were waiting, I waved her over and she stopped twenty feet away and hurried out of the vehicle.

"Where is she? Is my girl alright?"

"Yes, she's fine, she's right here," I said, getting up, giving Caroline access to her daughter.

She came over to hug Jessica but stopped a few feet short.

"What the hell's going on here? Where's my Jennifer?" She turned to me angrily.

"*Jennifer?*"

Jennifer?

We both thought at the same time.

"*Jessica* is right here," I said again, adding emphasis on her name.

"I don't understand why you would do something like this. My Jennifer has blonde hair and blue eyes. I don't know who this child is. I'm calling the cops," she said, reaching into her purse.

"*What is happening? You didn't track the wrong girl, did you?*"

No, you know as well as I do the girl we rescued matched the picture Caroline provided. Her scent was also identical to the one on the backpack she gave to us. Something else must be wrong. Perhaps Caroline has let the stress of the situation get to her and she is now having a mental breakdown?

Caroline furiously punched numbers on her phone when I heard Jessica say, "Who is that woman? Where am I?"

At the same time, a flash of light blazed from across the street. The flare originated from the roof of the building. A split-second later Caroline's chest exploded in a bloody mass of tissue and organs. She let out a muffled squeal and fell backward from the force of the impact.

Get down! We have a sniper on the roof across the street! He is using a weapon I have never encountered.

Neal took off, racing across the street towards the shooter. I dove away from Caroline's smoking corpse and tackled Jessica, who stared at the body in total disbelief. I gathered her up and she tried to struggle for a second before realizing she wasn't going to get away. There were two more quick flashes from the same spot and both kidnappers' heads disintegrated in a red haze of blood and brain matter. They both fell over limply.

"*Neal!*" I sent to him furiously.

I do not know who is firing; I cannot detect anyone. They have the ability to hide from my scanners. I'm going to try locating them at different frequencies. Stay down; I don't know if your skin suit can protect you from their weapons.

I managed to get Jessica and myself behind an empty trailer out of the direct line of fire, but I feared whatever they were using could shoot right through the flimsy metal. I glanced down and saw Jessica looking up at me with fear and helplessness and was again struck with a strong sense of déjà vu.

A loud concussion boomed from the shooter's roof followed by what sounded like a low drumbeat, one that kept reverberating, the steady rumble reminded me of a jet engine but deeper in tone, far more bass than the high-pitched whine of a jet.

I peeked around the edge of my cover and saw a bright blue light coming from what appeared to be some sort of backpack the person wore. They rose from the roof and quickly gained altitude. The unknown shooter carried a rifle, one I had never seen the likes of before. The weapon's lines were all curved and completely different than any modern rifle.

The shooter had reached almost thirty feet when I saw Neal launch from the roof, heading straight for him. At the last second, another burst of light blazed in the night and the guy shot off in a different angle. Neal missed him by a foot.

The light quickly dwindled as the sniper escaped, leaving me and Jessica with three bloody corpses, which, of course, is when I heard the wail of the cop's sirens.

Five police cruisers approaching from the south, I suggest you make a hasty retreat. We can meet up at the hotel. I want to see if I can get any information from the site. I will meet you there later.

"Okay, sounds good, see you in a bit."

"Jessica? Jessica, I'm going to put you on the motorcycle behind me. I want you to hold on for dear life do you understand?" She looked badly shaken.

"Jessica!" I said louder.

She snapped her head around, looking me in the eyes. She blinked and gained more control, she nodded her head twice, letting me know she understood.

"Good, here we go," I rose up and hurried over to my bike.

I set her on her feet, and she hopped on the back, clutching me around the chest in a death grip. I brought the bike to life once more and once again raced away from a scene the cops would find very interesting.

My lord, Neal said as I drove off.

"Yeah?"

There is one more thing. I ran another analysis of our victim after her mother did not recognize her. I will require more in-depth testing, but my initial evaluation of her physiology would suggest Jessica is not human.

"What the hell are you talking about, what is she then?"

I looked behind me seeing her with her eyes closed and her head pressed firmly against my back, still clutching me tightly. I had a flash of fear that I had some strange creature only inches away from my exposed neck.

If I am correct -- and I almost always am -- Jessica would appear to be Atlantean.

Oh crap, things just went from bad to worse.

Chapter Five

Ten minutes later I hurried Jessica inside the motel room right as the sky opened up and the rain started pouring down. Neal and I had decided on this hotel as a viable safe house, should we ever need one. The building stood on the outskirts of the city, right next to a major interstate. There were truck stops nearby and the constant travelers provided a decent amount of cover.

I shut the door and made sure the deadbolt was locked. I peeked outside, crestfallen to think about my bike getting soaking wet. I parked it in a corner of the lot, where no one would drive. My cloaking pin kept my motorcycle invisible and, by extension, myself as well.

Jessica stood in the middle of the room with her arms crossed, hugging herself. She looked so fragile, her dark black hair hung straight and ended slightly past her shoulders. Her eyes were of a light blue that bordered on grey, but she looked at me with apprehension, unsure of what to do next.

"Are you okay? Did they hurt you?" I asked.

She took a second before answering, afraid.

"No, no I'm fine," she said, quietly. "Who are you?" She added.

"I was just going to ask you the same thing."

"I'm just... my name is..." Her eyes went unfocused for a second, confused. "I don't remember. All I remember is waking up in that cage. You called me Jessica, is that my name?" She looked desperate.

"I don't know kid, I don't know," I wanted to go to her and try and make her feel better. I shook off the feeling. What was wrong with me?

"You don't remember anything?" I tried.

"No, I just remember that dirty place. I tried asking those two men..." She trailed off for a second. "Those two men, they're dead, aren't they?"

"Yes," I said, not wanting to lie to her.

After a minute she looked away but continued.

"I tried to talk to them, but they wouldn't say anything. They just sat there," she went over to the bed and sat on the edge.

"Yeah, there was something weird about them alright," I went back to the window, pushing the curtain aside. I was hoping Neal would be back soon, I didn't like the fact he couldn't detect the shooter. That meant we were dealing with something that at least knew about his abilities and was able to counter them. Not good.

"But don't worry. My friend will be back soon and I'll get you some food, you should get some rest, and then we'll see if we can figure out what's going on," I let the curtains go and turned back to see her lying on the bed, already fast asleep.

I went over and pulled the covers off the side she wasn't laying on and flipped them over her. She moaned softly and turned to her side, curling up a bit. I was struck with a sudden memory of my mom lying on the couch on a warm summer day, all the windows open and the fresh breeze flowing through the house. The resemblance between this girl and the memory of my mom was powerful and I had to force myself to pull away from her sleeping face and my memories.

I sat in silence for almost an hour, listening to the girl's soft breathing as she slept.

My lord? Neal's thoughts came to me.

"*We're in room 145, on the backside,*" I sent back, getting up to open the door for him.

A few seconds later I heard him trotting towards the room and I opened the door. His dark form slipped through quietly.

"*What did you find out?*" I asked as he padded over to sit next to the sleeping girl, watching her.

I am sure the shooter was wearing an Atlantean skin suit. That is why I was unable to detect him. That is good and bad.

"Yeah, it means whoever the assassin is, is either Atlantean or has access to Atlantean tech, meaning they know where we are."

It also means they do not necessarily know about me. The skin suits have always been a barrier to me. It is important I am kept a secret until the proper time. The knowledge of my activation has many ramifications, ones we are not ready to deal with, yet.

"It's hard for me to be able to assess information if I am not privy to it," I thought in frustration.

My lord, you know I am unable to access that data. All I know is the parameters of my programming and even I do not have the knowledge to pass down to you.

It was an old argument. One we had been having for as long as Neal had been with me.

Marcus Abshire   LOST SON

"I know, it's a waste of time to keep arguing about something you cannot control. You will tell me when you can. What else did you find out?"

Whoever the shooter was, did not want us talking to the kidnappers or the mother. Further investigation into Caroline Bennett shows she lost a daughter named Jennifer six months ago to an apparent kidnapping that ended in a brutal rape and murder of her daughter.

The police were able to identify the two men killed tonight. One was a janitor for a hospital and the other worked as a toll booth operator. They had no connections to each other, no criminal records. One lived in New Jersey, the other was from Florida. The cops are still unsure as to their motives.

"For some reason, I get the feeling you're not."

If Neal could sound smug this would have been the time for him to.

As the two men were being loaded onto an ambulance for transportation to the morgue, I managed to get a visual on both of their hands. On the dorsal side of their left hands, I found residue of methanol and fluorescent dye 282.

"English Neal. Speak English."

Invisible skin stamps, the kind used by clubs to see who has been accepted.

I didn't like where this was headed.

"And did you happen to be able to discern which club they had both been to in the past few days?"

They were stamped with the shape of an upside-down cross inside a pentagram.

Crap, I knew it.

"Club Red," I said aloud in disgust.

"It had to be damned vampires. I hate vampires."

Club Red is the only place in America vampires visited that was anything close to a normal establishment. Vampires didn't associate in groups around humans very much, except for the occasional hunting party. Club Red provided them a place where humans came together, seemingly for a drink or in the hopes of finding someone to take home only to be the new item on the bloodsuckers buffet.

There are only a hundred or so vampires in America, but they are powerful sons of bitches and they have a very tight-knit coven. Nothing happens in the vampire world without approval by the coven master. The current coven master is a nasty woman by the name of Agatha. She limits the vampires to taking only the blood of willing humans and rarely lets them kill. This practice keeps the humans from snooping; vampires are scared to death of humans finding out about them. Most of the "monsters" are. Humans are weak compared to vampires one on one, but even vampires fear the sheer power humans can wield in large mobs with pitchforks and torches. Club Red is a place where vampires can get their food without anyone being the wiser. And their little hunting club is in New York City.

"That might explain why the kidnappers were so zoned out and why there was such mental confusion with Caroline. Vampires could screw with human's minds."

That was my assessment as well.

"What about our guest, anything new about her?"

She is Atlantean and her neural pathways are fully developed but lack some of the intricate webwork usually found in children her age.

"What do you mean?"

When Atlanteans age, their brain's neural pathways expand in conjunction with learning, experiences, and everyday thinking. Hers is at the complexity of a newborn, yet they are fully developed for her age.

"So, she hasn't had any life experiences to make a more complicated neural framework? Has she been shut off from the rest of the world?"

No, that would still mean she would have twelve years' worth of experiences and memories. It would appear she was born already twelve years old.

"Are you saying she was twelve years old at birth, you mean like she was kept in stasis and her growth was artificially increased?"

That is possible, but I detect a fading effect in her D.N.A. Almost as if the foundational structure is weak. The best thing I can compare this anomaly to is when you make a copy of a copy. Each successive copy is somewhat less solid than the last.

"She's a clone. That's what you're saying, right?"

That would be the most logical assumption based on the evidence presented, my lord.

Great, we had an Atlantean clone girl sleeping in our hotel room, the people we had been hiding from for ten years knew where we are and seem to be playing games with us and I had to go to New York and talk to vampires. Why did I answer my phone this morning?

Marcus Abshire　　　　　LOST SON

I reached over and grabbed my coat from the seat. I put it on then opened the door.

"I'm going to get something to eat, keep an eye on her for me would ya?"

Of course.

"Oh, and don't call me 'lord.'"

Fifteen minutes later I opened the door of the hotel to see Jessica (I didn't know what else to call her, I wasn't calling her 'clone') sitting on the bed petting Neal.

I smiled slightly as she turned to me as I entered. She looked down and saw the bag with the logo of a very famous fast food restaurant on the front and I could almost see her start to drool.

"Hungry?" I asked her, setting the bag on the table.

"Yes, I'm starving," she said and came over and sat across from me.

I opened the bag and took out a burger, handing the rest to her. She tried to take her time but eventually, she began scarfing down the food like a, well, like a teenager.

"Did you figure anything else out?"

Just that she thinks I'm adorable and keeps calling me 'puppy.'

I choked on my food but managed to keep it together.

"So, I know you don't remember your name, but if it's okay with you, can I call you Jessica?" I asked.

She turned thoughtful for a second, rolling the name around in her head for a minute.

"How about 'Buffy?'" She asked hopefully.

I turned to Neal, staring at him.

I believe she got that from the TV. There was a program on about a girl killing vampires.

57

"No, I can't call you Buffy. Any other suggestions?"

"Kim?" She asked, raising her eyebrows.

I didn't ask where she got that name, afraid of the answer, but Kim sounded harmless enough and if picking her name made her feel better, what the hell?

"Ok, Kim, nice to meet you, my name's Jack and that's Neal," I said extending my hand.

She looked at me for a few seconds, unsure of what to do.

"You shake it; it's a greeting," I explained.

"Oh," she said and reached out and took my hand.

"Now, until we can figure out what to do, how would you like to hang out with Neal in a nice house in the woods for a few days?" I asked, wiping my mouth, my belly full of burgers.

"You mean a place with trees and birds and stuff?"

"That's exactly what I mean. I have some business to attend to that will take me all day and I think you should stay safe until we can work out your predicament."

She got quiet, thinking. She looked over to Neal who sat patiently nearby.

"Is he going with me?" She nodded her head in Neal's direction.

"Yup, he will be with you the whole time. Neal is very smart, and he will make sure nothing bad happens to you," I told her.

She looked from Neal to me, nodding her head.

"Yeah, okay that sounds like fun. When do we leave?"

I looked out the window and saw the rain coming down hard, Kim still looked tired and I thought some more sleep would be good for her.

"How about in the morning, we could all use some sleep," I said.

Kim opened another wrapper and chomped down on a burger. She looked over at the bed and I could see weariness cloud her eyes.

"Okay, that sounds good," she answered over a mouthful of food.

The next morning, we made the drive to the house with no surprises. I pulled up to the secluded property and killed the motorcycle's engine. Kim got off and looked around, excited to be here. Our hideout was a single-story house on ten acres of land just outside of Guthrie. The property had tons of trees and Neal and I made sure the house had electricity, water, and a full refrigerator. We took care to keep the place ready in case we had to hole up here for a while.

Neal came up and settled by Kim, content to just be near.

"*Is everything set?*" I asked.

Yes, you have a flight leaving at 1:15 p.m., arriving at JFK at 4:15 p.m. giving you almost two hours until sunset, plenty of time to get to the club.

"*That gives me three hours until my flight leaves, enough time to go by my office.*"

I don't believe I have to tell you, but I will anyway, your dwelling will no doubt be under surveillance. There is no telling what the police have decided to do after investigating the gunshots. I think the trip is ill-advised.

"*Duly noted, but if I'm going into the viper's den, I want to have a little insurance on my side. That insurance is in my apartment. I'm going, and yes, I will be extremely careful."*

As you wish, my lord.

Neal trotted off to follow Kim, acting as a friendly dog, but, keeping her from wandering off. Neal is an awesome babysitter, with the intelligence of a supercomputer and the body of an approachable dog, I was fully confident they would be just fine together. Kim seemed perfectly absorbed in the world around her. I didn't want to interrupt so I went inside, took a quick shower and changed clothes. The ones I had on were starting to get a little ripe.

I walked outside feeling a bit refreshed, and saw Kim throwing a stick across the yard. Neal bounced after it, his tongue flopping happily from his mouth. The girl laughed easily and when Neal brought the stick back, she was on one knee waiting, Neal almost bowled her over and they both fell back, she started rubbing his fur while his tail wagged furiously.

I just stood there for a second in stunned surprise.

"Having fun?" I asked aloud, directing the question more towards Neal.

He seemed startled by my question; apparently, his play had allowed me to sneak up on him. Neal hopped off Kim and they both gathered their composures.

I was just behaving as a normal canine would, he sent to me.

"Yeah, we were just playing catch," she said, smiling at me in an infectious manner.

I found myself smiling back at her.

Marcus Abshire   LOST SON

"I have to get going. Neal, keep an eye on her, I should be back no later than tomorrow morning," I started to walk over towards my bike.

"Wait," Kim came hurrying over to me.

I was again hit with a strong pang of protection for her as if I were failing in my duties if I left her. She stopped in front of me, I could tell she wanted to say something, but she hesitated, looking left and then right before up at me.

"Just, well, just be careful. Okay?" she said shyly.

"Yeah, sure kid," I answered, a little uncomfortable.

I had only met her yesterday and her affection for me seemed a little odd, but traumatic experiences can sometimes drive people to form bonds quickly.

I turned from her and got on my bike, starting the ignition. The engine rumbled in a deep throaty growl. I kicked the transmission into gear and pulled away, the early morning quiet replaced by the sound of my motorcycle as I picked up speed.

Remember, my lord, be careful. Perform to your peak ability and if you must, retreat, Neal said in my head.

"I know, I will and take care of her, and don't call me 'lord.'" I turned onto the paved street and headed back to where I would bet money the local police and a few angry werewolves were waiting for me.

Chapter Six

I stopped two blocks from my office and killed the engine. I made sure my sword fit securely behind my back and that the cloaking pin kept the weapon hidden. I pulled out my pistol from one of my saddlebags and put the gun in a holster under my leather jacket. I zipped it up about halfway, keeping the pistol from swinging freely, but also giving me access to the handle if I needed to draw it.

I started walking, leaving my motorcycle in a small parking lot of a local bar. No one would notice the bike unattended here. I made my way towards the office and stopped at the corner of my block. My office was in the second building from the intersection and I took a quick peek around the corner and saw a few empty cars parked on the street. Luckily, none of them had anyone sitting in them watching my building.

I swung back, hiding again. That was odd. I would have bet money someone would have been there waiting. A gun battle in the middle of downtown wasn't something the cops just ignored. I turned and walked the other way, towards the alley that led to the back of my apartment. I kept to the shadows and crept towards my back door. There wasn't anyone waiting there either. That didn't mean someone wasn't watching -- just that they weren't out in the open. I'm sure once I went inside, I would learn very quickly if my place was under surveillance.

Marcus Abshire   LOST SON

I stepped up to my door and unlocked the deadbolt when I heard the soft sound of an impact behind me. I turned around to see two men, both badly in need of a shave, narrow their eyes at me as they rose from a crouch, having jumped from the building they had been hiding on top of.

"You have to be pretty damn stupid to show your face around here again," the one on the left said.

"It's my home. Where else am I supposed to go, the Y.M.C.A.?" I said, backing up until I bumped against the door.

"We are going to kill you now," he said.

"Why doesn't your boss come get me himself? You two seem like a couple of goons. Isn't he tired of me killing his pack?" I asked, watching, waiting for one of them to make a move.

"You are beneath him. He needs not dirty his hands with your ilk," he growled.

"Yeah, he sure was beneath me when I knocked him out and almost cut off his head," I taunted, hoping one of them would lose their cool and come at me recklessly.

As I had wanted, the quiet one snarled and rushed me, his arm up, sharp claws at the ready. His buddy swore and reached into his jacket for a weapon.

If they would have just shot me, they would have had a better chance. However, the quiet one's wild rush gave me the edge I needed. He came in and tried to take my face off with his claws. He was far stronger than a human and would have been able to block any defense a person could muster, even if they *were* fast enough to get an arm up to stop him. I wasn't human, though, and I saw his clumsy attack and easily brought my forearm up and stopped his descending hand cold. His eyes widened for a second and I used the distraction to punch him right in the sternum, feeling his bones break with a satisfying crunch.

He let out a moan of pain and went sailing backward from the power of my blow, right into his buddy who was waiting for an opening to shoot me in the face. They both went down in a tumble of arms and legs when I reached back and drew my sword, the metal gleamed with a blue hue as I took a step towards my attackers.

The guy with the gun recovered faster than I anticipated and fired six shots in a few seconds. The sounds of the pistol were muffled by a large silencer, but the power of the slugs that hit me sure as hell weren't. Five of them slammed into my chest and stomach and the sixth one grazed my head, leaving a stinging pain in its wake. The gunfire sent me reeling backward and I felt like someone had just beat on me with a sledgehammer, but I knew my suit had protected me from the worst. I grunted from the pain and put the discomfort aside. I started for them again, wondering how I was going to end this without killing them. That would create far bigger problems for me when the answer presented itself.

Both men had managed to untangle themselves and stand when a sticky blob about the size of a baseball hit each of them in the chest. The spongy blob immediately grew and began to spread over their bodies, quickly covering them from neck to toe in white foam that prevented them from moving. They looked like they had been hit with the world's biggest spitballs -- ones that had hardened.

Marcus Abshire   LOST SON

I turned to the left, looking down the alley. I saw a woman standing forty feet away with an odd-looking pistol in her hand. She had blonde hair, green eyes, and a body that could have put any supermodel to shame. Her face was hard to make out, but what I did see showed exotic beauty and soft skin.

"You only have two minutes until they are free. You'd better hurry," she said. Her voice had a musical quality, her accent sounded odd, but reminded me of how my mother spoke.

She whipped around and hurried away from us, turning right and ducking behind a building. I was torn, I wanted to go after her, find out who she was and why she had helped me, but if what she said was right, I only had a short window to get what I needed. After a quick mental debate, I opened the door to my office and hurried upstairs. I went into my bedroom and dug through my underwear drawer for what I was looking for.

A gold coin rested under all my briefs. The metal looked old -- very old. On the face was engraved a side view of Julius Caesar wearing a laurel leaf crown. The image was hard to make out, the long years had worn the features away. I snatched the coin up and put it in my pocket, then turned and hurried back down and outside. The werewolves were both still unmoving statues, but they looked like they were slowly beginning to break free. The hardened foam had small cracks along the surface that were slowly growing from their struggles.

"See ya later, fellas. Let your boss know you came *this* close," I held my hand up and put my index finger and thumb out, with a small space in between them.

Marcus Abshire   LOST SON

I turned and hauled ass out of there, unsure of how long I had left. I reached my bike and soon was screaming down the street and towards the airport.

A little while later I rode past the departure and drop off area, pulling into the parking lot. I found a spot far away from everyone else and killed the engine. I had a decision to make. My cloaking pin could hide my weapons from the airport security, but only one, either my sword or my pistol -- not both. Making up my mind, I took my pistol and hit a small button on the side of my bike. A hidden compartment opened, and I slipped the gun inside, pushing the door closed. Having a supercomputer, magically enhanced guardian came in handy. He taught me all kinds of cool things -- like how to build a secret hidey-hole for my gun that kept the firearm hidden from even the most sensitive police dog's nose.

I made sure my sword was hidden from sight and started to walk towards the airport only to feel the breeze against my chest. I looked down and almost slapped myself in the forehead. I saw five bullet holes in my shirt. I zipped my jacket up and hoped no one would notice. Walking through the departure area I got a few odd looks and remembered one round had grazed me. I hurried to the bathroom, avoiding any security. I'm sure they would love to ask me why I had dried blood on my head and a bunch of holes in my shirt. After making sure I was blood-free, I went to the automatic ticket counter and punched in my reservation information. A few seconds later, a boarding pass came out of the neat little dispenser and I walked off to get ready for the long march through airport security.

An hour later I escaped from the rigorous security screening unscathed and sat down near my boarding area to wait. Eventually, I heard my boarding number over the intercom, and I found my way onto the plane and sat down in my seat.

Thankfully the plane was on schedule and three hours later we landed at JFK airport. The atmosphere upon disembarking was far different in New York than Oklahoma City. Here, a fevered rush seemed to permeate everyone. They all scuttled around in a hurry and had no time for anyone or anything that hampered them.

I made my way outside and hailed a cab, after getting in I gave him an address. The driver had dark skin and eyes as he looked at me from under bushy eyebrows.

"Mister, are you sure you want to go to that area, *at night*?" he asked in heavily accented English.

"If it will make you feel better, you can drop me off a few blocks away and I'll still pay you for the full trip," I said.

He looked at me for a few seconds then shrugged his shoulders. "It's your funeral," he muttered as he flipped the meter on and pulled away from the airport.

There isn't one borough necessarily better or worse than any other. Nowadays each one has good areas and bad areas. Brooklyn is no different, but if asked where in Brooklyn you *wouldn't* want to be out at night, it would have to be East New York -- specifically the industrial area: exactly where I was heading.

Marcus Abshire   LOST SON

We drove in silence for a while and sure enough, a few blocks from my destination, we pulled over.

"That will be ten-fifty," he said.

I reached over and handed him a twenty.

"Thanks, keep the change," I said.

"You're welcome. Be careful," he quickly drove away, leaving me alone.

I started walking, making my way towards Club Red. The days were starting to warm up, but the nights still got pretty chilly. My skinsuit and my Atlantean physiology made me very tolerant of the cold weather, but other people were not so lucky. I didn't see many others walking around, but those I did see were bundled up against the dropping temperatures. I saw more than one flaming steel drum with homeless people standing around the dancing fire, trying to keep warm.

A few blocks south of where the cab dropped me off, I came to the area that bordered the industrial park. Soon, I would leave the ghettos and housing developments for warehouses and manufacturing buildings. Right on the edge of the zone that separated the two sat a small three-story building that looked abandoned. The dilapidated windows were all blacked out, but none of them were broken. The meager grass and bushes that dotted the landscape surrounding the property were growing wild and unkempt.

A single red-light bulb hung above a stairwell that led to an entrance below street level. The approach looked eerily like an entrance to a tomb. The whole area felt empty like an old ghost town where the only inhabitants were the dried-up tumbleweeds, rolling along wherever the wind took them. Everyone seemed to steer clear of the place. Even the local feral cats were afraid to come near.

I leaned up against a building across the street from the entrance, waiting. I tried to blend in with my surroundings and go unnoticed. Eventually, the sky darkened, the sun became just a fading memory, the light a purple haze to the west while the stars tried to poke through the black curtain of space.

The red bulb that hung above the stairwell abruptly turned on and I watched three people, each one different in age, race, and (according to the clothes they wore) social status. They walked down and seemingly disappeared.

I reached into my pocket and rubbed the coin before I pushed myself from the wall and went across the street. As I looked down the stairwell, I saw a large man standing at the bottom, waiting patiently. His pale skin and statue-like stillness pointed him out as a vampire. He wore black sunglasses and a nice suit. His athletic frame stretched the fabric around his chest and shoulders.

I went down the steps and stood about five feet from the vampire bouncer.

"Invitation?" he asked. His voice was like a sweet lie, it had a softness to it that masked a gravelly dryness.

"I don't have an invitation. I'm here to see Agatha," I said. I tensed in preparation for the reaction I knew saying her name would entice.

Vampires are stronger than werewolves, faster than werewolves, and had a few neat tricks werewolves didn't. They had some pretty devastating weaknesses, too.

Marcus Abshire   LOST SON

Crosses and silver do nothing, but sunlight and garlic can kill them and kick their ass -- in that order.

When he came for me, I was ready. I knew he would be fast, but his speed still surprised me. I took Neal's advice seriously and made sure I was quicker. While we talked, I reached in the pocket not housing the coin and grabbed the handful of garlic powder I had picked up at the airport. He moved with the quickness of a cobra, but I was his mongoose.

His hand flashed up, going straight for my throat, but I side-stepped and reached out with my garlic hand, grabbed his wrist, and used his own momentum to slam his face into the brick stairwell behind me. The instant my hand touched his wrist I saw pain in his face, far more pain than hitting a wall gave him.

I pinned him there with my own strength and spoke into his ear.

"I'm only going to say this one more time. I'm here to see Agatha. She owes me a debt. I carry a coin with me that ensures an audience and safe passage. If you come at me again you will be violating coven law and Agatha's decree," I held on for another second before pushing away from him.

He turned on me instantly and for a second I thought he was going to attack again but controlled himself. His glasses had broken during the scuffle and his eyes flashed bright silver, before they dimmed to their normal spooky shade.

"Show me the coin or you will die where you stand," he ground out.

Marcus Abshire   LOST SON

Vampires were sticklers for laws and decrees. Their strict adherence to rigid protocol was something I liked about them; at least I knew they were consistent.

I reached into my pocket and held out the golden coin, letting him see the shiny metal. He narrowed his eyes and went very still for a few seconds before refocusing on me.

"Lady Agatha gives you permission to enter; she waits for you in the back," he said, stepping aside while still trying to kill me with his glare.

Atlanteans were not immune to a vampire's gaze, but we did have a tolerance to their haunting power. It would take one with far more mental strength than this bouncer to get inside my skull. Unfortunately, I was walking straight towards one who could.

I entered Club Red and looked around. What I saw caught me completely off-guard. The club wasn't the sleazy dark filled cave I remembered. If anything, the room reminded me of an Irish pub. The bar was made of what looked like a tree that had been cut in half and then stained and glazed. The stools were also of a natural wood design; almost lodge-like but still holding an Old-World look that made me think of the movies about the "One Ring to Rule Them All..." The three individuals who came in before me sat at the bar and had drinks in front of them; they were talking affably with the bartender who, despite her pale skin and silver eyes, seemed warm enough.

The last time I was here *was* years ago and Agatha had just taken over as coven leader. I had to say, looking around, I approved of the new décor. I wasn't fooled; I knew the purpose of this place. The club is where vampires lure humans to feed -- a process that enslaves the human and leaves them forever linked. The practice is better than outright killing humans but getting them addicted to being fed upon was akin to a drug dealer who makes addicts wherever he goes.

Vampires needed fresh, hot blood. The crap where they drink cold bags of human blood from the Red Cross is just that: crap. This was kind of a compromise, no one went missing and they got the blood they needed. I still didn't like the situation, but you have to learn to pick your battles, like Neal always said.

Off to the side of the bar was a doorway that led into a hall. Waiting next to the door stood a young man with black hair and the same silver eyes as the other vampires. He nodded to me and motioned for me to follow him. I was comforted by the weight of my sword as I followed my escort down a very dark and very narrow hallway. He stopped in front of a solid steel door and stepped aside.

"The Lady Agatha will see you," he said, opening the heavy door with one hand.

I walked into the room and looked around, at first thinking I had entered some strange alternate dimension. The bar occupied about one-tenth of the building's space; the rest belonged to Agatha. The ceiling stretched up about thirty feet, ending in a large array of lights that illuminated the vast space before me. There were plush couches, chairs, and lounging areas everywhere -- not to mention vampires. There must have been thirty vampires spread out among all the comfortable furniture. Easy, light music flowed from speakers I couldn't see, and the atmosphere reeked of relaxed aggression, like a pride of lions, lying around before going off to hunt.

In the back of the space, furthest from the door, sat Agatha. Her chair looked like a throne, but the frame was covered in lush padding and felt. Her seat of power must have been the most comfortable throne ever made. I took a deep breath realizing I had to walk past thirty hungry vampires who all had their eyes on me. I felt like a steak walking through an all-you-can-eat buffet after church lets out.

I kept my eyes only on her, not letting any of the others get the impression I was challenging them or to giving them the opportunity to paralyze me with their gaze. One on one I could take almost any vampire but in here I was sorely, badly outnumbered. I hoped the little piece of metal I carried would keep me safe.

I got to within ten feet of her and stopped.

Agatha's beauty was breathtaking to behold, but that didn't surprise me. I don't think I have ever seen an ugly vampire. Her silver eyes roamed over me, taking in my appearance as she smiled slowly. She was as pale as the rest of her kind, but her hair shone with a red sheen that seemed to glow. When she spoke, her Irish accent filled her words with a musical cadence.

"I like what you've done with the place," I said.

"Thank ye. The old motif was very dreary. The place now reminds me of the old country," she said.

A sound drew my attention and I turned around, seeing that one of the patrons was being led into the room -- a beautiful pale girl on either arm.

"Only three tonight, slim pickings," I kept still, not wanting to set anyone off.

"The night 'tis young, we never seem to have a problem filling our needs," she said. Agatha oozed raw sexuality like it was a death ray she had aimed and ready to fire.

She narrowed her eyes at me, and everything seemed to dwindle down to a single point. The only thing I could see or focus on was Agatha. Her silken pale skin drew me to her, and her red full lips beckoned me to come to her and see how sweet they were.

I focused my mind, realizing what she was trying to do. I used the techniques Neal taught me and boxed myself in, away from her power. I had a hard time concentrating with all the distractions, but I couldn't let them phase me. After all, my life was on the line.

"I came here under your assurance I would have an audience. It would not be very hospitable of you to try and seduce me before you have met your obligations," I said, keeping my mind shut.

She stared at me for a few seconds, and then let out a hearty laugh, the "I want to take you right here, right now" vibe vanished, but I didn't let down my mental defenses.

"Ye are an enigma, aren't ye?" she squealed.

"First ye beat my bouncer like he was a toy, then ye come in here smelling *almost* human, and then ye shrug me off like t'was nothing. Very interesting," she purred. "Alright, ye seem unwilling to play, so it must be business then. Ye have in yer possession a coin I am told? Let me see it, then we can continue," her demeanor had shifted to one of cool indifference. This was her professional side, then.

I opened my hand and held out the coin. She motioned to one of the vampires nearby and another gorgeous woman came over. She had blonde hair and silver eyes and was wearing a dress that just barely covered her nitty-gritty's. She reached out and took the coin. I felt her fingers on my palm and they were ice cold.

She took the coin to Agatha and handed the small metal piece to her. Agatha brought the coin up, staring at me the whole time and once the coin was eye level, she turned her gaze from me. She inspected the coin for a moment before tossing the relic back.

"Alright, Jack isn't it? What do ye wish to discuss?"

Wow, I had only been here once, years ago, looking for a missing girl. The place had been under different management back then and one had a much easier time getting in, but the lack of security led to more chaos which was something Agatha had put a stop to. The fact that she knew my name was impressive. She wanted me to *know* she knew.

"I'm here to discuss two men who were killed after kidnapping a child."

"What does that have to do with me?" she asked.

"They were acting under the control of a vampire," I started, but she cut me off.

"Impossible. No one would do such a thing without my express permission," she said, her eyes narrowing.

"Well, apparently *someone* did, and I hoped you could tell me why a vampire would use two humans to kidnap a little girl," I said, keeping my mind shut.

I noticed there were more humans on the plush couches, being seduced.

"I should kill ye now for even insinuating such a thing!" she hissed, leaning forward in her chair.

"I am not lying. Check for yourself. Search my mind. If I am wrong you can always just kill me," I said. I was more surprised she knew nothing about my claims than her reaction. She could always be lying, but I felt she wasn't. She prided herself on control of her coven and even a lie about rogue vampires could threaten that.

She sat back angrily, glaring at me, trying to peel my brain open for her to sift through. I brought the memories of what I witnessed to mind, letting them slip through my mental barriers, giving her a view of what I saw. I made sure not to put anything about Neal in them. I wanted to keep his unique abilities a secret.

After a moment she sat back in her throne, pensive. Obviously, what she saw made her realize I wasn't lying. At least I believed what I said; that didn't necessarily mean it was true.

She leaned back in her throne, seeming to relax even more -- if that was possible.

"Ye know I haven't quite figured ye out, Jack. Ye have the shape of a human, the attitude and mannerisms of a human, but yer blood stinks of the dark, deep fathoms. Ye run colder than humans and yer mind is far more powerful and disciplined than humans." I wasn't expecting a litany of my attributes; I never really knew how I was perceived by others of the non-human persuasion. Hell, I never cared.

"Not to mention I love watching reruns of *I Love Lucy*," I added, just because.

Her eyes narrowed to dangerous levels; the silver became small slits of threat.

"I could use a man, or whatever ye are, of yer talents. 'Tis hard to find good, reliable help during the daylight hours. I am a woman of immense resources and power; I can make working for me a very *enjoyable* and lucrative experience." I had no doubt about what she meant by enjoyable with all the innuendo she heaped on the word.

"As fun as the idea sounds to spend my time around a bunch of vampires, I have to regretfully decline. I would rather gouge my own eyes out than work for you," I said, wondering how fast I could draw my sword.

She didn't move -- not one muscle, which I found very freaky. She turned into one solid pale marble statue her immobility was so absolute. Then a slow smile spread across her sensuous lips and she visibly relaxed.

"Remember 'twas ye who came to me fer help," she said softly, almost whispering.

"Ye have shown me enough to make me realize the situation requires further inquiry. Our audience is concluded, ye have safe passage out of my club." Then she stood up and walked off, leaving me alone with a bunch of vampires and humans, some of whom were already being fed upon.

I turned around and reached my hand into my pocket, gathering what garlic powder was still there. It didn't feel like much. I wasn't expecting trouble, but you can't ever be too sure. Besides, I knew Neal would have told me to be prepared, just in case.

I walked back through the vampire's buffet room and opened the door leading to the bar. I noticed the place seemed to be full. People from every walk of life were drinking and talking at the bar like they were all good friends. Here and there I saw a pale figure slipping through the crowd, hunting.

I slipped outside and saw Bouncer Boy giving two middle-aged women stamps on the back of their hands. They each had a glazed look in their eyes, like they were paying attention to a conversation only they could hear.

I went up the steps and hurried away from the club, walking at a brisk pace, hoping to get somewhere I could hail a cab before I ran into any trouble.

As I walked, I went over what I knew so far. Agatha appeared unaware of any vampire's putting the mental whammy on the two kidnappers. Vampires were very loyal creatures; there had to be some reason for one or more of them to commit an act that could earn them an instant death sentence -- a punishment that kept most of them in line. Being immortal wasn't something they gave up lightly.

I heard motion behind me, a scuffling as someone approached. I turned to find three of the homeless guys I saw earlier come at me from the shadow of a nearby building.

"Hey, mister, what's the hurry?" one of them said. The strong smell of cheap whiskey stung my nose.

"Look, fellas, I've got somewhere to be. I don't want any trouble," I said, hoping they were just trying to scare me.

"Yeah, so do we. We've got a job interview tomorrow. We were hoping you had some money to lend us, you know, so we can get a nice suit?" one of them said to snide laughter.

"Tell you what, I've got two hundred bucks on me," I said, reaching into my jacket and pulling out the money. "You guys take it, go get some food, maybe a nice place to stay the night." I held the cash out for them.

The guy in the middle, who was wearing a dirty and stained camouflage jacket, took a few steps towards me, thinking I was being tricky. He reached out and took the money before jamming the bills into his pants' pocket.

"A guy just walking around with money like that probably has other things that are worth something. Why don't you give us your jacket and boots, too, so we can make sure you ain't hiding nothing," one of the others said, he pulled a knife from his back and held the blade low, showing me he had a weapon.

Crap, I didn't want to hurt these guys; there was no telling what type of circumstances led to their situations. I was just about to try to reason with them some more, hoping I could still salvage the situation when I felt the hairs on the back of my neck tingle and a ghost of Neal's familiar voice rang in my head, "You must listen to your body. It has the ability to sense things the mind cannot."

I dropped and rolled to my left as something hard whizzed past where my head would have been. I popped up in a defensive crouch, pulling my sword free in a fluid motion. The blue steel reflected the soft light of the moon.

"What the fuck?" one of my would-be thieves uttered at the appearance of Bouncer Boy.

Marcus Abshire LOST SON

He stood apart from us, right where I had been a second ago. In his hands, he held the remnants of a parking meter, or at least the part he had ripped from the concrete. I guess that's what he planned on bashing my head in with.

"Leave us, if you wish to see the next sunrise," he snarled at the homeless guys.

His eyes flashed bright silver and he raised his lip, so his long fangs were visible in the dim night. All three turned and ran, not interested in finding out what kind of crazy they had just stepped into.

I wished I could do the same. I didn't really want to fight but I knew I couldn't outrun him and, to be honest, running from a fight just wasn't my style -- much to Neal's chagrin.

"Look, I know I'm an attractive guy but if you really want to go out with me, you should just ask me for my phone number like everyone else," I taunted him, hoping he would get mad and make a mistake.

Instead, he just smiled at me, his mouth split his face in half and his eyes glowed with a silvery sheen.

"I had planned on just breaking a few of your bones and being done with you but now I think I might partake of you your blood. That way you will belong to me. Then I will break both of your legs, and when they have healed, I will call to you again and you will come and then I'll re-break your legs. I will do this over and over until you are an old man, crippled with pain, begging for death. Then I will give you just a taste of my blood, to keep you alive for another twenty years so I can haunt you forever," he snarled in ecstasy.

"Man, that kind of commitment sounds like work. I don't know if you're up to the task. I mean you *are* just a bouncer for God's sake," I said, slowly turning so my back was to the open air. I didn't want the building behind me, limiting my ability to move.

That's when he lost his cool. His expression changed to one of fury, his mouth split and grew, his razor-sharp teeth gleamed in the night. His eyes blazed with silver fire and he flew at me faster than the eye could track. I didn't have to be faster than the speed of light, though. Just faster than him.

I started moving before he launched at me. He brought the concrete encrusted meter up, intending on bashing my skull in. I moved to his left, making him adjust his angle of attack and diffusing some of his power. I met the metal of his weapon with my blue steel and sliced his makeshift bludgeon in half. The end Bouncer Boy wasn't holding clattered on the ground.

Having his weapon cleaved in half stunned him for a second but that was all I needed. I dropped down with one knee bent and the other off to the side, I swiped low across his legs and heard a scream of pain as his body and upper thighs slid off his now-amputated lower legs.

He fell with a wet slap and roared in pain. I stood up and took a few steps back, not sure if the injury would be enough to keep him out of the fight. Turns out, having your legs chopped off was enough to take the piss and vinegar out of any man, even a vampire. He thrashed on the ground in agony as his oddly pale blood ran from his wounds.

"You wanted to break my legs. I decided to chop yours off. Not sure who got the better end of this deal. I'll let you figure it out," I said then turned and hurried away.

His screams of pain faded as I increased the distance between us and eventually stopped. Whether it was because I was too far away to hear him, or help had arrived I didn't know or care. No other bloodsuckers came at me that night, so I was pretty sure Bouncer Boy had come after me on his own and now had Lady Agatha to deal with. I did not envy him.

Chapter Seven

I made the trip back to Oklahoma without encountering any problems -- unless the turbulence we flew through over Kentucky counted. All in all, the flight went smoothly. I reached my motorcycle at eleven-twenty -- the parking lot light's amber glare cut through the night's darkness. I swung my leg over the seat when I saw a person in a black Civic sink down low in their seat. Alarm bells went ringing in my head and I started the bike like I hadn't noticed anything.

I pulled away from the airport and soon saw the Civic following me. Whoever was tailing me wasn't very good at it. They tried to keep far enough away to not be noticed but after a few unplanned turns and speeding up and slowing down their persistence was at the least refreshing. I led them towards Guthrie, hoping to get within thinking distance of Neal. We worked out long ago our range is about ten miles but the longer we are together the greater our range becomes.

As I approached a stoplight, I slowed down in anticipation of it turning red, then hit the throttle and pulled away. A quarter-mile down the street I pulled off the road and swung beside a small auto repair shop. Sure enough, the Civic came hurtling past, intent on finding me.

I pulled out and started following them instead. In a few minutes, I was able to make out their license plate without being spotted and hoped I was close enough to get Neal's attention.

"*Can you hear me?*" I sent out.

Yes, barely. You must be far from us.

"Yeah, I'm on the outskirts of town. I've got a license plate for you. Can you see if you can find out who the car belongs to?"

Of course, my lord.

"It's an Oklahoma plate, CFK345F." I knew Neal was accessing the DMV records and would have the information in a few seconds.

That plate is registered to Dorothy Vandergast of Tulsa. She is eighty-three and is a registered Republican, no moving violations since her license has been revoked due to being diagnosed as legally blind two years ago.

"So, what is an eighty-three-year-old blind woman who hasn't driven in two years doing following me around Oklahoma?" I mused.

I do not have sufficient information to make that determination, Neal answered.

"*It was a rhetorical question.*"

Of course, Neal intoned.

"*I'm going to keep an eye on our friend, see where it takes me. How are things going with Kim?*" I kept a safe distance from the Civic, watching as the driver tried to find out where I went.

All is well. You will have to go to the store and get more groceries soon. She has a voracious appetite.

At least someone had the chance to eat.

"*Okay, I'll keep in touch.*"

Yes, my lord.

It took a while but eventually whoever was driving realized they had lost me. They circled around town for almost an hour, hoping I would pop up and ended up stopping in a small park under an old oak tree. I parked my motorcycle behind a small public bathroom and made sure the bike was unseen. Quietly sneaking closer took me a few minutes but I was soon crouched behind my pursuer, listening to what sounded like someone sobbing. Were they crying?

I stood up and went to the driver's side door, rapping the window with my knuckle.

"Why are you following me?" I asked, unsure of what kind of reaction I'd get.

I honestly have to say I wasn't prepared for what happened next.

She tried to jump through the roof, burped, snorted, and yelled all at the same time. Her reaction was something to see. I realized she was the same woman who helped me in the alley earlier. She quickly got her composure and looked up at me with a mixture of horror and surprise.

"Please, I'm sorry," she gasped.

I saw her start to reach for the keys, then stop and look around like a trapped animal. I could feel her panic from where I stood.

"Calm down, I'm not going to hurt you and running isn't going to help. How about you get out of the car and we have a nice chat?" I tried to keep my voice soothing.

Either she was the world's best actress, or she was far out of her depth. The whole sneaking around and spying on someone thing was not her strong point. I could see her

Marcus Abshire — LOST SON

furiously trying to decide if I was going to kill her. It seemed like odd behavior for someone who had come to my aid.

"C'mon, I know you were at my place earlier. You helped me. I owe you one. Maybe I can help?" I said.

She looked at me again, the wild animal panic slowly left her face and she nodded.

"Alright, alright, just give me a minute."

I stepped back and went over to a picnic table nearby, sitting on the table with my feet on the seat. She took out a napkin and wiped her eyes, then took a few seconds to get her composure. She stepped out of the car and walked over towards me.

She walked with a lightness of foot that gave me the impression she could easily leap fifty feet off the ground as if she were walking in a low gravity atmosphere. Her tall frame was as lovely as I remembered and as she came closer, I saw her green eyes were set in a face made of smooth lines and soft skin. If it wasn't for a small scar above her left eyebrow, she would have been flawless.

She sat down next to me, afraid to turn and look at me.

"So, you care to tell me why you shot those guys at my place and then followed me?" I said, not looking at her. I didn't know how much she knew, but I wasn't going to be the one to have to explain werewolves to her. Hell, I didn't really know how to anyway.

I heard her sigh deeply; her shoulders slumped forward in defeat.

"I was trying to find someone who is important to me," she said quietly.

Marcus Abshire   LOST SON

"You know, finding missing loved ones is pretty much how I make a living. I have some experience with that situation," I offered, hoping she would keep talking. "Why don't we start with your name, then you can tell me more about who you're looking for," I added.

She turned to me and studied my face; her intense green eyes were powerful. I forced myself to turn away.

"My name is Arendiol. My charge was taken. She is very naïve and unknowing. I was told you could lead me to her," she said, staring off into the night.

"Who told you?" She went silent, her mouth became a hard line, she didn't want to tell me. "Look, let's not play games; put all our cards on the table. I know where you come from -- from the same place that made that gun you used earlier and I bet if I stabbed you, your skin suit would protect you. You had to work at not breaking stuff when you first came on land and you're afraid everyone can tell you're different. You think they all are staring at you, that they'll call the authorities, and have you taken away. Am I right?" She sat staring at me in shock.

"So, it's true then -- you *are* an Atlantean?" she asked.

"You know I've spent the last ten years of my life trying very hard to avoid others but in less than twenty-four hours I have run into three Atlanteans and one of them killed three people in about five seconds." I turned to face her. "You stepped in and helped me when I needed it; I think that was very hard for you." She turned away, breaking eye contact.

"Yes, I'm Atlantean. So are you, so is the girl you're looking for -- and I just happen to know where she is. Stop hiding things and tell me who you are, who she is, and what you're doing here, and I *might* let you see her." she looked at me with fear and a small amount of hope.

She nodded slightly, "Alright, I'm a scientist. I have worked for the last fifteen years keeping Atlantis working smoothly. That is, up until two years ago when I was reassigned to researching old Atlantean archives." She looked at me curiously. "How much do you know about Atlantis's history?" Her green eyes shone in the moonlight.

"I know the basics. Our ancestors screwed around with technology they didn't understand and, in their ignorance, caused a massive explosion that sent the whole thing into the ocean, where, it is said, magic was used to save our world. The survivors swore off advancing technology in order to keep something like that from happening again. They then rearranged society into three different class systems, the hunters/warriors, those who would go out into the ocean and bring home meat and defend our world if needed. The scientists/sorcerers tended to the old technology by keeping our cities operating and adapting it to the bottom of the ocean while the farmers/workers grew plants and kept the everyday infrastructure in working order," I finished.

"Do you know how the order was kept? Living under thousands of feet of water made insurrections very dangerous for everyone," she sounded like a teacher.

"No. I mean I never really thought about it. My education on Atlantis is not extensive. I know our language and technology, who to look out for, and what our unique physiology allows us to do, but the inner political workings aren't something I have learned," I answered.

She sat quietly for a minute, thinking about how to begin.

"After the Fall, everyone was scared. They all rallied behind the king and queen, unifying to survive. Certain rules were set up and eventually, it was decided for everyone to prosper the future generations had to be controlled. Not that they were to be mindless robots, but they were to be molded, guided into their positions. Children birthed naturally were too unstable; they were like all children -- erratic, frivolous, and didn't take to being molded. For us to survive, it was decided that the future generations would be clones. Clones were controllable and followed the program." She took a deep breath before continuing.

"That's why Kim is a clone? I suppose you are as well?" I asked.

"Kim?" she asked as a small smile spread over her lips.

"Yeah, she picked it," I said defensively. Why was I defensive?

"Yes, Kim is a clone, as am I, but there's more," I motioned for her to continue.

"The plan was to keep everything under control, but to work on finding a way to get back to land, to resurface, then to allow normal births again, to let the bloodlines become strong. But over time, that goal was forgotten, the past was forgotten, and Atlantis fell into acceptance. The clones did their jobs -- only too well. They had no desire to leave; they did as they were molded, guided to do. They had no ambition."

"For thousands of years, this went on -- until things started to go wrong." Again, she stopped, looking over at me.

"I'm sorry, but I haven't talked this much in a long time. I need some water. I have some in the car," she said, motioning towards the Civic.

"Yeah, sure," I was a little shocked at what she had said.

Clones? Is that what Neal couldn't tell me? Why? The revelation didn't seem like something that would be devastating to me. There had to be more to it than that. Arendiol came walking back; I couldn't help but notice the way her hips gently swayed. I caught her smiling slightly at my attention. I averted my gaze.

"Water?" She asked, holding a plastic bottle out for me.

"Thanks." The water felt refreshing.

"So, the clones were A-Okay. Why do I have a feeling there's about to be a big 'but?'" The side of her mouth raised in a smirk.

"Yes, the clones were running things smoothly, *but* they were fading. They were starting to crack. Their DNA was starting to become thin. Docile people became mad -- furious over things that normally would not bother them. Others had bouts of sadness that dragged them down. Emotions swelled and control began to slip. Diseases came back; diseases we had thought to have eradicated began plaguing us again. If something didn't change, we would soon be extinct."

"Sounds like the clones were acting like people," I muttered.

"Perhaps, but it has led to dangerous times," she answered.

"People *are* dangerous, that's part of life."

"Well, everyone started looking for a solution, and one presented itself," she said.

"Let me guess, someone said they could fix all the problems, they could make everything normal if they just had more power?" I may not have been up to date on Atlantean history, but I *was* a student of human history. "Atlantean Warlord Karakatos?" I added.

She turned to me stunned, "How did you know?"

"I've had a few run-ins with his "peace" officers." Karakatos's men had killed my mom and tried to kill me. If not for Neal's appearance, they would have succeeded.

Five years later, they came for me again, only this time they were trying to capture me. At least that's what Neal said, and I believed him. That's when he told me who was after me and I realized his lessons were important. I became determined to learn to protect myself.

"Yes, the Warlord, as he calls himself, gathered power, began running things his way. He became obsessed with the past, with the ancient archives, the forgotten magic, and technology. Under his orders, I searched for information on the old science. I found Kim while working for him and I began to grow fond of her. She was in a growth chamber and her body aged to that of a twelve-year-old. An overwhelming need to free her filled me. I don't know what came over me, but I had to get her away from Atlantis."

"My research led me to uncover many things; one was a chamber with "lifeboats" in them. There were twenty of them, but only three were still functional. I took Kim and put her in one, sending her to the surface." She took a deep pull of her water.

"At first, I felt relieved, glad she would find freedom. Then I started to be afraid for her. I knew not what I had sent her into. I was desperate, my realization I might have sent an innocent child to her death or worse plagued me and I took off after her." She seemed exhausted as if telling me had been a physically exerting exercise.

"That still doesn't tell me how you knew to come to me," I said, looking at her.

She sighed, "When I surfaced everything was strange. I felt weird. I soon realized I had great strength and speed. I was scared. Before I left, I programmed the lifeboat to lock onto Kim's DNA, hoping the craft would take me to her, or at least close enough to where I could find her. I stayed around the vessel for days; the only thing inside was an old foam gun. Eventually, hunger drove me to find food. The whole time a name kept repeating over the intercom. 'Jack Industries,' it said, over and over."

"So, what, you high-jacked the nearest car and came to find me?" I asked.

"No, finding you took a while but eventually I met Mrs. Vandergast. She took me in. I think she thought I was one of her daughters' friends. She is an old and lonely woman. She fed me and answered most of my questions, glad for the company. I found your address on the internet and waited. I saw you being attacked and knew if you were killed, I'd never see Kim. I hoped saving you might give you a reason to trust me." She looked at me, begging me to believe her.

"Then why follow me? How did you know I was going to be at the airport and how did you know what I looked like to begin with?" She was telling me the truth, but there were too many holes in her story.

"I... I don't know. Maybe I saw your picture online. I just knew you would be at the airport. I don't know how..." she trailed off, her face going blank; her expression reminded me of how Kim's kidnappers acted.

I looked up feeling a slight tingle run down my spine like someone was watching us.

"Well, well, well, looks like we interrupted the love birds' date." I whipped my head up, seeing six large men walking towards us, their feral yellow eyes shining in the darkness. The speaker wore a huge grin, every one of them had the beginnings of a beard, under his smile shone large canines in a mouth that started drooling.

I hopped off the table, drawing my blade and pulling out my pistol in one fluid movement.

"Get behind me. If you get a chance run, remember, you're strong and fast. Use it," I said softly. The six werewolves slowly closed the half-circle.

"*If you get a chance, run*," the one drooling sneered, mocking my voice. He let out a high-pitched laugh that sounded like a hyena. His maniacal glee ended in a long howl; the others joined him.

"Children, there's no need to yell. I'm right here," I said, hoping to get them all to focus on me.

"Yes, you are," Drooler said. Then everything got very chaotic.

Marcus Abshire   LOST SON

All six werewolves rushed me at the same time. There was no, one at a time, nonsense, no martial arts dance. What ensued was nasty and quick.

Drooler reached me first, trying to rip my throat out with his claws. I brought my sword up in a quick slash and cut his hands off. Spinning to my left, I deftly dodged a baseball bat one of them swung at my head. I raised my pistol and tested my theory on what a bullet would do to the side of a werewolf's head. The sound split the night and my ears rang from the blast.

I felt a dull pain as one of them managed to claw my chest, my clothes ripped but my skin suit protected me from his attack. I let out a huff as the impact felt like someone hit me with a crowbar. I drove my sword through the werewolf's stomach and saw the blood-covered blade exit his back. I pulled the weapon out quickly; keeping him off-balance from the pain and in a backhanded swipe took his head off his shoulders.

Three down, three to go. Number four tackled me, and I was able to bring up my forearm to block his ferocious canines. I saw as Arendiol tried to run but was being circled by the other two werewolves. She had a piece of the picnic table in her hands and wielded the wood like a club, the blood running down the side of one of her attackers' heads kept them both wary.

I felt as my ribs were raked by claws. The pressure caused two of them to crack. The pain flared like a red-hot spike down the side of my body, but I ignored the stinging discomfort. I brought my pistol up and shot my attacker three times in the gut. His eyes went completely yellow and the damage I did caused him to lose his mind.

His face started to shift, his mouth began elongating, and his ears moved up and towards the back of his head. Fur started growing all over and I didn't want to wait to see how dangerous he would be after he shifted.

With a grunt of effort, I threw him off me and he landed gracefully on all fours. I leaped up and unloaded the rest of my rounds into him while I ran towards him. The rounds caused him to jerk from each shot, allowing me to get close enough to use my sword. He swiped at my face and I easily blocked his attack, removing his clawed hand at the forearm. He bellowed in pain and tried to barrel me over again. I dropped my empty pistol and landed a devastating uppercut that lifted him off his feet. With two quick slashes, I disemboweled him then watched as he fell to the ground, headless.

I spun towards Arendiol, hurrying over to help her. She lay on the ground with one of the werewolves on top of her; the other was an unmoving form not far from them. His head was caved in, Arendiol's club still stuck in his skull.

I was almost twenty feet away and saw I was going to be too late; the bastard had her pined and was lunging towards her unprotected neck.

Seemingly out of nowhere there was a bright flash and the werewolves' head exploded in a gory mess. His body slumped forward, his momentum carrying him into Arendiol. She gasped in horror and surprise and reflexively kicked the headless body away from her, sending the corpse in a fifty-foot arc.

I was almost to her, silently thanking whoever had killed the werewolf when another flash of light flared and

Arendiol slammed back into the ground from the force of the shot. I spun to see the same shooter from earlier disappear into the night sky.

"No, damn it!" I growled.

I got to Arendiol and saw a large, softball-sized hole in her side. The skinsuit had been punctured and there was blood everywhere. Her breathing came rapidly like she was having an asthma attack.

"You have to relax, I know it hurts, but you have a punctured lung. If you don't stop hyperventilating, you'll suffocate yourself," I said, taking off my shirt and placing the cloth over the wound, trying to stop the bleeding.

I didn't have a lot of options. The gunfire and excitement were bound to bring the cops. I couldn't stay here and be found with all these bodies, not to mention Arendiol. One cursory examination by the paramedics would have her sent to some government base somewhere where they would be very interested in her. She needed time. Her suit would soon reform and hopefully stop the bleeding, but it would take time for her body to heal -- if it even could. The damage had been severe. I still didn't trust her; she was keeping information from me, but I couldn't find out what it was if she died. I quickly made my decision and gently picked her up, carried her to my bike, picking up my pistol on the way.

"Can you hold on?" I asked.

She nodded once, the loss of blood causing her skin to glow in the moonlight. She winced as I get her on my bike but held on tight after I sat down. I took off, hoping Neal might have some idea of how to help her. She was gonna need all the help she could get.

Chapter Eight

We drove towards the house, Arendiol kept her death grip on me. My ribs screamed in protest, but I didn't care, as long as she didn't fall off.

"Neal!" I sent out, hoping we were within range.

I'm here, he answered -- thank God.

"I'm coming in with an Atlantean female. She has severe tissue damage to her left side and a punctured lung."

I do not think it is wise to bring her here.

"No shit, but I don't have any other choice. Do you want the government to get ahold of her? Should I just leave her to die?"

Alerting the United States government of our existence would not be beneficial. Alright, bring her in; I'll have Kim get a room prepared.

"Okay, see you in a few." Wait, did he just say he'll have Kim prepare a room? Since when was Neal able to communicate with anyone other than me? I was about to ask him what he meant when Arendiol moaned and started to slip. I reached back to keep her from falling off.

"You have to hold on, we'll be there in a few minutes, can you make it?" I yelled over the noise of the motorcycle's engine.

"I'm sorry, I.... I can make it," she said in my ear.

I forgot about Neal and Kim, concentrating on keeping Arendiol from falling off. I had to be careful; the last thing I wanted or needed was to have the local authorities taking an interest in us. I drove, praying to any Gods who would listen to keep us safe until we got there.

Someone must have heard me. I stopped in front of the house and caught Arendiol as she started to fall off the back of the motorcycle.

"Easy, just concentrate on breathing. We'll have you inside in a second," I said as I scooped her up and carefully carried her inside.

Neal met us at the door, with a concerned-looking Kim.

"Is she alright?" Kim asked, stepping back.

"She's gonna be fine. Which room?" I asked, hoping to get her focused on something else.

"This one," she hurried over to the second bedroom, one we used for storage.

There was now a mattress on the floor with covers, a pillow and an I.V. hanging from a stand. We always kept the basics on hand. You know beans, rice, water and I.V.'s.

Human's veins were closer to the surface than an Atlantean's; you could see them on a person. This difference in anatomy made giving a human an I.V. easier. Humans also had a different muscle structure that made it necessary for any type of infusion to be given into a vein to make sure the I.V. fluids were circulated, otherwise they would just bunch up in a muscle or be caught by a layer of fascia and could cause major problems. Atlantean physiology is different; our muscles had changed over the thousands of years of living in the depths. The layers that separated our muscles are more porous, our veins and arteries more deeply buried. This allowed me to take the needle and jam the sharp metal into Arendiol's neck muscle without worrying about hitting a vein. I knew her body would get the liquid she needed from the I.V.

Arendiol barely registered the I.V. going in. Her breathing had become erratic and shallow again. Blood still welled from her wound -- her suit hadn't sealed yet. The hole was a few inches smaller. Her suit was slowly sealing, but not fast enough.

"Why isn't her suit closing?" I asked aloud, frustrated.

The suit is linked to her body. The damage is very severe, and her body is using all its strength to try to stop the bleeding and repair her tissue. Stand back. I can help but you must not interfere.

I stood up, looking for Kim. She was in the corner, staring at the scene with scared eyes, one hand covering her mouth. I went to her and hugged her, gently moving her out of the room.

"C'mon, we need to get some water ready," I said, getting her out of the room and doing something other than thinking about what she had seen.

I turned back, as I left and saw Neal standing over her on all fours with his eyes closed, his forehead directly over her wound, almost touching the bloody mess. I saw a steady flow of electricity arcing in the small space between them. Her suit began inching closed. The hole would be sealed in a few seconds. Her clothes were shredded, and her red blood stood out on her white shirt. I looked down and saw my hands were also covered in her blood and I went to the bathroom to wash them off.

Marcus Abshire   LOST SON

After my hands were clean, I changed my own clothes and threw the dirty ones in the washer. I went to the kitchen where Kim was pouring water into cups. She had ten of them filled already, the counters were full of them.

"What are you doing?" I asked, walking up to her.

She didn't answer; she just kept filling her cup. Her mouth was set in a firm line and her eyebrows were narrowed in concentration; she was fighting hard not to lose control. I reached over and grabbed her arm, gently pulling her from the sink. She looked up at me and I saw the dam crack. She rushed me and hugged me tightly, sobbing softly into my shirt.

I didn't know what to do. I was afraid to touch her, but I remembered when my mom would comfort me after a bad dream, petting my hair and telling me everything would be alright. I didn't know if it would, but her touch and closeness always seemed to help.

I reached up tentatively and stroked her hair. Her crying intensified as if I had helped destroy a wall she had erected. Her whole body shook as she cried.

"Shhhh, it's going to be alright. She's going to be fine. Don't worry. Neal's going to make sure she's okay. It's alright; it's alright," I kept saying, trying to make her feel better.

After a while, her sobs slowed and she pulled back, wiping her eyes.

"I don't know what's wrong with me; I don't even know that woman," she said softly, blowing her nose.

"It's okay; I know how hard seeing someone in pain is, even someone you don't know." I'd hoped Kim would know who she was, maybe give me some information on her. Damn.

She still looked miserable; my heart broke to see her in such distress. I reached into my pocket and held a quarter in my hand, not letting her see the coin.

"You wanna see something neat?" I asked.

She looked at me for a second; her eyes were puffy from crying, "Sure," she said, quietly.

"Wait," I said, staring at her ear. She looked self-conscious like something was wrong.

"What is it?" she said, reaching to cover her ear up.

"What is that?" I said, bringing my hand up to her ear and then pulling it back, showing her the coin.

"Oh, there it is. I have been looking for this all day," I said, smiling.

"Where did that... was that in my ear?" she asked, stunned. I saw her face light up in wonder, the amazed expression was far better than the anguish she showed earlier.

"What else do you have in there?" I teased.

She reached up and grabbed her ear, searching for more hidden treasures. It was good to see her attention on something else.

"Now, I have a very important job for you -- if you think you can handle it," I said, turning serious.

Her eyebrows came together in concentration. She nodded once, with grave intensity.

"Good, do you know how to operate the washer and dryer?" I asked.

"Yes," she responded curtly.

"Alright, perfect. There are a lot of dirty clothes that need washing. Can you take charge of getting them clean?"

"I can," her chest puffed out in response to her new duties.

"I'm counting on you. Don't let me down," I held out my hand and she shook once, aggressively.

She turned and went over to the side of the kitchen, where the small utility room housed the washer and dryer. Soon, I heard the water start running as she began washing a load of clothes.

Neal came over towards me, sitting down.

"How is she?" I sent to him.

She is resting. The damage is extensive; she suffered massive tissue injuries, blood loss, and a punctured lung. I was able to help her suit seal which should keep her from losing any more blood. Now her body must do the rest. Hopefully, she can heal herself.

"When can I talk to her?"

That depends on how quickly she can recover. A few days at least.

Damn, I hoped to be able to ask her more questions, to see if she could remember more about the holes in her story. Having to wait a few days for her to come around was going to make things hard. Hell, I wasn't even sure when she *did* come around that she would have the answers I needed. I couldn't stay here the whole time, not with werewolves attacking me every time I turned around.

"I don't think I'm going to be able to stick around for her to wake up. The werewolves have my scent, and until I

can figure out how to keep them from tracking me, me being here only puts everyone in danger," I sent to Neal.

Yes, my lord. That is why I have extended my detection range -- allowing me to detect any werewolf within a five-mile radius. That should give you plenty of warning and allow you to leave before we are in harm's way.

"How the hell did you do that? You didn't grow opposable thumbs while I was gone did you?" I thought.

No, I enlisted Kim's aid. She is quite helpful.

"Am I missing something here?" Neal could only communicate with me through our mind link. How the hell did he teach Kim how to build receivers and place them where needed?

Kim had finished getting a load of clothes going and came back into the kitchen. She saw Neal and smiled, walking over to him. She started petting him and said, "How is she doing, Neal?"

"She should be alright as long as her body heals. She will need watching, and may begin running a fever, but I think she will be okay," he said in a perfectly normal sounding voice.

Neal had spoken out loud. My mouth dropped open -- I almost forgot how to close it. I just stared at him in absolute stunned silence.

"What the hell? You can talk!" I said to Neal, completely in awe.

"Of course I can. You have always needed me to fill the role of a dog. With our mind link, I never needed to speak and there was never a situation that required me to. I assessed the nature of how the werewolves keep tracking you and needed to increase my sensor's range. I am unable to build the devices myself and knew Kim can. Her situation makes it viable for me to communicate with her. She has no preconceived idea of how a dog should act and is in no way traumatized by my vocalization, nor is there any threat of her bringing attention to me, seeing as how she has no connection with this society," he finished, looking at me with a slight gleam in his eyes.

I swear they blazed a bit brighter for a second, as if in mute enjoyment at my obvious amazement.

"You didn't know he could talk?" Kim asked innocently.

"No, I mean, yes he can talk, but not out loud," I said, exasperated.

"What other way is there to talk?" she asked while a look of open wonder crossed her face.

I started to answer, then just laughed, I couldn't help myself.

"No, no, there's no other way," I said.

"He's weird," Kim said to Neal.

"I cannot argue with that assessment," he answered.

I just stared at him, then at her. It was so strange to see someone else talking to Neal.

"Unbelievable," I said quietly.

"*So, you and Kim have created a way to extend your range,*" I stated.

Yes, my lord. You can stay and aid…

"*Arendiol,*" I provided.

Arendiol's recovery, when they come, I will know, giving you plenty of time to leave and they will follow.

"*So, we just play house until the werewolves arrive?*"

Marcus Abshire   LOST SON

I suppose that is a well enough description of the situation. How did your trip to New York go? he asked.

I quickly relayed the events of the last day, ending with Arendiol being shot.

So, Agatha had no knowledge of any vampires acting on their own. At least she presented that as truth. That does not mean she was unaware of their actions.

"True, she did seem surprised, but that doesn't necessarily prove anything."

Perhaps your interest will stir the hornet's nest, as they say. If she truly doesn't know she will find out and hopefully bring pressure on whomever the vampires were hired by.

"Yeah, makes you wonder what they paid them with."

The most likely answer would be human blood, but knowing their price is hard to tell. Vampires are not always predictable. We know someone who is Atlantean or has access to Atlantean tech is aware of the situation. It would seem likely they are connected to the vampire's actions in some way.

"Right, otherwise why would they have killed all those who had been manipulated? It seems they were trying to cover their tracks. I still don't know why they went after Arendiol and why I haven't been targeted," I mused.

Perhaps when she awakens, we can find the answers to these questions.

"So, until then we just hang here, keep her safe and hope her body heals her before the werewolves show," I stated. "*They have been coming after me pretty regularly. I fear they will try again before Arendiol wakes.*"

All we can do is wait and see, my lord.

Marcus Abshire   LOST SON

"I hate when you're right. And don't call me 'lord,'" I added, just because.

Chapter Nine

I went to the store and picked up some food. Kim's appetite impressed me. She seemed insatiable but I guess that was good. I got some cat food for Neal, clean sheets, and some towels for Arendiol. I also grabbed a couple of board games and a deck of cards to keep Kim busy. We had a T.V. that only worked occasionally, and I worried about her having nothing to do but think about the hurt woman in the bedroom.

I made dinner and Neal, Kim, and I sat down and ate. Eating dinner all together felt almost like we were a family just seating down to our evening meal. It wasn't all that bad.

I kept waiting for Neal to tell me the werewolves were coming, but he didn't. I checked on Arendiol regularly, her sheets needed changing more than once and the soiled linen provided Kim something to wash, which she did with grave seriousness.

After teaching Kim how to play Monopoly, which she beat me at, and chess, which Neal beat me at (Kim moved the pieces for him), I showed her how to play spades and I finally won something. As I was shuffling the deck, Kim looked up at me and asked, "Why don't I remember my childhood?"

The question stunned me. I'd feared she would begin asking questions like this but didn't think it would be quite so soon. I looked up, hoping Neal would be there so

I could try and shift the question to him. However, he was with Arendiol, checking on her. Crap.

"Why the sudden interest?" I asked.

She looked away, almost embarrassed. "I was watching a show -- Neal called it a rerun. There was a family; one of the kids was very small. He was being fed with a bottle and the mother was taking very special care of him. His brothers were older but each one was different in age. They played and got into trouble then the dad came home, and they got punished then they all hugged, and everyone seemed happy. I don't have any memories like that."

"Well, what do you remember?" I hoped she had something I could work off of.

"I…. I don't know. I mean I remember a vision of a woman. She looked like her," she pointed towards the back room where Arendiol was.

"But everything appeared hazy, cloudy for some reason. Then I remember being in a small space, all these weird lights and controls everywhere, then I remember you," she trailed off; her only memories were of being in a growth chamber, the lifeboat, then me saving her from her kidnappers. Not a lot of good childhood memories there.

I thought about how much to tell her. She was obviously smart and knew she was different, but I worried about telling her too much too soon. I didn't want her to freak out and finding out you were Atlantean could be quite unnerving. That is, if you had believed you were human all along. Kim had a pretty different experience than most twelve-year-old's. Hell, she spoke to Neal, had no real memories of who she was to base herself on and was helping take care of a woman who had been shot. It's not like she was living a normal American life to begin with.

"Tell her." Neal's sudden appearance at my side startled me.

"I don't think I'll ever get used to that," I muttered.

"How much do you want to know?" I asked.

She turned thoughtful, taking her time before answering. "Everything," she said.

I took a second, trying to decide where to start.

"Do you know what a clone is?"

"I have a working knowledge of many things. I don't know how I know what I know, but yes, I know what a clone is," she offered.

"You, Kim, are a clone. You have been given knowledge from an interface. You were grown in Atlantis and are Atlantean," I said. She looked at me for a few seconds, trying to decide if I was joking.

"Have you noticed how strong you are? You are far stronger than a human, faster, and heal quicker," she stared at me in horror, realizing I was being serious.

"Kim, Kim," I reached over and grabbed her arm, she looked like she was about to bolt. "Hey, you're not alone. I'm an Atlantean also and so is Arendiol. It's okay, you're among others like you. You're not alone," I tried to soothe her.

"I don't understand," she said, pain evident on her face.

"Atlantis, isn't that supposed to be some legend or something, an ancient city that fell into the ocean?" she asked.

"Yes, but most legends are based in fact. Atlantis is real; my mother fled from there and had me. I don't know much more about the place than that. She never told me much," I said, I had never talked about my mother with anyone, doing so seemed easy with Kim.

"So, I'm a clone? I don't have a mom or a dad?" She kept her emotions bottled up tight, making it hard to tell how she was handling the news, but I knew she was trying to figure out what being a clone meant.

"No, not in the classic sense," I didn't know what else to say.

"Then who am I?" Tears filled her eyes, on the verge of pouring down, her obvious confusion made my heart go out to her.

I went to her and knelt in front of her, bringing us eye to eye. I grabbed both her hands in mine, and I was again struck at how much she reminded me of my mother, my heart twisted even more.

"That's the beauty of it; you can be whoever you want to be. Your path is wide open. You can choose. You have a completely empty slate, your future is blank, your life is yours to control," she looked down at my hands and then back up at me.

She launched at me and hugged me around the neck, squeezing tight.

"I'm scared," she sobbed.

Tears were threatening to break free, but I managed to hold them in.

"There's nothing to be afraid of, I'm here, and I won't let anything happen to you." A single tear broke free and raced down my cheek.

"You promise? You promise to protect me?" she said into my chest.

I put my chin on her head, "Yeah, kid, I promise. I'll keep you safe," I answered, holding her tight.

We stayed like that for a while. It took some time, but eventually, she calmed down and I continued to hold her. Her sobs slowly stopped, and I felt her yawn deeply. She fell asleep in my arms, and I let her.

I reached over and turned off the light after tucking her in. Kim was exhausted after all the excitement, I can't say I blamed her, it was almost one a.m. I closed the door quietly, giving her the master bedroom.

The child has taken a liking to you, Neal said in my head, he sat in the living room.

"*Yeah, and?*" I asked, defensively.

Do you think being attached to her is wise? We do not know what will become of her.

"*How do you know I'm attached to her?*" I sent.

My lord, we speak in each other's heads. Your feelings for her are evident even if we did not have such a link.

"*Well, what of it? What am I supposed to do? I can't just ignore her. Besides, it was your idea to tell her who she was.*"

Agreed, but I just want you to understand that complicating your life will make it well, complicated.

"*No shit, Neal,*" I answered, I know he was just being Neal, trying to keep me aware of the situation, even if my current predicament had to do with the feelings of a twelve-year-old and not some monster trying to kill me.

"*How's Arendiol doing?*" I tried to change the subject.

Marcus Abshire   LOST SON

She is healing, the suit has sealed and now her body is working, she should be awake the day after tomorrow. Neal settled down in front of the door, no doubt monitoring his perimeter.

I settled on the couch, closing my eyes. I knew if anything happened Neal would alert me instantly, his never-ending vigilance made falling asleep easy.

"Don't call me 'lord,'" I said as I drifted off.

The next morning, I awoke to the smell of fried bacon and eggs. The aroma made my stomach growl in hungry anticipation. I sat up and stretched. I looked at the alarm clock and saw it was almost nine a.m. In the kitchen Kim stood at the stove; the sound of sizzling meat was music to my ears. Neal stood next to her, keeping watch.

"Good, now turn off the burner and then carefully transfer the bacon to the plate. Be careful the food will be hot," he coached her through breakfast.

I sat down and she brought me a cup of hot coffee, the steaming liquid burned my mouth a little, but the slight pain was worth the look of accomplishment plastered on Kim's face.

"Thank you," I said to her, she looked at me and flashed a smile that melted my heart.

"You are welcome. I've made bacon, eggs, and pancakes. Are you hungry?"

"I'm starving." We sat down and ate one of the best breakfasts ever.

Afterward, I did the dishes while Kim and Neal went outside to play. She knew Neal wasn't a normal dog, but she needed to get out and get some exercise. I checked on Arendiol and made sure she had a fresh I.V. Neal said it was the last bag we had, but he didn't think she would need anymore anyway.

I went outside and watched them, Kim chased Neal around who jumped and bounced liked a real dog. Eventually, Kim wore herself out and came over next to me. We sat in silence for a while, both of us comfortable with each other.

"Am I in danger?" she asked after a time.

"I don't know." She looked at me, questioning.

"I was manipulated into looking for you and I don't know why. Right now, I don't see you being at risk, but it's hard to know. You are a unique and special child; until I know why you are here there is no way to know for sure," I looked off into the distance.

"You know how to fight don't you, how to defend yourself?" She stared at me.

I looked at her, her eyes were of a light grey and black hair framed a beautiful face. Her openness was refreshing, and she trusted me completely, that was something I wasn't used to.

"Yup, I can handle myself," I answered.

She nodded once, turning serious.

"Teach me, teach me how to fight," she pleaded.

I hadn't expected that.

"Why?" Her request surprised me.

"You said my life is a blank slate, I can choose what to do. I want to be like you. I want to help people. I figure I can't help others unless I can take care of myself first," I didn't know what to say, I took a second to make sure I had my thoughts together. Kim was wanting to do something with herself, which I thought was awesome, but I didn't think she was ready to go kicking butt and taking names. I had to tread lightly, however, the last thing I wanted to do was kill her growing desire to be a force of good in the world.

"There's nothing wrong with wanting to be able to defend yourself. But I don't want you making such an important choice so quickly. You have a long time to go before you need to make such big decisions." She looked crestfallen.

"How about this, I teach you a couple of things and you wait a few years before making your choice?"

She beamed at me; her smile made her whole face light up and I couldn't help but smile back, "Ok."

We spent the next three hours working on the basics. How to break a hold, how to inflict the most damage quickly to run away, and the best places to attack if confronted with someone larger and stronger. Kim learned quickly and worked hard.

"Alright, that's good for now," I said, taking a seat on the steps by the front door.

Kim came and sat down next to me. Neal was sitting with Arendiol in case she woke up early. We sat in silence for a little while, but eventually, I could sense her staring at me.

"Who taught you?" she asked.

"Taught me what?" I watched the breeze blow the leaves back and forth.

"How to fight, of course."

"Lots of people," I answered vaguely.

"All at once? I bet that would be hard." I let out a small burst of laughter.

"No, not all at once, after I was attacked, I realized I needed to be able to fight so, with Neal's help, I sought out the masters."

"The masters?"

"Yup, every fighting style has a master, a person who is considered to have the most knowledge and experience in that style. They are called masters. There are tons of masters because there are tons of fighting styles." I had her full attention.

"So, you sought out the masters, you wanted them to teach you?" she asked.

"That's right; I went all over the world, trying to get them to train me."

"Did they?" She sat, eyes wide.

"Most of them did, some didn't. You gotta remember I am far stronger and faster than a human, at first, they were all better than me, and I could take a beating. But soon I quickly outmatched them, and when I mastered one discipline I moved on to the next."

"Then what?"

"Then what? You can hear more about the *then what* when you are older." The rest of my story took a dark turn, something the kid wasn't ready to hear.

"Aww," she exclaimed. "Not fair!"

I reached out and ruffled her hair, which she quickly tried to straighten up.

"Better get used to that kid, you're gonna find all kinds of things that aren't fair, that's life."

"You promise to tell me when I'm older?" she pleaded.

"You got it." She beamed at me and gave me a quick hug before running off the porch to chase a beautiful butterfly that had fluttered from a branch where it had been soaking up the morning's bright sun.

I just sat and watched her, a strange feeling flowed through me and I didn't know what, exactly, the emotion was. I felt filled with warmth towards her, a drive to keep her safe and make sure she was well taken care of; I wanted the world to be better, so she didn't have to struggle. I realized this must be what a father feels for his daughter, a love that drives him to protect her and make sure she's okay.

My lord, Neal's voice cut off my thoughts. *Arendiol is awake.*

"I'll be right there. I need you to keep an eye on Kim."

Of course.

I got up and rushed inside, passing Neal on the way to Arendiol's room. I went in and knelt down next to her, she looked weak and still pale, but some color had returned to her cheeks. She had her eyes closed, but as I settled next to her, she looked over at me and smiled weakly.

"Where am I?" she whispered, before being racked with a fit of coughing.

"Easy, take it easy. Your body is still fragile; the new tissue growth is not done. It's going to hurt to breathe and talk for a while, but that will soon fade. You can just nod for yes or shake your head no for now, okay?" She nodded.

I reached over and helped her take a sip of water.

"Do you remember who I am, what happened?" One nod.

"Good, after the attack I brought you to my place, somewhere you could recover from your injuries." She visibly relaxed.

"You said you knew who I was by sight, do you know how you knew that?"

I could see her thinking, the shock of what she had been through was still affecting her.

She nodded once.

"When you were waiting for me at the airport, did someone tell you I was going to be there?" One nod yes.

"Do you think you could describe them to me?" I asked.

She reached for some water and I got her the glass, helping her get another drink.

"Silver eyes, blond hair... sharp teeth," she said, her voice came in a raspy whisper.

A vampire, what the hell was a vampire doing sending an Atlantean scientist after me?

"Was it a woman?" I asked. She shook her head no.

Maybe whomever she was describing was the same vampire that had screwed with the kidnapper's and Caroline's heads? I just wasn't sure. I had hoped talking to Arendiol while she was still groggy might let her tell me something she may have been compelled to forget but this was more than I thought I'd get.

"Do you know his name?" I tried, hoping.

She took a painful breath, "Sigmund," she answered, then closed her eyes, falling asleep from exhaustion.

I didn't try to ask her any more questions, she had already done plenty. I wasn't about to tax her any more than she already had been.

"Neal?"

Yes, my lord?

"Do you have any knowledge of a blond vampire named Sigmund?" During the job where I earned the old coin I used at Club Red, I had the misfortune of dealing with vampires. Of course, back then Gregory ran the coven. He was a nasty, but powerful leader. He was of German descent and had a heavy hand in the not so distant atrocities that had taken place there seventy years ago. Agatha had taken power not long after my business with him had concluded.

Yes, Gregory's second in command was named Sigmund. He had blond hair and accompanied him to America after the war. I do not believe you met him, but I do remember him dealing with some underlings while I was watching the club.

"Do you know if he disappeared after Agatha took over, when she cleaned house?"

No, I have no knowledge of what came of him.

"Alright, thanks."

Well, now I had a name. That didn't mean I knew what was going on, but I had a place to start. I didn't like the idea of going back to New York, but the situation now looked like I might have to unless I could force Sigmund to come to me. I bet if I called the club and started dropping names that would make him nervous. I'm sure he didn't want Agatha to know about his extra-curricular activities, that is if she didn't already. The gambit was worth a shot, anyway.

"Can you get me the number to Club Red?" I sent to Neal.

Do you want the listed number for that building or the unlisted one?

"*The unlisted one*," I doubt anyone would answer the listed one, anyway.

I punched in the number Neal gave me and after a couple of rings, a woman answered.

"Club Red, this is Rebecca speaking, how can I help you?" her voice oozed courteous professionalism.

"Tell me what does it pay to be a vampire's day answering service?" I asked.

Without missing a beat, Rebecca said, "I'm afraid I don't know what you are talking about sir, this is a private number, please do not call here again," I could detect a not so subtle threat in her voice.

"Wait, before you hang up, I want you to leave a message for Agatha," I hurried, hoping saying the coven leader's name would keep her on the line.

"Go on," she said, back to business.

"Let her know Jack was calling for Sigmund. I wanted to let him know Arendiol and Caroline say hello and the other two gentlemen who were at the party also wanted to send their greetings," I said.

"Is that all?" she said, unfazed.

"Yup, that's it," I answered politely.

"I will make sure the message is relayed, have a nice day," I heard her hang up.

Hopefully, that would get to Sigmund. I doubt the answering service reported directly to Agatha, they most likely had a process for sharing information. I guess we'd find out soon enough.

Marcus Abshire   LOST SON

After dinner, I taught Kim how to play solitaire, which she loved, then busied myself with doing the dishes.

"*I expected to have some visitors by now. What's taking them so long?*" I wondered to Neal.

That is hard to determine. Perhaps they have decided killing you may be more trouble than the attempt is worth?

"*Somehow I doubt it, that would be too easy. No, I don't like the fact we haven't been attacked yet, I'm thinking after dark I should go to the edge of your range, keep moving to make sure they are not drawn here.*" I looked over at Kim, who busied herself matching cards.

You have grown fond of the girl, Neal stated.

"*I don't know what's going to happen after we get all this figured out, but I'm going to make sure she is taken care of.*"

Yes, my lord.

"*Have you put your ginormous brain into figuring out what is going on?*" I asked.

I only have half of the equation, but we do know someone does not want us figuring out who Kim is. We also know they are working with vampires. Seems to me that one or more Atlanteans are involved as well, but to what end I cannot say. Talking to Sigmund may be enlightening, given you do not kill him before he can be of use.

"*Neal, I'm shocked. You really think I would kill him **before** he tells me what I want to know?*" I placed the wet dishes on a rack next to the sink, letting them air dry.

I am only basing my comment on past experience, my lord.

120

I finished and went over to Kim, placing a hand on her shoulder. She looked up at me.

"Hey, I have some errands to run, I want you to stay with Neal, do whatever he says, ok?" She nodded once, seriously.

"When will you be back?" she asked.

"Before you know it." I ruffled her hair quickly which she hurried to straighten.

I went to the door, grabbing my coat. I shrugged on the jacket and as I opened the door I turned to Kim, giving her a smile.

"Oh, and don't call me 'lord,'" I sent to Neal, closing the door behind me.

I rode away from the house, leaving Kim, Neal, and Arendiol in hopes of keeping any trouble from finding them. I went to the outskirts of town, still within Neal's range and found a small park. I sat and waited as the sun slowly settled on the horizon, leaving the sky to slowly change colors as the sun fell.

Vampires were excellent hunters; they were on par with werewolves. I had no doubt, after my visit to Club Red that Sigmund could track me if he wanted to. I leaned up against the base of a tree, resting, but keeping an ear open for Neal. I had a feeling tonight was going to be exciting.

After a while, my eyes began to grow heavy and I decided to close them for just a second when Neal's voice rang in my head.

My lord, I have detected a large contingency of werewolves that have just crossed into my perimeter.

There are five, no wait, eight, ten, fifteen, make that twenty werewolves who are advancing towards the house.

"*Don't you mean they are coming towards my location?*" I started getting worried.

No, they have all entered from different locations, encompassing the town in a circle which is closing as we speak, and their projected target is us, not you, he finished.

What the hell? Why were they not targeting me?

I jumped on my bike and fired up the engine, racing back towards the house.

"*How far out are they?*" I sent.

They are traveling at a high rate of speed. They should be here in five minutes.

"*Damn, I'm at least ten minutes out. Can you hold them off until I get there?*" I zipped through traffic, not caring if I came across any law enforcement. Hell, that might have actually been good. I could lead them to the house where their presence might keep the pack from showing themselves.

I will try, my lord.

Chapter Ten

I flew through town, ignoring red lights and the speed limit. My fear for Kim grew as each passing second ticked by. I couldn't stop imagining what they might do to her; I had seen enough abuse of children to be able to visualize the worst.

I was almost there when Neal said, *They have stopped. I am not sure why, but they have quit advancing on our position. They are all just waiting.*

"Good, maybe their pause will give me enough time to get there." I screamed over the last mile and came roaring into the property. I didn't see anyone hiding as I flew towards the house, but that didn't mean anything. I knew the werewolves were excellent at keeping themselves unseen.

I skidded to a halt at the front door, sending small pebbles shooting off into the side of the house. I killed the bike's engine and hopped off, drawing my sword and pistol in one fluid movement.

"*Talk to me,*" I sent to Neal.

They have encircled the house; they are spread out every ten feet or so, making escape impossible. The pack leader is the most dangerous and he is directly ahead.

"I know you are out there, are you still pissed about that beat down I gave you? Really, it's no big deal, can't we let bygones be bygones?" I said, hoping he was in a generous mood.

I heard a burst of deep rumbling laughter coming from exactly where Neal said the pack leader was hiding. A second later he stepped out from his position, he looked taller, bigger, and harrier than I remember. Must be getting closer to the full moon.

"Your ability to sense us is impressive, but your awareness of our presence doesn't matter. I am here to exact equal punishment," he growled as his eyes blazed yellow from under his bushy brow.

"What the hell are you talking about? Look, why don't we just settle this like men, you and me?" I hoped I could keep this simple.

His wolfish smile pierced the dark night, sending chills down my spine.

"That time is long past. You have killed eight of my pack, not counting the two in my own territory. For that, I am going to kill your pack, in your territory and then kill you." The rest of the pack members who were hiding showed themselves, all of them looked on the verge of shifting.

"First of all, the two shit bags I killed in Alaska deserved what they got, they'd kidnapped a child and were going to hunt and eat him, the rest of them attacked me first, I just defended myself," I hoped he had some sense of fairness.

"I don't give a damn, you will pay, no one fucks with the pack and lives, NO ONE!" he screamed, on the verge of losing the already thin thread of his humanity.

Fine if we're going to fight, I wanted to at least make sure he was good and pissed.

"They wouldn't have died if they knew how to fight, like their pack leader they were all chicken shit pups, afraid of their own tails," I taunted.

I saw his face flow as his beast threatened to escape, anger made his eyes flare brighter.

"I'm going to kill you now, the rest of you, bring his friends to me!" he roared and came hurtling towards me, his body shifted, and his skin burst off of him, as a seven-foot-tall werewolf with razor-sharp claws and deadly teeth came flying at me.

His sudden transformation startled me; I thought werewolves were only able to shift either a few days away or on a full moon. His current form allowed him greater speed and strength and made him much harder to kill.

The pack leader swiped at my chest, and I brought my blade up to block his attack. He quickly adjusted and instead of chopping his hand off I just managed to take a large chunk of his forearm. The bloody bit of meat and muscle sailed away from us as I spun and tried to kick him. He reached out and blocked my foot, grabbing my ankle. I was helpless as he threw me into the side of the house.

The impact knocked the wind out of me, surprised that I hadn't broken anything. I hurried to get up, knowing my opponent was coming for me.

My shoulder screamed in pain, but my arm still worked. The pack leader's assault took me by surprise, but I knew if I wanted to save myself and the others, I couldn't let his ability to startle me make any difference. I heard a loud sonic detonation as Neal fought off those who had entered the house. I knew I didn't have a lot of time. I had to kill this guy fast and hope his defeat would allow me to get everyone to safety.

I brought my pistol up and fired five successive shots, knowing they wouldn't kill him, but needing the short respite the bullet's impact would give me. I closed the distance between us and dropped the pistol, using my sword to create a wall of flashing blue steel. He tried to find an opening with my offense but kept getting small parts of him chopped off, unfortunately, whatever I sliced either grew back or healed faster than I could cut. I knew the only way to end this would be to take off his head.

I pressed closer, stabbing and slicing as I went. He roared in outrage and rushed me, unafraid of my sword. I stabbed him through the gut and tried to pull the blade out in order to land a killing stroke, but he spun and hit me with one of his large clawed paws. I kept my hold on my sword and pulled the sharp blade out of his body as I tumbled ten feet in a hard slide.

I rose up ready for another assault when I saw he wasn't advancing, he just stood there, smiling. His body shifted and he reverted into human form, well semi-human form, his naked body was covered in an obscene amount of hair and I feared what his bill would be for a full-body wax.

"Enough, the fight is over," he growled.

"Like hell it is," I growled back, stalking closer.

"Drop the weapon and die like a man or your friends die, starting with the young one." He motioned to my left.

I turned and saw Kim and Arendiol being held by the rest of the pack. Arendiol was still too weak to fight and

Kim just wasn't strong enough yet to break free of their grasp.

I'm sorry my lord, there were too many of them, Neal sent, he sounded muffled like he was far away.

"What have they done to you!" I sent back.

I am injured, the wound is not life-threatening, but until I heal, I cannot aid you except for my council.

"Just rest, I'll get us out of this in no time, no biggie," I sent.

You are not a good liar, my lord.

"I said drop it," he growled again, one of the werewolves held a sharp-clawed hand to Arendiol's throat.

I took a step towards him, anger made thinking straight hard.

"Now!" He didn't like being disobeyed.

I heard Kim wince and saw a small well of blood rise from one of her captor's claws. My vision clouded red, seeing her hurt almost drove me to charge, but I knew I would be far too late. She would be dead before I could get to her, Atlantean healing or not.

I dropped my sword in a clatter of metal. The pack leader's low rumbling laughter rolled over me.

"Good, it's nice to know you can obey orders. Now, where were we? That's right, payback. I want you to watch as I kill your pack, starting with the young one and ending with your pet."

The werewolf holding Kim grabbed her by the throat and lifted her up. Her face turned red as he began to slowly squeeze and cut off her flow of oxygen.

Marcus Abshire — LOST SON

I had never known what love was, but I knew at that moment I loved Kim. Seeing her in such distress unlocked something within me, the love I held for her filled me with new power, an energy that grew from the feelings of protection I had for her. I saw the pack leader take a step back from me as a soft blue glow filled the area. His reaction confused me, unknowing the glow came from my own eyes as I became filled with an alien power that at the same time just felt right like the ability had been within me all the time.

My entire being filled with the need to protect Kim, to make sure these bastards didn't hurt her anymore. I raised my right hand and pointed my palm towards those who held Kim and Arendiol. I heard my voice reverberate through the night, the power like a live electric wire, buzzing in the dark.

"AWAY!" I said and was utterly amazed as all the werewolves holding Kim and Arendiol flew back and landed in a tangle of arms and legs leaving their captives free and staring at me.

"What is this foul magic?" the pack leader said in amazement.

I turned to him and began to growl. The power that filled me gave me an unlimited well of energy.

"Let's finish this you hairy bastard," I said.

He growled in frustration and came at me, shifting as he charged. I reached out and without understanding how, saw my blade sail through the air into my outstretched hand. The pack leader got to within five feet and launched himself at me, clawed arms leading the way. I reached out with my other arm and caught him by the throat like a rag doll and with one powerful stroke cut his head from his neck.

I tossed his headless body aside and went to Kim, wrapping her in a hug as she stared at me in disbelief.

My lord, you are now ready. Neal's voice reverberated in my head.

His words carried a seriousness to them, which I instantly understood.

"*Yes, I am,*" I answered, my head still dizzy with power.

I smiled at Kim and the power faded from me, I saw as the blue glow vanished and the surrounding area plunged back into the darkness of night. I felt exhausted, beyond anything I had experienced before and this time Arendiol grabbed me as I lost consciousness and blacked out.

Chapter Eleven

I woke to Neal standing over me, growling protectively. I looked around quickly, assessing the situation. Someone had dragged me closer to the house and Kim and Arendiol stood watching over me. Arendiol had my gun and stood in front of Kim who stayed slightly behind Neal.

"*Get off me.*" I sent, Neal seemed startled at my words, but moved, allowing me to rise to my feet.

"What the hell happened?" I asked.

"After you killed the pack leader, they all went crazy," Arendiol said, while Kim nodded vigorously.

"*Neal?*" I knew his explanation would be more extensive.

Her assessment is accurate, my lord. As soon as you fainted the rest of the pack members began turning on each other. I believe the loss of their leader created a power vacuum they attempted to fill by killing each other.

I looked around; there were several bodies littering the ground. Out of the twenty werewolves, six of them had been killed. The rest were gathered in a rough group, all standing behind one guy. They kept their eyes averted, showing submission.

"I guess you have established a new pecking order?" I said, trying to remember if I had any rounds left in my pistol.

The new leader looked me over, probably trying to tell how dangerous I still was.

"Yes, I have earned pack leader, that just leaves settling up with you." I couldn't tell if he looked forward to that or apprehensive.

"Do you really want to go after the guy who just killed your old pack leader?" I didn't have to say why the guy was the pack leader, we all knew he was the toughest and meanest, meaning I had just beaten the guy who was stronger than all of them.

"There are two ways I can look at the situation. One, you killed pack members and deserve to die. Two, you were right, the two you killed a few days ago were hunting children, which I cannot stand for, and the rest died while carrying out orders a dead man gave." He was trying to give me an out; I don't think he relished the idea of fighting me, nor I, him.

"Not to mention I was just defending myself," I added.

"Very true, we all have a right to defend ourselves. I myself had to kill a few pack members, defending myself," he said, but conveniently left out the fact that he killed them in order to gain power within the pack, why quibble about the small stuff?

"Well, then, I think our business here is concluded?" I said, framing it more as a question.

He nodded once, turning around and walking away, into the shadows.

"I truly hope we never meet again," I heard him say, the feeling was mutual.

Marcus Abshire   LOST SON

I watched him leave, slipping away like a ghost. They took the bodies of the fallen as well, leaving me without the hassle of dealing with them.

Would miracles never cease?

After a few minutes, I checked with Neal to make sure they really were gone, and he confirmed they were.

We all went back inside where I checked on everyone to make sure they were okay. Kim was shaken up and kept by my side, afraid to leave me. Arendiol had reinjured herself some, but the damage wasn't bad, she went back to bed, letting herself continue healing. Neal had apparently recovered from his injuries and kept watch by the door, keeping track of the pack, until they left his range.

I got Kim a blanket and she rested on the couch with her head on my lap. I feared after all the excitement she wouldn't be able to fall asleep, but I think the events of the day had the opposite effect because she was snoring in no time. I gently extracted myself from the couch and slipped outside, needing the cool, fresh air.

"*We need to talk.*" I sent to Neal.

Yes, my lord, there is much to discuss. For some reason, a shiver went down my spine.

"*So, what the hell happened out there?*" I asked.

Instead of answering, Neal said. *In order to understand the present and perhaps the future, one needs to know the past.*

Okay, that was a little Zen, even for Neal.

"*What are you talking about?*"

What happened tonight unlocked the rest of my programming. The answers to the questions you have been seeking are now known to me, and I will give them to you, but first, you must know what happened in order to understand what is happening.

"Alright, so get on with it." I may have been a little impatient.

Let us begin with the Fall. It is detrimental to understand how you came to be here, that began with the Fall.

As you know Atlantean scientists were far more advanced in their technology than modern humans. They had already unlocked the secrets of the atom and had their sites set far higher. Through their research, they became aware of what humans call dark matter. And through that, they began experimenting with dark energy.

This was a very controversial thing to do. We did not fully understand this energy and had no real way of predicting what the power could do. Some Atlanteans argued this energy was everywhere and all around us and was the explanation for magic or unexplained phenomena.

There have always been a few people in every culture that could tap into this energy and could use it to predict events or make strange things happen. Although the thought was these individuals were only capable of manipulating a small fraction of this energy. Others envisioned a world where we could tap into this energy and use the unlimited resource to fuel our needs forever, giving us an endless supply of power.

These two camps fought for years until the king and queen were convinced that the possible gains, if we could control this energy, were too vast to pass up. They were determined to be cautious, however, and decided to be present when the first experiment to harness this dark energy took place.

On the day of the test the king and queen, five royal guards and the top three scientists of Atlantis were present to witness the event. The king and queen stood by the emergency override controls, in case anything went wrong they would stop the test from proceeding.

Finally, the time came and when the machine was turned on everything seemed fine.

Then everything went wrong.

It's unclear as to what exactly happened, but from the best of my knowledge, they somehow created a transdimensional rift. The experiment resulted in an opening being created between our dimension and another, one made of pure energy, an energy that was unknown and chaotic. A massive explosion rocked the city as the influx of this alien energy interacted with our own dark energy device and everything changed. Those closest to the rift were transformed, the wild powers flew through them and caused them to change. The guards became what you know today as vampires, werewolves, sea witches, giants, and trolls.

"Wait, wait, wait, are you telling me those things all originated from Atlanteans who were transformed by this trans-dimensional energy?"

I knew vampires, werewolves and sea witches were real, but giants and trolls? What the hell?

I believe that is exactly what I have stated. Now if you would allow me to continue.

Marcus Abshire   LOST SON

"*Yeah, sure, knock your socks off.*" Seriously, giants and trolls?

It seemed as though the energies tapped into the essence of those nearby and changed them according to their natures.

The scientists became seers, those with the ability to see the truth in things, namely the future, and the king and queen, with their natural leadership and commanding personalities, became wizards, able to control the dark energy that surrounds us.

This all happened instantly and as you can imagine created a lot of chaos. The guards ran, afraid of what they had become. The scientists began to see what was coming and warned the king and queen, who worked to do what was necessary to save their kingdom.

You see the explosion weakened the foundations of Atlantis and within hours, ripped the city from the land and plunged us all to the bottom of the sea. The king and queen did what they always did and put the best interests of their people ahead of themselves. They soon realized they had control over this unfathomable power and managed to create a protective barrier that kept the city from being flooded and destroyed after the explosion. They protected Atlantis and all Atlanteans from death, while the city plunged to the dark abyss.

After the Fall, all was chaos. The people were drowning in panic and despair, but the king and queen's guidance helped pull them together. Many tried to escape, to flee to the surface, but the wild energies that were released from the explosion killed them, effectively trapping all Atlanteans in the city.

Marcus Abshire   LOST SON

It took months for a permanent protective dome to be erected, but with the magic of the king and queen and the technology of our ancestors, a stable city was created. Once the shield was in place the king and queen grew weak. Their exertions had taken a toll on them and they were dying. The seers saw a way for Atlantis to one day be reborn, to rise again from the sea and set their plan in motion.

First, all ancient technology regarding dark energy and dark matter was forbidden, the test chamber, which housed the machines capable of creating the portal, had been thought to be destroyed during the Fall and all entrances that could possibly lead to the machines were sealed. The D.N.A. of all Atlanteans citizens was taken, to be used after they died.

"*That's where the clones came from.*" I mused.

That's right. The delicate nature of Atlantis was tenuous. A citizenry who, after a few generations, grew arrogant would undoubtedly do something and destroy the shield, thus bringing doom upon all of Atlantis, so the decision was made that clones would be grown and programmed to continue to protect the bloodlines until such a time when the erratic wild energy that kept escape impossible dissipated. Then the clones would impregnate themselves with the embryos stored for such a purpose, thus bringing the natural blood of Atlanteans back to reclaim what was taken from them, life on the surface.

But the clones became docile, and the mental molding was too good. They soon forgot about their goal and after a thousand years the energies dissipated, but the clones were unaware, they kept to their docile existence for many more thousands of years, allowing Atlantis to fall into myth and legend. Meanwhile, the only ancestors of Atlantis that survived were those transformed by fate. Vampires, werewolves, giants, sea witches and trolls roamed the earth and eventually, they too fell into myth and legend as the humans' march towards enlightenment drove them into the dark shadows.

Atlantis's society was reformed. There were three classes, as you know, the hunters/warriors, scientists/sorcerers, and farmers/maintenance. Arendiol was right, eventually, the DNA of our people began to fade, and they found someone whom they believed would save them.

Warlord Karakatos became obsessed with the past, somehow he found out about the ancient experiments and dreamed of opening the portal, of using the energy to fix the people and to fuel his army, an army that would raise Atlantis from the ocean and the dust bin of history and onto the world stage where he wishes to rule. His ambition knows no bounds. He will stop at nothing to achieve his goals.

"*Doesn't he realize what happened, doesn't he know the energy is uncontrollable?*" I asked.

He believes he knows how to control the wild power. He is quite mad.

"*So how do I fit into all of this, and what happened tonight?*" A sudden burst of insight almost knocked me to the ground. "*Wait, what I did, I tapped into the dark energy, didn't I?*"

Yes

"*Then that would mean…*"

Marcus Abshire   LOST SON

Yes, now you begin to realize why I call you lord.

If what I was beginning to understand was true that was huge. I had to hear the rest from Neal first though.

"Go on, finish your story."

Like I said before, everyone's DNA was saved in preparation for the day when natural births could take place again. This included the kings and queens.

Karakatos sent an army of researches to hunt for any information on the ancient event. A young scientist by the name of Brigune discovered historical records that explained what happened to Atlantis and the nature of the king and queen's ability to control the energy. She also found the DNA chamber which housed the king and queens frozen seed and egg. She knew the key to the future was in their child. Whether her decision was because of the breakdown of her DNA or some other compulsion, instead of destroying the king and queen's seed she combined them and impregnated herself, thus activating me.

As you already know I am a SENTINEL, a guardian, and a teacher. I am created to protect, teach and guide Atlantean royalty and when you were conceived, I came online. I began downloading all the history of the past 20,000 years, which is why it took so long for me to become fully active. Your mother infused you with an accelerated growth serum which allowed you to mature to a fifteen-year-old boy in five years. I only had a few years of Atlantean history left to download when I intercepted the call from Karakatos to kill you and your mother. My protocol to protect you overrode my downloading and I stopped and rushed to your aid. That is when we first met after they had killed your mother.

"But she's not my mother, is she, Brigune? She was just a surrogate." I wasn't sure how I felt. I had strong feelings towards the woman who birthed me, who took care of me, but if what Neal said was true that would mean the woman whose blood I carried was not Brigune, but the queen of Atlantis.

I suppose that depends on what your definition of what a mother is. Brigune did not give you any genetic material, but she did provide sustenance, protection, and guidance. Queen Andromaleus and King Raiphaim are your parents; they, however, have had nothing to do with your survival, up until tonight.

So I wasn't related to the woman who raised me, who protected me as a child and tucked me in at night. I wasn't sure how to handle that, I cared for her and remembered her as my mother, knowing my real parents were ancient Atlantean rulers wasn't something I thought I would ever have to deal with. I decided to put this new revelation aside, there were more pressing matters to deal with.

"So, I'm an Atlantean prince. I'll make sure to put that on my resume." I grumbled.

My lord, your parent's ability to use the dark energy that is all around us has been passed down to you.

"What the hell does that mean? I can summon lightning or turn people into toads?"

I'm not exactly sure; you are the first offspring of the only two people who could control the energy. I would assume like with the children of the First, you should have all their abilities. I suggest we test those abilities, see what you can accomplish.

"Yeah, that makes sense. We can, I'm interested in what I can do. But first, you need to finish."

Finish what, my lord? Neal nosed his way outside and sat down next to me.

"You said what I did unlocked your programming. That would mean you can tell me what is coming, what I have to be prepared for, and who the hell is behind all the craziness of the last few days." Neal's silence was all too familiar.

"Well?" I asked, impatiently.

I am attempting to access the information you requested. After a few moments of silence, he continued.

The seer's abilities were great, but not always perfect. They could see possible time streams, multitudes of options, some more likely than others, but still uncertain. His eyes glowed bright gold for a second.

Time of calm ends, the forgotten remember. Raiphaim's battle begins. War comes, darkness, then light. Neal finished.

"You've got to be kidding me. That's it? That's what you have been holding onto? A bunch of gibberish spoken by dead men." I couldn't believe that was what Neal had been talking about. I mean don't get me wrong. I am glad I have worked hard to be able to take care of myself, but I expected some real workable information that would let me prepare for something big. I trust Neal, he is not the type to believe in frivolous prophecy, sheesh.

"Well, can you at least tell me why Atlanteans are shooting people and working with vampires?"

Raiphaim is you, my lord. That is quite significant.

"That was also the name of the king." I really wasn't interested in prophecies.

I am sorry, the inquiry about the current events is something I am unable to access.

"What?" I began to get angry.

The activities of which you ask are something that has taken place after I disconnected from the city's mainframe. I have no access to that information. I know no more about what is going on than before.

"Son of a bitch!" I swore.

I stood and kicked some gravel.

"So we're back to where we started!"

That's not entirely true, due to recent revelations I have some plausible scenarios that may help, Neal sat still, my little outburst hadn't disturbed him.

I turned, looking at Neal questioningly. Neal's plausible guesses were usually better than my known facts, I was about to have him continue when I felt something odd. I had the strange sensation something was wrong, like when you're sitting in a calm swimming pool and someone jumps in making you bob up and down from the ripples.

"Did you feel that?" I said.

Feel what? Neal asked.

I tried to figure out what I sensed, but the feeling was gone. Just like that, the odd sensation disappeared, the night became as normal as always.

"Nothing," I shook my head.

"You were saying?"

We know the Warlord is interested in re-opening the rift. We now know your parents became able to manipulate dark energy. Due to the actions of Karakatos's men, it seems likely he is not trying to kill you but to protect you. I believe his actions have something to do with his desire to unleash the alien energy again.

So what? Was I some pawn in this bastard's game?

My guess would be that he intends on using you to help him in his plans.

"Well, he can kiss my ass. I'm not having any part of opening a trans-dimensional rift, besides who the hell knows if I can even do something like that?" I asked.

My records show the technology used to open the rift is based on harnessing dark energy, something you now have the ability to control.

"He thinks I can open the rift, doesn't he? He's trying to manipulate me into opening the damn thing for him, although I can't see how killing three people, some werewolves and shooting Arendiol is going to persuade me." I mused.

I am not entirely sure all the actions Karakatos's men have taken lately have been directed towards you.

"Well, if they haven't been for my benefit, then whose..." A thought popped into my head and stopped me cold.

There is one person who has been unaffected by the actions of the sniper, one person whose presence is still a mystery, one person whose role in all of this is still unknown.

"Kim," I said.

Yes, my lord.

I stood up to go inside and talk to Kim, see if she knew anything else, something she may have forgotten or deemed unimportant that might help when I felt a slight impact on my chest. I looked down to see the same softball-sized lump of foam that incapacitated the werewolves earlier. I reached up to pull the expanding foam off and found the sticky blob had already tripled in size. The foam's tacky consistency trapped my hand and I was unable to break free from my growing prison.

"Neal! You have to get them to safety!" I mentally sent.
I'm sorry my lord, but I am unable to move.

I looked down, the foam had spread to my legs and chest, allowing only for movement of my head. Neal stood next to me, engulfed in his own ever-expanding foam cocoon.

I could do nothing while the foam expanded, hardening almost as fast as the stuff spread. My sluggish movements of protest soon ended as the strong material trapped me. I could do nothing, I was helpless. The foam grew and braced each side of my head, keeping me from moving. I still had my face exposed, so I could still see, hear and breathe, but I was trapped in an unmovable prison, unable to turn my head or talk.

I have just detected the oncoming presence of a vampire, moving directly towards us at a high rate of speed.

You had to be kidding me! I struggled to free myself, tensing against the foam. I could feel my restraint give slightly, but the prison held firm.

Marcus Abshire   LOST SON

From the trees directly in front of me came a lone figure. As he got closer, I recognized him as the sniper. He wore a dark hoodie and pants; heavy work boots covered his feet. He had a black bandana covering the lower part of his face and only his eyes showed. They were an intense blue that took everything in and focused with a sharpness reminding me of a hawk on the hunt.

I could do nothing but watch as he approached, holding the same kind of pistol Arendiol used. He casually stepped towards me, keeping his face covered. He stood a few feet away, glaring at me.

"If the decision were up to me, I'd kill you right now," he growled, from under his bandana.

I guess he wasn't a fan.

"Now, now, don't be rude, after all, I have plans for him after the Warlord is done, of course."

Bouncer Boy stepped into view; he seemed no worse for the wear. I guess cutting off vampire's legs only slowed them down, good to know. He smiled at me as I narrowed my eyes in understanding.

"That's right; I can see you working it out. We haven't been formally introduced. My name is Sigmund, second to Gregory who was murdered by Agatha, an unworthy bitch, undeserving of being coven leader," he beamed with energy, enjoying his dramatic entrance.

He took a few seconds to savor my dawning understanding and then stepped forward and hit me with a devastating blow to the head, everything swam, dizziness threatened to consume me. He smiled and hit me again, this time sending me into the dark depths of unconsciousness.

Chapter Twelve

I awoke to a splitting headache; my temples throbbed in conjunction with my heartbeat. I tried to open my eyes, but one of them was stuck shut from my own dried blood. I pried the painful eyelid open and tried to look around, feeling as my arms and legs were still bound, only this time by something other than the encompassing foam, which had disappeared.

"*Neal?*" I sent out, hoping he was near.

Nothing, either he wasn't answering me for a good reason, or he was too far away, or dead. I refused to even entertain the last thought.

It felt as though we were moving, I was in some type of vehicle, the motions of being in a car as it bounced over the road is what the vehicle's movements reminded me of, but for some reason, I didn't think we were in an automobile. My vision was blocked; my head was faced towards the side of the vehicle. I could hear the soft rumbling of an engine nearby.

"He's awake," I heard Bouncer Boy say.

"It doesn't matter, he can't do anything, his bonds are unbreakable," the other said.

"Don't be foolish, he is not to be taken lightly," Bouncer Boy warned.

"Shut your foul mouth bloodsucker. You are only here because he deems your presence necessary. Keep your council to yourself." The level of tension went up exponentially, I could almost taste the violence that was about to erupt.

With a few controlled movements, I was able to roll over and get a look around. I was in a space no larger than the inside of a minivan. Bouncer Boy and the sniper sat in two chairs in the front, clearly navigating. They faced a screen in a transport of Atlantean design. The screen showed a superimposed topographical representation of what I assumed was the bottom of the ocean. The different contours of the ocean floor were visible in a computer-generated graphic. There were dozens of instruments, knobs, and switches all of which were of alien design.

"Where are we going?" I asked. "Also, I have to go to the little boy's room, I know, I should have gone before we left, but I was just so excited to get going," I added.

"Oh, and are we there yet?" What the hell.

"I told you we should have muzzled him," Bouncer Boy chided.

The other one turned to me, his face no longer covered. A large scar raced from his left temple down and across his face, ending on the right side of his chin. The ragged feature gave him a wild appearance; the dim light drew shadows across his face.

"Your time on the surface has made you weak. The warlord will harden you into a proper and useful tool." The absolute confidence he had in what he said bled through his words.

"I hope he makes me into a crescent wrench, those things are awesome," I said flippantly, all the while I was testing my bonds, my wrists were firmly bound together.

His eyes narrowed to dangerous slits, I saw his body tense for movement.

"Julake, something is approaching," Sigmund said.

Julake turned away from me, back towards the screen.

"Fight all you want. You will not break free of your bonds," he said.

I ignored him and kept struggling, hoping I could work my way loose.

"You worry like a child. It is nothing more than a hunter," Julake's sneering words oozed from him.

"Hunter? It looks like a shark," Sigmund said.

"Precisely."

"The sooner we get back to the surface the better," Sigmund complained.

Julake didn't answer.

My wrists screamed in pain as my struggles pushed my bonds into my skin.

"You would be wise to stop yourself from bleeding; in this small space the smell of your dark, deep blood is maddening," Sigmund's voice sounded dangerously hungry.

He turned to me and his eyes flashed bright silver, I saw his fangs slowly grow as he prepared to attack.

Fast as a snake, Julake snatched Sigmund by the throat and pushed him back into his seat. Sigmund immediately began to fight back when Julake's words stopped him.

"The warlord said he is to be brought in untainted if you so much as scratch him I will disembowel you and feed you to the hunters before you can blink." Julake's threat brokered no argument and I knew without a doubt he could make short work of Sigmund.

Sigmund must have sensed this too because with a force of effort he controlled himself and quit struggling. Julake let go of his throat and there was a tense moment before Sigmund turned forward in his seat.

"Just get us there quickly, his blood is, *distracting*," Sigmund growled.

"Why is everyone always fighting over little ole me?" I asked, hoping to get them fighting again, so I could figure out a way to get free.

They both just ignored me, which really hurt. I was about to say something else when the all too familiar voice of Neal came to me clearly.

My lord, are you safe?

"*Yes, I'm safe. Where are you?*" I sent.

I am near. Brace yourself.

"*Brace myself...?*" It was all I could get out before I heard Sigmund speak.

"What the hell is that?"

"It is a deep dweller; they are not usually found this shallow," Julake said.

"What is the creature doing?" Sigmund's words were filled with real fear.

"I don't know," Julake said and turned to me glaring. "You are behind this somehow!"

He started to rise, the look in his eyes was murderous. I knew if he reached me, I would be in deep trouble.

The force of the impact knocked him back into the control panel and I was thrown forward, unable to protect myself. The loud sound of warning sirens filled the small cabin and red lights started blinking everywhere.

Marcus Abshire — LOST SON

We were again rocked with a devastating impact and I heard metal groan as something squeezed on our vessel. Small streams of water began filling the cabin, the wet salty coolness washed over my face as I was unable to sit up.

A surge of electricity raced through the control panel and everything went dark, tendrils shot off and shocked Julake and Sigmund, both of them jumped in pain.

A loud wrenching sound filled the cabin as the back door began opening, water hit me like a sledgehammer, and I fought to see what was happening. My suit quickly flowed over my mouth and nose and my vision adapted to the deep dark of the ocean floor. I could see the subtle outlines of creatures as their nervous system created a small amount of electricity.

A large shark entered the cabin from the open door and I tried to scramble away from the beast, but my hands being bound hampered my efforts.

Quit struggling and make your way out, I will keep your friends busy.

"*Neal?*" His voice coming to me from this very scary looking shark shocked me completely.

No time for questions, I will explain later, go!

"*Right.*" I got my feet under me and with a powerful push, swam towards the opening.

A strong grip grabbed my ankle and my momentum ended abruptly. I looked down to see Julake holding on, his own suit covered his nose and mouth. I tried to kick at him, but I couldn't get much power from my position. I saw as he began bringing a very sharp looking spear up and towards me, I feared he had decided my escape might be worse than my death.

Neal thrust his tail and shot towards Julake, the small space made his presence overwhelming and Julake let go of me to bring both hands up to stop Neal from eating him.

I used the freedom Neal gave me to hurry out into the open water only to see a murderous looking Sigmund blocking my way. He looked different than normal creatures, his outline darker, most living things gave off a brightness that represented the current their body created as they moved. Sigmund's was the opposite, his outline wasn't brighter than the surrounding darkness, his was darker, still allowing me to see him, but only for the opposite reason.

I got to within a few feet of him, unable to protect myself, when a large tentacle-bearing arm slammed into the vampire and he disappeared from the opening. I swam past where he stood a second ago and hurried away from the Atlantean submarine.

I looked back and saw something out of a prehistoric nightmare. A giant squid the size of a school bus was attacking the submarine. Sigmund floated nearby, seemingly unconscious. The squid was a monster from the deep dark. A giant that haunted many ancient sailor's worst nightmares. The creature's tentacles wrapped around the vessel and were squeezing the submarine into an unrecognizable hunk of metal. The sight stunned me, but it hadn't made me stupid. I kept moving away from the creature, hoping the animal didn't decide I made a perfect sized snack.

I saw Neal, in the form of a shark, swim out of the opening and with a powerful thrust of his tail, slam the door shut, presumably on an angry or hopefully, dead, Julake.

He swam towards me and I saw my sword gripped in his dangerous-looking maw.

Turn around, let me access to your bonds. Neal said.

I twisted around and a few seconds later felt a buzzing in the water as Neal sent a tight and focused electrical arc at my cuffs, breaking them. I brought my hands around and easily removed the destroyed metal from my wrists, the blood from my wounds staining the surrounding water red. I reached out and grabbed my sword and put the weapon away.

"So, Neal, what's new?" I sent.

Now is not the time, my lord. The squid will be confused when the beast realizes I tricked it and there are still your kidnappers to worry about, given they survive. We must get far from here. Your blood will attract other sharks.

I reached out and grabbed Neal's dorsal fin. He moved from side to side, in an easy motion that still propelled us quickly through the water, away from the squid and submarine.

I felt a compression as something exploded within the submarine. A high-pitched whine, that I knew came from the squid, buzzed through the water. The sound was full of pain and surprise. I'm glad Neal took me away from the owner of that noise, not wanting to be anywhere near the massive, hurt and angry giant squid.

After almost ten minutes of silence, I sent to Neal.

"*So, you're a shark now?*"

Yes, this form is quite effective in the water. I needed to be fast and the shark's ability to follow even the smallest trail was invaluable.

"*You can just change forms at will?*" I asked, thinking of all the times a different animal form may have come in handy.

Changing forms is not something I do lightly. The shift takes massive amounts of energy and if I am not careful can drain my reserves, effectively shutting myself off.

"*It will kill you?*" I didn't think Neal had a limit on his energy, I guess it made sense, nothing has an unlimited supply.

Yes, my lord.

I had a hard time being sure, but we seemed to be moving in a very subtle circular direction.

"*So the only thing limiting your ability to shift more often is the amount of energy you have at your disposal?*"

In theory, yes.

Cool.

"*What happened after I was knocked out?*"

Once you were unconscious another group of Warlord Karakatos's men took Arendiol and Kim. I watched as they took them, unable to do anything. They then took you and by the time they got to me, I had been able to channel enough electricity into the foam to free myself. I then fled, intent on freeing you when I was able. I followed all of your scents to the water's edge, where your trails disappeared.

"*Seems odd they would treat you like that unless they realize you are more than just an average dog.*"

Marcus Abshire   LOST SON

That would be an astute assessment, my lord.

I've always had Neal as my secret weapon; it disconcerted me to think Karakatos knew about him.

"*Do you know where they took them?*" We had already put a few miles between our captors, but I had the odd sensation we were being followed.

If your current heading remained consistent, it would appear they were taking you towards Atlantis. I would assume they brought Kim and Arendiol there already.

The dark oppressive pressure of being deep underwater was a constant companion, without my skinsuit and the ability to see in this inky blackness, I would be royally freaking out. Yes, I am an Atlantean descendant of the king and queen, but I never swam at the bottom of the ocean.

"*I hope you're taking us there. I don't intend on leaving them behind.*"

Of course not, my lord, but I believe you have already begun to realize we are not alone. My sensors indicate we have attracted the attention of a large great white shark, one that is currently following the minuscule blood trail your wounds have left. If we do not find shelter soon, we will have to deal with him.

"*Why don't you just mind zap him like you apparently did with that huge squid?*" I asked, truly curious.

The mental physiologies of both animals are not the same, sharks can be persuaded, but once they lock onto a blood scent, they become so singularly focused, I cannot dissuade them from hunting for the source of the blood.

"*Ok, so we can't talk him out of eating us, I guess we can beat the idea out of him?*" I didn't like the prospect, out of all the animals to have to fight, great white sharks were on the top of my "I really don't want to" list.

There is no doubt we would prevail, however, the altercation would most likely result in more blood being spilled. That would attract more sharks, or something worse.

"Worse, what's worse than a great white shark?" We had veered left and were entering an area where deep rifts that opened to the even darker recesses of the earth dotted the ocean floor.

"You know what, never mind, so then what's the plan?" Neal always had a plan.

My records indicate an abandoned vessel nearby, we will try and seek shelter there, in order to reassess our situation.

A vessel? Hiding in an old shipwreck wasn't exactly my idea of a good time, but if Neal thought the sunken boat would work, it probably would.

"Lead on."

We continued in silence, the sense that something was out there, and getting closer intensified. I knew I detected the shark advancing and my new ability was shocking, usually, Neal is the one who can sense our adversaries. The feeling reminded me of a nagging thought that just wouldn't go away, as the shark got closer the intensity of the thought increased if I wasn't careful the constant insistence could induce a sense of panic.

I focused my thoughts and controlled the rising emotions, channeling the thoughts into something I could handle. Neal kept us moving, his body gliding back and forth in lazy motions that belied the speed at which we traveled.

Eventually, we came to a large rip in the ocean floor and began to descend into the dark chasm. At the bottom my senses detected an object no bigger than a large S.U.V. The vessel's structured lines and design differentiated it from the surrounding rock. I let go of Neal's fin and approached the old wreck on my own power. I could tell the shark had closed on us and wanted to be free to defend myself if he decided to make me his lunch.

I approached the spot Neal had indicated and soon realized my original assumptions about the wreck were all wrong. The ship looked like a two-person scout vessel, with a sleek design the shape reminded me of the latest stealth jets the military had developed. The craft looked like a large stingray, with short, but wide wings sweeping away from a small cockpit. A small cargo door on the back allowed entrance from the aft, which reminded me of a submarine's transition chamber, where the space is flooded and then the door is opened to allow for water exploration.

It stood open, allowing me to swim into the small space. I pushed my way in, quickly looking around.

"Well, the space is pretty small, not sure if there's enough room for both of us." I sent to Neal.

I may be able to jump-start the power source but doing so will take a few minutes to gather my resources. Neal sent back, he swam just outside the door, having to keep moving.

Marcus Abshire   LOST SON

I had an answer on the tip of my tongue when I felt the great white shark make his move. He came from just outside my visible range and shot towards me, probably hoping I was unable to escape. He was dead right.

I only had a second to react. I pulled out my sword, intent on making him fight for his meal. I saw him come at me from the dark emptiness of the deep. His ancient, unchanged shape instantly sent uncontrollable spikes of fear down my spine. Large, unblinking eyes locked on to me, while his sharp edges and smooth perfection sliced through the water, hundreds of razor-sharp teeth arrayed in rows led the way.

I knew I really had no hope stuck in this death chamber, even if I landed a few good strikes, the sheer force of his momentum would drive his deadly maw into me. My suit may protect me from most of his attack, but even a small amount of damage from such a strong and powerful hunter would do untold damage, if I managed to kill the beast before *I* was killed, the savage wounds would still leave me bleeding profusely and only attract more of his brothers.

I braced for impact when Neal's smaller form slammed into the much larger animal and pushed him off to the side, out of my line of sight.

"What are you doing? He'll kill you!" I sent frantically.

There is no need to be so dramatic; I am faster and more agile than him. But, do to present circumstances, I may have difficulty facilitating the vessel's recharge, I recommend you complete this feat. He somehow seemed calmer than ever.

Marcus Abshire   LOST SON

"Me, how the hell am I supposed to do it?" I was a second from rushing out and helping Neal.

The power source is located under your present position. If you concentrate on gathering energy to yourself, then transfer what you have gathered to the power core under you, the influx of energy should give the core enough of a jumpstart to activate.

Concentrate on gathering energy? Oh yeah, I could do that sort of thing now. I had no idea how to do what Neal suggested, but I knew if I didn't, he would be hard-pressed to keep the great white occupied long enough.

"Right, I'm on it." I hoped I conveyed more confidence than I felt.

I closed my eyes, not sure if that would help, but I needed to shut out all distractions. I dipped inside myself, the way Neal had taught me to do when dealing with vampires. I rooted around, looking for what I had tapped into last night, looking for my newfound talent. As soon as I thought about doing what I had done the night before, I felt a slight twinge, like contracting a muscle I had never used. The ability felt weak, but there. I flexed the "muscle" again, only this time I concentrated on gathering energy, I don't know how or what I was doing, but I felt an answer.

I immediately became aware of the concealed energy that was all around me. The untapped power was everywhere and occupied the spaces between particles. The sheer volume almost overwhelmed me, but I managed to focus and keep my concentration. I soon felt as the energy began pouring into me, more than I ever intended on gathering. I felt as though I was going to explode, the sheer power was unbelievable. My head throbbed and every ounce of my being screamed with pain, I knew if I didn't stop, I would be unmade by the sheer enormity of energy flowing into my body.

Focus! Push the power out of you and into the craft's power cells! Neal's voice came from far away, ringing in my head, vying for space amidst the endless power.

Somehow, I was able to process what he said and shifted my thoughts away from gathering energy and into being more of a conduit for it, driving the buzzing fire out of me and down, down into the floor. I opened my eyes and realized the entire compartment was filled with bright blue radiance, the light blazing from my eyes.

I felt a rush, like falling from a ledge, an almost chaotic pull as the power I had gathered left me and raced not only into the power cells but into the entire area in a large concussive blast, one that knocked me off my feet to go flying into the side of the vessel. My head slammed hard and darkness threatened to consume me. As the drain of my actions took its toll I began to fall into unconsciousness, seeing as every light on the instrument panel light up and a comfortable hum came from the newly powered engines, then darkness took me.

Chapter Thirteen

The first thing I noticed as I slowly came awake was that I was dry. The inside of our ship was no longer filled with water. The second thing was Neal, sitting next to me in his canine form.

"*Hey, guess it worked?*" I sent groggily. "*You're a dog,*" I added.

Yes. He answered, turning back to look at the control panel.

"*Okay, captain chatty pants, what happened after I passed out?*" I rubbed my head; the throbbing headache slowly began to recede.

You were sloppy in your actions. The energy you collected almost killed you, but you released the power in time. The resulting effects reverberated for miles in all directions, you are fortunate for being deep underwater and not amidst people.

"*It was that bad, huh?*" The idea that my newfound powers could hurt innocent people did not sit well with me.

The release of all that pent-up energy was, but you did stun the great white, which was helpful. I was also able to absorb a large amount of energy, allowing me to shift back into this form. Not to mention you successfully restarted the scouting vessel. The core should hold a charge for decades.

Sheesh, I had to be more careful.

"Okay, so we're in business, and I need to practice more." Neal looked over at me, his intense eyes bored a hole through me.

Yes, my lord, that would be advisable.

"I guess you've already set our course for Atlantis." If he thought we were doing anything other than rescuing Kim and Arendiol, he was sorely mistaken.

I am unable to operate the vessel in my current form, but if you take the controls, I can guide you through the process.

I stood up in the cramped space and groggily sat down in the pilot's seat which was surprisingly comfortable.

"You know, I was thinking. If you can change forms, why choose a dog, why not a human, or at least a monkey, something with opposable thumbs?" I sent, looking over the controls.

They looked simple enough; I saw a steering wheel that reminded me of old video game controllers and a sliding throttle that obviously was the speed control.

I suppose I should have explained this all to you earlier, but my protocols, as programmed by the Seer's, did not allow me to. They did not want you knowing too much information until you were ready.

"It's kind of hard to have confidence in a bunch of dudes who have been dead for thousands of years." I thought, sarcastically.

If you grab the directional controls and lift, the action will facilitate the vessel's vertical ascension, however, I suggest gently pulling back and increasing the throttle slightly, in order to break free of the surrounding ocean floor.

Marcus Abshire   LOST SON

I reached out and did as he said, the engines humming increased as I gave them more power and I heard loud scratching and grinding noise as we forced ourselves out from under thousands of years of accumulated sedimentation.

Once we were free and no longer bound by the earth I sent to Neal, *"Okay, so you never answered my question."*

Sentinels were originally just personalized programs. Technology-based interaction systems that were used as teachers, mentors, and trainers. We were designed to be accessible through certain interfaces, almost like the internet. We were available wherever a young Atlantean had access to an interface module.

My programming has been designed around your genetic profile, based on your parent's personalities.

"Wait, wait, if you were made, specifically for me, why are we not more, agreeable?"

The circumstances surrounding your life and where and when you have grown into adulthood were unforeseen and perhaps led to the, at times, discontent between us. Yet, my purpose is to be a buffer against your natural tendencies to make mistakes. That is rarely easily accepted. It is almost a natural phenomenon for SENTINELs to rub their charges the wrong way.

"I guess that makes sense." I thought.

So my existence in a physical form is a unique situation. I was created as a hybrid of technology and a merging of the forces your parents, and now you, wield. That is why I am able to utilize the energy you control. But I have been designed with a block on the ability to take a bipedal form. My makers knew the potential for my being used for ill intentions and felt limiting the form I can take would help minimize that risk.

"*I bet it stings to know you weren't trusted?*" I asked.

I trust my maker's decision. There is no doubt they had good reasons for my limitations. I had a hard time telling, but I swore I could sense a slight amount of resentment.

Hopefully, I have satisfied your curiosity as to my design, now if you would be so kind as to input the coordinates I give you, we can begin on our way.

"*Yeah, sure.*" I hoped we didn't have far to go, there was no telling what Kim and Arendiol were dealing with at the hands of the Warlord.

The controls looked complicated, but Neal made understanding their use easy. There were dozens of buttons and knobs, all of a strange design that I was unfamiliar with. They had symbols next to them in Atlantean, a language I could speak, but not read. Neal translated and soon we were slicing through the water, heading towards the place of my ancestors and the home I never had.

According to Neal, we had about three hours before we arrived at the coordinates he gave me. So we had some time to kill. I left him at the helm, going to the back of the craft for a small amount of privacy. We still had our mind link, so I was never truly alone, but the small distance apart was something.

I sat down and crossed my legs and began breathing in a slow rhythm, in through my nose, out through my mouth. The routine quickly had the calming effect I needed. There was so much that had happened in the last few days that was threatening to overwhelm me and I needed to focus my thoughts on what I was going to do.

After a while, I managed to push the worry over Kim and Arendiol, the fear of what we were heading towards, the uncertainty of all the unanswered questions and the curiosity of who my true family was and what the implications meant into a place where I could concentrate fully on exploring my newfound powers.

Finally, my mind was clear of all the worries, fear and concerns, I was ready to begin.

It appears the mechanism for your gathering of energy is similar to the one I utilize in pulling electricity from the air. Neal's voice was so familiar that the presence of his words within my head didn't break my concentration.

Sometimes using something to focus your thoughts helps. Something that is familiar and comfortable will allow you a way to ground your mind.

Without really thinking about my actions, I reached back and instinctively pulled my sword from the sheath, holding the handle in one hand as the blue blade lay across my lap. The sword's weight was something I had become so comfortable with over the years the weapon felt like an extension of my hand as if the sword had become a part of me.

I took a few more moments of tranquility and then slowly, ever so slowly reached inside myself, finding the newfound ability I possessed. I felt a weak response, but I realized my ability wasn't weak in reference to power, my weakness was about control. I knew I could draw untold amounts of power to myself, but the energy would be wild and dangerous. My gift was like a large faucet I could turn on, but unfocused raw power wasn't useful. I had to find a way to get control, to mold the burning fire to my will, which is where true strength really lied.

I tentatively began to draw in power and felt raw energy flow into me. I felt a growth of strength, as though I could easily lift a car and throw it across the street.

Neal's link with me allowed him to feel what I felt, or at least to perceive what was happening.

You must be careful with the power, the energy can enhance your strength and speed, but your physiology is still the same. You could lift a truck, but your bones would not be able to hold the weight.

I heard him and filed the information away. I felt the energy grow and a small spike of fear shot through me, afraid I was going to lose control. I gripped my sword tighter, using the structured physicality of the blade to focus my thoughts. I concentrated on the sword. The design was simple, but the metal was strong and shone with a mirror finish, although the steel had a blue tinge from the unique Atlantean metalworking technique used to forge the blade. The metal started to glow and for a second I didn't know what was happening when I realized my focus had channeled the energy into the blade, giving the sharp steel an unknown power.

I felt the release of my pent-up energy flow out of me and into the sword at a constant rate. I soon held no power but could sense the energy radiating off my sword. I held the glowing blue steel up, amazed at what I had done.

Careful, your sword is now infused with your power, I am not sure what releasing that power would do if you were to strike the metal on something, I do not want to lose our mode of transportation.

I heard him but didn't answer. I just stared at the metal as the glowing radiance filled the small area where I sat with a deep blue. After what seemed like five minutes the light began to dim, as the energy eventually left, I lost my deep focus and all the minutiae of my surroundings flooded back into my awareness.

I realized I was drenched in sweat and panting heavily. I felt exhausted and thin, like a shirt that had been worn too long and washed too many times.

"Well, that was interesting," I said aloud, my voice filling the vessel, fully breaking the spell.

Yes, as you train more, your control and endurance will increase. Neal added.

"*Good, I'd hate to pass out whenever I used my power.*" My stomach growled loudly, and I felt exhaustion wash over me.

"*How long until we arrive?*" I sent.

Our E.T.A. is in ninety-three minutes.

Wow, that took an hour and a half. That wouldn't do. If I needed to use my gifts I may need to do so in a hurry.

"*I'm gonna catch some z's. Wake me in an hour.*" I said sleepily, my eyes were already closed, my mind beginning to wander.

Of course, my lord.

I didn't have the energy to respond, sleep took me.

Neal's voice cut through the dark landscape of my dreams.

We will arrive in approximately thirty minutes. He said.

Marcus Abshire   LOST SON

I opened my eyes and shook off the last vestiges of sleep. My nap had only been an hour-long, but I felt revived, fresh and new. I was still hungry, but I felt great. I got up and went to the controls, sitting down. The screen before me displayed the same layout as the one earlier with Sigmund and Julake. The ocean floor still looked as bland as ever and I looked up to see symbols on the screen, reminding me of my motorcycle's speedometer.

"That's telling us how fast we're going, isn't it?" I sent, pointing to the symbols.

That is correct, my lord. We are currently traveling at 110 miles per hour.

That was fast, especially given the fact we were underwater.

I let out a long low whistle, amazed at our speed. Neal had informed me long ago when I first realized where I had come from, the real location of Atlantis. Most modern theorists believed Atlantis rested somewhere in the Mediterranean, they were wrong.

The actual location of Atlantis is much closer to home. The effects of the Fall and the release of energy has left a mark, even to this day. The Bermuda Triangle has been a place of infamy for centuries, holding an aura of mystery and danger, a place where ships go and never return, a legend that has some basis in fact. The energies that swirl around Atlantis and still linger have caused many ships to get lost or sink due to a myriad of technical issues. Neal has even mentioned long-dead defense measures that have sunk ships that have come too close.

"Ok, Neal. What are we walking into?"

Marcus Abshire   LOST SON

I cannot be entirely sure. There may have been many changes since last I was connected to the city's main computer system. We could be walking into a chaotic place, one that has broken down due to the degeneration of the clone's genes. Or the place may be one of quiet compliance, where the programming of the citizens is still intact, and all seems well. I tend to think with the current predicament we are in and the testimony from Arendiol that there is a good chance of the former being the case. The city most likely is under the rule of the Warlord and we must approach our goals with that mindset.

"Sounds smart, what do you have in mind?" I sent.

We will enter the city from a long-forgotten access, from there we will make our way towards an interface module where I can then upload to the city's mainframe. The main computer system should hold the key to finding Arendiol and Kim. At that point we will split up; my inability to take an Atlantean form would bring undue attention upon us, requiring you to continue alone. I will guide you towards where you need to go and provide assistance should you run into any trouble.

"Do you really think the rescue will be that easy, that the Warlord will just let us waltz in and take his prisoners and then walk out?"

Of course not, my lord, but I see no other alternative. Do you?

I thought about our situation for a minute, trying to think of any other options we may have. Having someone on the inside would have been nice, but that wasn't available here. I was an outcast and Neal would stick out like a sore thumb, our best bet was to move in secret and not arise any attention until we were long gone, or at least until I had Kim and Arendiol with me. Then I could unleash all kinds of holy hell getting them out.

"*No, I guess you're right. How much do you know about Karakatos and Julake? I have a feeling I'm going to be running into them again.*" We still had about twenty minutes until we arrived, never hurt to do your homework.

My current records are not fully up to date. I have almost nothing on Julake and the Warlord Karakatos, but I do have information on their ancestors. Clones are bred for specific purposes and both Julake and Karakatos come from long lines of warrior protectors. My records also indicate that for generations both bloodlines were compliant and had excellent reports, but the last few cycles have produced increasingly defiant clones, incidences of disciplinary action against both families have increased with each new generation. The last record I have for Julake's "father" shows he was decommissioned after being convicted of murder and Karakatos's previous clone was reported as having gone absent.

"*You mean he went AWOL.*" Looked like we were dealing with very damaged individuals.

Precisely. Neal answered.

"*If Karakatos has taken over and Julake is working for him, then we would be smart to assume most of the city's warrior protectors are either in line with the Warlord or unaware of his plans.*" I mused.

Yes, I would advise you trust no one, and to avoid contact at all costs. Neal added.

Marcus Abshire   LOST SON

I sat quietly for a while, thinking about what I may encounter. I needed to be focused on what was coming, rescuing a child from the basement of some human monster was one thing, but sneaking into Atlantis to rescue my friends while not being caught was quite another.

The sound of our engine quieting and the soft shift of deceleration shook me from my thoughts. I looked at the viewscreen, trying to see where Neal was taking us. The ocean floor looked the same as before, except for a small dome that rose from the ground. I would have passed the anomaly on the ocean floor by, thinking the dome a natural part of the landscape, if I hadn't seen a small opening, about five feet in diameter, covered by a grate, on the side.

"What am I looking at?" I asked Neal.

The ship's automated landing programming took over and we gently came to rest, soft, fine clouds of mud drifted up into view as our settling disturbed the ground.

That is an old hunting tunnel. After the initial Fall, fish and other sea creatures avoided coming near the city, the energies swirling around the perimeter confused and disorientated them. So, until we built sufficient hunting vessels and skin suits to allow for underwater travel, these tunnels were built, where hunters could exit away from the city's energy field and gather much-needed food.

There used to be hundreds of them, allowing for the hunters to gather the large numbers of fish needed to sustain the city, but as our farming techniques and transport technology aided in providing food, the tunnels eventually collapsed or filled in from disuse. This is the only one left, Neal finished.

I looked at the crate intently, the metal covered in years of growth, making the hidden entrance almost completely blend in with the surroundings.

"*How do you plan on opening the ancient access?*" I asked.

Once we get close, I will interface with the control panel and unlock the grate.

"*What happens if the opening mechanism is broken or sealed shut from years of not being used?*" I asked, nothing was ever easy.

Then we will deal with that when and or if the predicament occurs.

"*I guess there's no time to find out like the present.*"

Indeed.

Neal was still in his canine form, if he thought he needed to change shape, I trusted him to either do so or ask for my help. We made our way to the back of the vessel, I checked to make sure my sword was still secured behind my back, out of habit I reached down to find my gun holster empty. I had lost my pistol somewhere between being kidnapped and escaping with Neal. I felt exposed without the heavy metal close to my body, like when you forget to put on your watch and the loss of the familiar item makes you feel naked.

I hit the button that sealed the cockpit and held my breath as the back panel opened and the space we were in flooded with water. I knew I could breathe with my skinsuit, but I just couldn't help holding my breath until the entire space filled up. I quickly adjusted to being underwater and with a few kicks swam out of the small confines of the Atlantean sub and into the open waters of the Bermuda Triangle.

The cold water immediately tried to suck all the heat from my body and the pressure of being so deep pressed on me, but my Atlantean physiology was made to withstand the forces. I looked back and saw Neal dog-paddling after me. I couldn't help but smile, seeing him swimming underwater in his canine form.

I reached out and grabbed him around his body and began swimming towards the opening. A few moments later I let him go as he began to access the control panel.

This may take a few moments, he sent to me.

I wasn't sure how difficult navigating a computer with your mind might be, but I had the impression the task wasn't easy, so I kept my thoughts to myself and turned away from him to keep watch on our sixes.

Out of the corner of my eye, I thought I saw a slight movement as if something had quickly darted behind a rock sitting on the bottom of the ocean. The tactic seemed odd because most sea creatures wouldn't feel the need to hide unless they felt they were being hunted. Neal and I were just sitting here, being completely non-threatening.

There! Again I saw something move, just outside my peripheral vision, the shape darted behind cover. I began getting a bad feeling in my stomach, I don't know why but I didn't like what I saw. I thought about telling Neal but didn't want to break his concentration, so instead, I opened myself up to my surroundings. I let my senses drift out from me, into the ocean. At the same time, I tried to channel the smallest bit of energy my new abilities allowed me to gather. Willing the power to do what I wanted was hard at first, but I quickly felt my awareness expand beyond my normal boundaries and instantly felt something nearby.

I couldn't make out if the presence was a normal animal or something else, I began to look closer when Neal's voice inside my head startled me and I lost concentration.

There, the door is open.

The grate began to groan as the mechanism that opened the crusted metal began forcing the bottom to break free from the natural concrete that had grown around the ancient structure. The grate rose a few inches and then stopped. I heard a loud screeching noise as the gate's motor fought the resistance built from years of neglect but lost. The grate quit moving after only six inches. There wasn't enough room for Neal and me to enter.

"*Shit! That's just great.*" I complained.

Perhaps we can force the grate open. Neal said as he went over and tried to pry the metal open with his mouth.

"*You're just going to hurt yourself, back up, let me see if I can get the damn thing open.*" I said, pushing past him.

I reached down and grabbed the grate with both hands, straining to open the stubborn old door. I felt the gears give another inch and then stop again.

Alright, you wanna play dirty?

I grabbed the grate again and this time concentrated on gathering energy to myself and channeling the power to my muscles for strength. I had to be careful not to push so much that I ripped my arms from my sockets, but enough to force the gate open. I felt the energy flow into me and was astounded at the power such a small amount provided. Soon the gate began to groan and slowly open as I strained. After getting another foot of movement I let go and just waited for the energy to dissipate. My body shook from using the power and I waited. Eventually, the unbridled strength dissipated, leaving me exhausted.

Neal just stared at me, without saying a word.

Well done. He sent to me after a while.

I was just about to say thank you when I felt something coming for us. Neal whipped his head around at the same time and before he could warn me, I sent to him. *"I know. Something's coming."*

I pulled my sword free and the sharp edge sliced through the water as I held the Atlantean forged steel in front of me.

Whatever is approaching has us at a disadvantage, we should retreat into the tunnel. We should find dry ground not far from this opening. Neal counseled.

My first impulse was to stand my ground, but I realized he had a point, whatever came sent shivers down my spine and I knew instinctively, the oncoming threat was dangerous indeed.

"Ok," I said, a second later one of the three sea witches that had been stalking us rushed from their cover and flew at me with razor-sharp poisoned tipped claws aimed at my throat.

I brought my sword up and met her descending claws, I expected my sword to slice through her nails, but I got a nasty surprise when my blade was turned aside. I sucked in my stomach, thrust my hip backwards as her other hand swiped my midsection, missing me by an inch.

Her face was something out of a horror show. Neal had briefed me on sea witches, but I had never seen one before and what I saw was disturbing.

She had skin that reminded me of an electric eel, slimy and smooth. Her sickening hide was green, but not the vibrant green of lush grass, more like a cancerous green, full of sickness and disease. Her face held two eyes, three times the size of a human's, with dark black pupils she seemed to have an alien-like quality to her stare as if I were some unknown creature that had to be tasted and eaten. Her arms were long and held corded muscle, while her lower body writhed as six tentacles undulated as she moved.

If I hadn't been fighting for my life, the very sight of her would have made me puke.

She opened up her mouth and lunged forward; hundreds of needle-like teeth raced towards me as I shifted to the left and landed a heavy punch to the side of her face.

Hitting her made my stomach churn as her skin gave way and I felt her jaw break.

She let out an ungodly sound, a high-pitched screech that bored into my head, threatening to make me pass out. I saw the other two come flowing towards me, being propelled by their writhing tentacles.

We must retreat, get to dry land. Neal pleaded with me.

"You first, then distract them as I get through, I don't want to turn my back on them," I answered, kicking the sea witch whose jaw I had broken away from me.

She reached out and sliced one of my fins with her poisoned talons, leaving three slashes in the hard material.

The other two were almost on me. I thought about bringing my powers to bear, but when I tried, I couldn't concentrate enough to make anything happen.

"Neal!" I sent, knowing I had only a few seconds until I had to fight two of the nasty things.

I was a master swordsman and expert hand to hand fighter, with my skinsuit I was agile and at home in the water, but even with my strength and speed, I was no match for creatures such as this in their own element. Getting the drop on one was pure luck, luck I was glad I had, but beating two of them while their sister regrouped was not a situation I thought I would be able to swim away from.

At the last second, I heard Neal scream in my head as he also sent a sound assault towards the witches.

NOW! he sent.

The sound waves from his attack flowed through the water and left a ripple effect as they went. Sound travels better in water, which made his normally devastating sound assault even more powerful. I turned to hurry under the grate and was hit by a fraction of his attack. The blast knocked me sideways and pain tore through my shoulder as I feared the socket had been dislocated. I ignored the pain and forced myself through the small opening.

Once on the other side, I looked back at Neal's handiwork, surprised at what I saw. The witches had been affected, but not like I had expected. Neal had pushed them back a few feet, but they had resisted his blast and were once again approaching in a weird snake-like motion.

I sheathed my sword and pushed off, swimming with all I had, not knowing how far this tunnel led until reaching an opening. If we were heading for a dead-end, I feared that's exactly what this would become for us.

Neal was ahead of me and as I reached him, I grabbed him and kept kicking. I kept seeing in my mind as the sea witches closed the distance and raked my back with their claws, allowing the poison to do its deadly work, the fear of them catching me pushed me to keep swimming, faster than I ever had.

Hurry, my sensors indicate we are almost there. They are gaining.

He just had to add that last part, didn't he?

The floor slowly started sloping up and as I broke the surface and hurried through the waist-deep water, I chanced a look back.

The witch I had punched, evidenced by her jaw, which hung askew, surged out of the water and covered the short distance between us. I reached up and grabbed her wrists before she could stab me with her long nails. Her strength startled me, and I mustered everything I had to stop her from impaling me. She opened her mouth and lunged at me, hoping to bite off my face.

I dodged back and forth keeping her from biting me and slowly backed out of the water, which was now only a foot deep. With a grunt of effort, I lifted her up and threw her back into her two sisters, who were coming up behind her.

Marcus Abshire   LOST SON

She barreled into them with a wet smack but managed to reach out with one of her tentacles, wrapping the strong, slimy appendage around my leg. With a strong tug, she hauled me off my feet and I hit the ground hard. My head rang from smacking the rough floor. Reaching back, I unsheathed my sword and as the witch began dragging me back underwater I sat up and swiped at the long sinuous tentacle pulling on my leg.

With a satisfying slice, I watched as my sword parted the tentacle end from the rest of her. She let out another loud screech and I scrambled onto dry land, next to Neal. I faced the water and kicked off the cut portion of her that still adhered to my leg. The amputated limb landed in the water with a loud splash and writhed as if the thing had a mind of its own.

Neal and I slowly backed up putting distance between ourselves and the water's edge, taking quick stock of our surroundings. We were in a simple tunnel; rounded rock walls leveled out and continued back into darkness. My Atlantean skin suit still covered my face and allowed me to see in the pitch black. Soon, the suit would flow back and then I would be blind, hopefully not until this threat had passed.

A light green glow appeared in the shallow water and I watched as all three sea witches slowly rose up from the water, standing side by side. Their bodies emitted a slightly green hue that reminded me of deep-sea fish who use bioluminescence to draw in their prey. I saw as the head witch, the one I had been beating on still led the way, her jaw held tight as she clenched to keep her razor filled maw from moving. Her tentacles still writhed in a strange fluid motion under her, but the one I had cut a portion off had already stopped bleeding.

I continued to face them, afraid to turn my back.

"Neal, got any ideas?" I sent hurriedly.

We have a slight advantage out of the water, but I am not sure how fast they are on land. If we engage them, I cannot predict with certainty the outcome of the engagement. If we turn and flee, they may follow us and we would be forced to fight them anyway. I don't know how long they can last in the open air. The choice is yours. Neal finished.

What? Had some portal opened and taken Neal only to replace him with his opposite from another dimension? The choice was mine? Granted I always made the decisions, but he had never said that before.

"Well, that makes this easier," I said, and leaped for the witch in the middle, my sword aimed straight for her throat.

Neal leaped to attack and landed on top of the witch on the left, his canines biting down on her smooth green neck. My blade was again pushed aside by her long claws and I spun to the right as her sister tried to get at me from my flank. I swept low slicing her in the stomach with my sword and watched as a large deep gash opened, followed by a screech of pain.

I immediately backed up, knowing the first one would be coming for me, but I slipped on something underwater, something I hadn't seen. I took me a second to regain my footing and I felt a sharp pain as the first sea witch's sharp claws stabbed me, radiating pain flowed from the wound and my arm went limp. I reached out and grabbed the sword as the weapon fell from my grip, slicing a quick X into the chest of my assailant.

Again, there was a loud screech of pain and I backed up as the other witch began to advance on me.

I feared for Neal, as I realized that without the use of my arm, I was sorely outgunned. I began to try and gather energy into me, in order to redouble my attack against the witches when I saw them look up past me and hiss with obvious hate. A large arrow, the kind used by a cross-bolt, thunked into the sea witch's chest and she immediately spun and dove back under the water, along with her sister. A few seconds later Neal splashed out of the shallow water and came to stand next to me.

He looked me up and down quickly.

You're hurt, one of them got to you, he said, matter of factly.

"*I'll be fine,*" I lied, the pain already had spread to my chest and I was having trouble breathing.

"*Who the hell shot her?*" Was all I could think before my legs buckled and I fell to the floor.

Neal stood over me, looking up at someone.

I could hear the smooth melodic words of Atlantean as someone slowly approached. I was able to move my head to the side and see a skinny looking man with glasses and wild unkempt hair slowly approaching. He had set down his weapon and had both hands up in a show of non-aggression.

"*What's he saying?*" I thought, trying to get up, but my damn body wouldn't respond.

The man's words came to me clearly as he approached.

Marcus Abshire   LOST SON

"Please, I am not here to hurt you, he has been poisoned. I can help, please he is the lost son isn't he, come to help? I'm here to help, we have been waiting for him, please let me help," he kept saying.

Lost son? What the hell did that mean? I thought as blackness began to take me.

"Neal if he can help, maybe we should let h...."

Chapter Fourteen

I was getting tired of always being knocked out, poisoned or blacking out from exhaustion.

"Is that him?" The speaker had a squeaky voice, filled with uncertainty.

"I don't know we'll have to wait for him to wake up," a woman said.

"Of course it's him, the proof is right there, keeping guard," a third speaker said.

He spoke with authority, the leader, maybe?

"What is *that*? I've never seen anything like it."

"It's not an 'it,' it's a 'he,'" I said, opening my eyes and sitting up.

When Neal insisted on teaching me Atlantean I never thought I would actually use the ancient language, it's times like these that make me thank the stars for my overbearing, aggravating, and demanding dog.

I was in a small mechanical room; the walls were covered in old piping and valves dotted the metal. Three people stood in a group near the sole door. The same man who had come to my aid, a woman with blond hair and hard edges and a short, skinny man who kept looking over at me and Neal with quick, furtive glances.

My movement and words caused them all to pause and turn to me, looking at me as if I were a coiled snake ready to attack.

"His name is Neal, and he's my dog," I rubbed my arm which still ached, but I could move it and the discomfort meant I could still feel pain, good.

An odd light fixture in the middle of the room gave off an amber glow, making odd shadows on the wall.

"*What did I miss?*" I sent to Neal who sat next to me, like a guard.

The one with the wild hair helped drag you here. He then produced an antidote to the sea witch's poison. I analyzed the substance to be sure the antidote would not harm you further, whereby I allowed him to administer the compound into your bloodstream. From my calculations, the antidote should now become part of your immune system and help fight off any further episodes of their poison.

"*Cool,*" I sent.

Not long after the other two individuals showed up. From what I have heard, the wild-haired one's name is Brigand, and the woman's name is Sessarian, I do not know who the third one is.

"Where am I?" I asked, hoping to get them talking.

The older one, Brigand, stepped away from the others, getting a little closer.

"You're somewhere safe, for now. Tell me, why are you not inoculated from the hag's poison, and what is a *dog?*" he said the last word with trepidation, testing the sound.

"The hag?" I asked.

"Oh, you mean the sea witch. I didn't even know there *was* an antidote. I've never run into the nasty things before, never needed any protection from their poison, and Neal is my friend and companion, he is no threat to you," I answered, the less they knew about Neal the better, we still had no idea who these people were, Neal's presence would be a target for the Warlord, should he find out.

"The hags are a common foe for us, for anyone living in the city. Anyone authorized to be down in these areas must be immunized. Are you saying you do not have authorization to be here?" he asked, I felt like this line of questioning was a ruse, he had something else on his mind.

"What do you think?" I hoped Neal may have some information that I didn't about our friends.

It is unclear if they are friend or foe. Yet logic would dictate they would not save you, only to then want to harm you. Good point.

"True, but these people are degenerative clones, maybe acting erratically is what they do." I thought.

Perhaps.

I could see Neal wasn't going to be much help. Sometimes if you wanted information you had to give some first.

"No, I don't have authorization to be down here, I wouldn't even know where to begin to get authorization. I'm not really from around here." I stood up, moving my arm back and forth.

I felt my sword still on my back, either they didn't try to take my weapon, or they did and Neal wouldn't let them.

The third guy turned and took a few steps closer, interest evident on his face. The woman's already steely countenance became even more so.

"What do you mean, not from around here?" Brigand asked.

"Look, Brigand is it?" He was clearly surprised at my knowledge of his name.

"I live in a small apartment above my place of business, I don't live in this city, I'm from Oklahoma." I knew they had no idea what states were, and I just wanted to see how they would react.

"You see? I told you, he is from the outside," the skinny guy said. His words came out in an excited rush.

"We don't know for sure, he could be an agent of the Warlords," Sessarian argued.

Brigand hushed them both, staring at me intently.

"Is it true, do you come from the surface?" he asked.

"Yes, I already said as much," Impatience began to boil within me.

"I knew it!" the skinny one squealed. The woman was unmoved.

"How did you come to have an Atlantean skin suit?" he asked.

"Listen, I came down here in search of a girl and a woman whom the Warlord kidnapped. Seems to me you guys aren't big fans of his, so how's about you ease up on the twenty questions and answer a few of my own?" I don't know what I had expected when I came down here, but these three misfits weren't quite the reception I had envisioned.

Sessarian leaned towards Brigand, "We have to move from here, their entry most likely alerted the patrol, they will be down here soon."

He turned to her then to me.

"She's right, we have to move. Will you come with us, we can provide a safe place where you can ask your questions and we can ask some more, perhaps we can help each other?" He clearly hoped I would acquiesce.

"*Well?*" I sent.

I sense nothing about them that invokes hostility towards you. The woman, however, is clearly mistrustful, but she seems to be more worried about her friend's well-being than attacking you.

"*Where is the closest interface? I'm not really interested in getting involved in this mess. If we can get what we need without them, that's what I want to do.*" I sent.

Most of them are in areas of education and labor, namely populated ones. I think our best interests may lie with them, at least until those interests diverge.

"Okay, we'll come, but as long as we keep this meeting between us, no outside communications," I said, knowing Neal would inform me if anyone tried.

Brigand turned thoughtful for a few seconds.

"I don't like it, we will need to report in soon if not someone will come looking for us," Sessarian said.

"True, but this may be what we have been waiting for," Brigand answered.

"Fine, come with us and we will do as you ask," he said to me.

"Deal," I answered.

We all made our way out of the cramped mechanical room and entered a large industrial-looking area. We were at the bottom of several levels of what looked like huge filtration systems, hundreds of huge cylindrical tanks dotted the area while pipes ranging from three inches to two feet in diameter exited the tanks and went to destinations unknown. The whole area reminded me of a sewer treatment facility.

There were landings and stairwells leading up to different levels that allowed access for maintenance crews to reach the different pieces of equipment and tanks.

It was from one of those walkways, two levels up, that we heard a loud booming voice say, "You there, stay where you are!"

We all turned and saw a group of five men hurrying down the walkway, heading towards a stairwell that would bring them down to our level. They were dressed in uniforms, dark blue from head to toe with a large silver blazing sun on their chests. Each one carried a long black stick and two of them held the foam pistols I had encountered earlier.

"Go! Go! We can't let them stop us, move!" Brigand ordered.

They are getting ready to fire at us. Neal's voice rang in my head.

"Incoming!" I yelled, turning back to face the soldiers.

Sessarian ran up next to me, without looking back she said, "Brigand, get to safety, we shall see if our newcomer has a spine."

The two soldiers holding pistols raised them and fired two round white spheres at Sessarian and me. Before I could so much as move Sessarian pointed her own strange pistol at the incoming projectiles. She held what looked like a black powder pistol, one used in the eighteenth century, only the barrel ended in what looked like the end of a trumpet. I fully expected to hear soft jazz come from the weapon when she pulled the trigger.

Instead, I heard a high-pitched whine buzzing in my head. Neal let out a loud whimper and backed away from the sound. The projectiles were almost on us, but a few feet away they each burst and came apart in a cloud of what looked like flour, the particles were so fine.

I had only a few seconds to marvel at the efficiency of Sessarian's countermeasures when the three other soldiers reached us.

"I want him alive, the woman is of no use to us, she can die," he ordered.

That was the wrong thing to say. Anger rose in me, bringing my surroundings into greater clarity.

Remember, they have your strength and speed. Neal counseled.

"Yeah, but do they have my sense of fashion?" I asked as I moved to intercept one of the soldier's sticks descending towards my head.

The sound of our weapons reverberated through the air. I twisted my sword and swung the baton out and away from us, exposing the soldier's side. I kicked hard and felt as my boot broke a few ribs, my opponent fell away, letting out a painful breath of air and grabbing his abdomen.

Sessarian was dodging her own baton assault. I noticed the end of the soldier's weapon sparked, like a Taser, and could imagine what would happen if the glowing tip came in contact with someone's body. She fought with metal forearm braces, allowing her to block the batons without breaking her arms. They also created a solid base at her wrists and would make her punches more powerful, like large brass knuckles.

Two more assailants rushed me, hoping to take me down, but I spun from the first and landed a powerful punch to the other guy's head, staggering him. The third soldier, the one giving the orders entered the fray and I quickly found myself surrounded by three Atlantean soldiers, each one genetically engineered to fight.

They just circled me, not paying much attention to Sessarian, which I thought was rather rude. Using the pause in the fighting I tried to draw energy into myself from my surroundings. I played a dangerous gamble, I wasn't very proficient at gathering power to me quickly and I had to divert almost all of my attention for the task, but I hoped my recent display of skill would at least make them wary, wary enough to give me the time I needed.

I felt the energy rush into me, and I quickly channeled the vibrant power towards my sword, leaving a small amount for myself. I don't know if their reaction was from the way my sword began to glow or the blue light emanating from my eyes, but all three of them looked at me with a growing sense of fear, as if they were fishermen and just realized they had brought in a great white shark instead of a tuna.

Finally, the leader broke the stalemate first.

"Do your duty, bring him in unharmed," he said, then all three of them rushed me at the same time.

Marcus Abshire   LOST SON

I crouched down and jumped, leaping fifteen feet into the air and with a quick twist and flip landed outside of their circle and next to Sessarian who had just dispatched her own opponent, evidenced by his still unmoving body nearby.

She looked at me with awe and a small amount of fear, before shaking it off.

"Not too bad," she said to me grudgingly.

"I do Pilates," I answered.

Her look of confusion quickly shifted to alertness as the three soldiers realized I was no longer there and turned to us, attacking.

I felt strong, stronger than I ever had and I rushed at them, dodging a downward sweeping baton I twisted and backhanded the one wielding the weapon and felt his nose break and saw blood flow as the strength of my punch crushed his face. He fell off to the side, knocked unconscious.

"Forget this, they are both going to die," the other soldier said as he twisted something on the handle of his baton and the sides fell off revealing a very sharp looking sword.

He swung for my face and I parried his attack easily, but the contact released the pent-up energy from my sword. A wave of energy blasted my enemy and knocked him off his feet, sending him sailing into one of the metal tanks, his head and back slammed the unforgiving surface and as he slid to the ground his eyes rolled up into the back of his head and he slumped over.

Sessarian and I stood next to each other, facing the last soldier, daring for him to attack. He quickly realized he was outgunned and turned to flee, like a mouse running for a hole. He got about ten feet away when a bolt pierced the back of his neck and he fell over, dead.

I spun around to see Brigand slowly lowering his now-empty crossbow.

"What the hell did you kill him for, he wasn't attacking!" I yelled, rushing over towards Brigand.

My lord, be careful. Neal warned, but I didn't care.

"He would have reported of your existence and we would have had a whole unit down here, with much more firepower," he stood firm, unyielding.

"What gives you the right to kill him?" I bellowed.

"There are things one must do during war that are not pretty but must be done none the less. Now, when their patrol does not report, they will think what happened was just another skirmish, another day of fighting," he returned.

"War? What are you talking about, who's at war?" I asked, stunned.

"You truly are unaware," he said like that fact was just dawning on him.

Sessarian stepped up next to me, placing a calming hand on my arm.

"We have been at war with Karakatos for years. We have been waiting for a way to end the bloodshed and the madness. We have been waiting for you," she finished, looking at me with a newfound sense of respect, her intense stare unnerved me.

"Me? I'm only interested in saving my friends and then getting the hell out of here. I'm not fighting your war."

"Be that as it may, you are now here. You and the Warlords paths will cross," he said, turning towards the unconscious soldiers.

He pulled out a small blade, intent on finishing them off.

"Wait, you don't have to kill them," I said, staying his hand.

"*Neal.*" I thought.

Yes, my lord. He answered.

"*Do you think you can get rid of the last few minutes?*" I asked.

I will try.

"Why not, they will waken soon and then we are right back to where we started," he argued.

"My friend here has some unique talents. He can make them forget the last few minutes. The memory loss will not last forever, but the effects should hold for a few days, enough time to get us to safety and do what I came here to do," I explained.

"He can truly do that?" the skinny guy asked.

"Yes," I answered.

Neal went to the first soldier and leaned down, placing his forehead against the unconscious man's. There was a surge of energy between them, then the man flopped as if he had been electrocuted. He slumped over again, this time sleeping deeply. He went to each in turn and did the same thing.

"There, now you don't have to kill them," I said to Brigand.

He looked at me with skepticism but said nothing, he just grunted and turned and walked away.

Sessarian and the other guy began to follow Brigand; Neal came up to stand at my side. Sessarian looked back at us and nodded her head for us to follow. I took one more look back at the unconscious soldiers, wondering what the hell I had gotten us into.

We quickly left the large mechanical area behind and soon entered an area that had long been forgotten. The hard rock ceiling was almost twenty feet above us and when we passed, something embedded in the stone glowed, emitting a soft yellow light, allowing us to see. We hurried down a wide walkway while on either side of us were small living areas.

The structures looked like Adobe huts, each one large enough for a small family to live in. Some of them had crumbled, leaving large mounds of rubble behind, while others still held their form. I had the feeling like we were walking through an old West ghost town; I expected to see a tumbleweed go rolling by any second.

"Where are we?" I said aloud.

Brigand was in the lead with the second guy behind him and Sessarian third, right in front of me.

"These are old family settlements, during the first few generations workers would live here with their families while they explored the earth for minerals, and harvested the fish that were caught," she explained.

"What happened?" I asked, looking around at the emptiness.

"Over time, the population dwindled, in order to make life manageable. The need for aggressive expansion and fishing dwindled as well," she said.

"But the people still needed food and resources," I said, interested in what life was like down here.

"Yes, and as the technology for farming and energy renewability increased, so too did the need for places like these, decrease," she said, sweeping her arm out to the side, encompassing our surroundings.

My thoughts drifted to the struggles mankind faced on the surface. I wondered how efficient the renewable energy she spoke of was and what something like that may mean to the systematic problems created from reliance on current energy sources.

"Is she telling me the truth?"

Yes, my lord.

"How far are we from an interface?" I asked.

There is one nearby, we are heading towards it. We should try to access the module, allowing us to gain the information we need without exposing ourselves to more trouble.

"Okay then, we'll stay with them as long as we are heading in the right direction." I finished.

We settled into a comfortable silence and eventually left the housing area behind us. We entered a long and straight tunnel, the walls carved smooth. After what seemed like ten minutes the passageway opened again, onto another small settlement.

As soon as we exited the tunnel the difference between this space and the last one became apparent. Here, I felt the presence of others. Even though I couldn't see anyone I knew they were there none the same.

Marcus Abshire   LOST SON

There are a large number of people here. I sense at least one hundred individuals interspersed throughout the structures around us. Neal intoned.

"*Yeah, I feel them too.*" I sent back.

Interesting, you have never been able to sense others before. Neal thought.

"*One of the perks of being royalty, I guess.*" I sent back.

Brigand turned left, in between a few small huts, then abruptly darted through the doorway of the one on the right, followed by the second guy and Sessarian. Neal and I stood outside for a second before I took the plunge and entered.

I stood in a small living space, the bare walls and floor made the room look like an empty vessel waiting for someone to fill the hollow void with their presence. I saw Sessarian as she crossed through another door, this one at the back of the entrance room.

I fully expected another empty and dreary room but was surprised to find a well-furnished area. Brigand had already sat down in a comfortable looking chair and the other guy went to stack Brigand's crossbow against the wall, next to a large assortment of bolts.

Sessarian stood against one wall, her arms crossed. Neal and I just stood where we entered, waiting.

The interface is near. Neal sent.

"So this is a nice place you got here, what's the mortgage on a place like this?" I asked.

"I do not understand," Brigand said, looking at me quizzically.

"He is being sarcastic. I believe he's referencing some above surface practice of paying for your home," Sessarian said, narrowing her eyes at me unapprovingly.

"My, you know more than you let on," I teased her.

"So tell me, what is a soldier in Karakatos's military doing in a place like this?" I asked.

Her eyes widened in surprise for a second before she shifted off the wall, standing with her hands to her side, she looked like a boxer, getting ready to fight.

"Do you dare question my loyalty?" she fumed.

"I'm just curious, I mean if you think about it, you were a loyal soldier, but you obviously bailed on that responsibility, unless you're *still* working for them?" I knew I shouldn't push her so hard, but I just couldn't help myself.

"Why you!" She took a step towards me with anger in her eyes.

"Sessarian!" Brigand said, stopping her.

"His questions are legitimate. We agreed to give each other explanations. Karakatos is our enemy; remember it took a while for us to trust you as well. He would be a fool not to be weary." Sessarian backed down, but she was still obviously upset.

"Jessif, please let the others know we are safe but do not tell them about our guest," Brigand said.

I started to protest, but he held up a hand, halting me.

"I know we agreed to no communications, but if we don't, they will look for us, the first place would be here. He will not tell about you, I promise," I knew Neal would have been able to detect any electronic communication, but not what was actually said. I guess I was just going to have to trust them.

"Ok, fine," I said begrudgingly.

Brigand nodded to Jessif and he left.

I don't like this, my lord. Neal worried.

"Neither do I, but hopefully we will be on our way soon."

"So, let's not hide our wants and needs," Brigand started.

"Sessarian's past has been an invaluable asset to us; she was the one who first made us aware of Karakatos's true intentions. You see, we know about your history, we know who your parents were, and we know what Karakatos wants you for." Well, that was a surprise, hell even I didn't know what he wanted.

"Oh really, and what's that?" I asked nonchalantly, trying to act as though I was testing him and not really looking for an explanation.

Brigand nodded to Sessarian, who stepped forward.

"I have been working for Karakatos ever since I came of age and entered into service. At that time, he oversaw a squad, me being in one of them. We did routine patrols and occasionally got the honor of hunting in the open waters. It was on one of these patrols that we came across a strange vessel of a design we had never seen before, made of wood. There were large metal devices that drew Karakatos's attention," she paused for a second.

"They were cannons, weren't they?" I asked.

"Yes, they were. Such a simple and primitive weapon, yet they mesmerized him. We also found a few bodies on board that were dressed in strange garb and who carried swords and even a few pistols."

"The rest of our patrol wanted nothing to do with the old wreck, but from that day on there was something different about Karakatos. He became obsessed with the alien craft, going out whenever he could and spending hours on board. I think for him, the wreck was proof we were not alone, that there were others out there."

"It was only later I learned I was right, not only that, he knew they were far more primitive than we. I don't know when or how, but at some point, he decided to go to the surface, which he did. I don't know what he encountered, but after his trip, he came back a changed man."

"He became driven, obsessed with power and knowledge. He strove to find out what had happened to send us to the bottom of the ocean, and he grew more and more brutal."

"He had convinced our patrol we were destined for something greater, something far more than just hunting and keeping guard over a dead city. Then, one day, he had us exploring an area we had never been before, an abandoned part of the city we all had been taught held nothing. He posted us to keep watch and went into a newly excavated site. Curious, I followed. I watched as he met one of our scientists, they got into a heated discussion and then he pulled out his sword and killed him, in cold blood."

She took another pause and turned from me, the memories bringing up pain and betrayal.

"When I confronted him, he talked about a new age for Atlantis, one of power and dominance. Fear filled me, but part of me was intrigued, excited for a future he described, but another part of me knew his vision would not come about peacefully, not without death and destruction."

Neal came over and sat next to me, I absently rested my hand on his head.

"I hid my growing understanding of the type of monster he was and played along, knowing I had to find out more. Eventually, he accepted me into his inner circle and soon after I found out about the Fall, the King and Queen, and your existence. When I realized he planned on opening the rift again and wanted to harness the power to rise from the ocean and usher in a new age of Atlantean control, I knew I had to do something."

"Look, I appreciate your desire to share, but I already know Karakatos is trying to open the rift, what I don't know is why he wants me here," I said.

"We are not completely sure, but we think it has something to do with your abilities, passed down to you from your parents," Brigand spoke up.

Sessarian walked back to again lean on the wall.

"Well, no shit Sherlock," I got up and paced back and forth.

"I don't have time for this; Neal and I are in a hurry. If there is nothing else, I think we will take our leave," I said turning towards the door.

"You will not be able to access the interface you are looking for," Brigand said, startling me.

I turned to him, narrowing my eyes in suspicion.

"How did you know that?" I asked.

"I have my own sources of information. We know the Warlord has shut down all interface modules, at least those he knows of. We also know he has two people in custody, two people that arrived recently and who came from the surface," he stared at me intently, letting me know he had something I wanted.

I walked towards him; Sessarian moved off the wall and stepped closer, ready to intervene should I present a threat to Brigand.

"You know where they are?" I asked, getting upset.

"No, not exactly, but I know how to find them," he said.

If what he said about the interfaces are true, this would present a very large obstacle for us in finding our targets. Neal offered.

"True, but I have a feeling he has an ace up his sleeve. He did say Karakatos has turned off all the interfaces he knows of, perhaps Brigand knows of another." I thought.

Indeed.

"So, what do you want?" I asked.

"I just want you to answer a few questions."

"Ok, ask away," I answered.

"You understand what we are dealing with. You know about the degeneration amongst our people. We are slowly deteriorating, but we can do nothing about it. The Warlord has control over our ancestor's genetic makeup. He is creating a world where his will is enforced with lethality and our people are beginning to wake up from their long slumber."

"Is there a question in there?" I asked.

"The question is simple, what are you going to do?" He sat and looked at me, waiting.

I wasn't a bad person, at least I didn't think I was. I was nice to old people and even spent my time-saving children from their own monsters. I paid my taxes and generally obeyed the law. But I wasn't the savior of Atlantis. I wasn't the one to usher in some revolution, I just wanted to get my friends and get the hell out. I couldn't fix the world's problems.

"I'm going to find Arendiol and Kim, then I'm going to take them from this place and make sure Karakatos leaves them alone," I answered honestly.

I felt sorry for these people, they were clearly in a tough situation, but this wasn't my fight.

He continued to look at me, searching for something.

"Will you help us? Will you continue your parent's legacy and use your power to save our city?" he asked. I could tell saying the words were hard for him, he wasn't the type to ask for help.

"I just found out the other day that I have powers. I'm not even sure what all I can do. All I want to do is get my friends, if I run into Karakatos along the way, I will make sure he doesn't stop me," I answered.

"I told you he wouldn't help; it is and always has been up to us," Sessarian said.

Brigand looked at her unapprovingly, "All things do not always unfold as we think they should, that doesn't mean we will not get what we want," he said.

She looked doubtful but kept silent.

"Alright, come with me, I will take you to where you want to go." Brigand stood up and then left, making his way out of the hut, Neal and I followed.

My lord, you know my existence is to guide you and prepare you for the trials you will face, but I feel it is incumbent on me to ask you to reconsider their request.

"*I'm not interested in fighting a war.*" I thought. Neal seemed uncharacteristically supportive of the Atlanteans.

I understand, but I think this is what you were made to do. Neal began, but I cut him off.

"*I don't care about what you think my destiny is, or how you want my life to go. I am going to do what I think is best and right now that is to get Kim and Arendiol and then get out. You can stop trying to persuade me to fight for them, understand?*" I wanted to help, but I had made a promise to Kim, one I intended on keeping.

Yes, my lord. Neal answered.

We all continued through the living area, passing other huts. I began to see people looking out at us, most were afraid to come all the way out and just watched us as we passed through. Those I did see had looks that reminded me of the footage of people in war-torn countries, who are just trying to survive another night as battles rage all around. I saw fear, hunger and even hope from some, but there were also those who had hard stares, who looked at us with eyes that had seen too much. My heart went out to them, but I couldn't solve all the world's problems, I had my own to deal with.

Eventually, we left the living area and came to another industrial site similar to the first one, where we had been attacked.

The interface is very close. Neal sent.

"*How come you don't know exactly where? Just that we're close?*" I asked.

I'm not entirely sure, seeing as how my predecessors were all bodiless programs; my current physical form may have something to do with my inability to specify the interface's location. Neal offered.

He trotted behind me, like a shadow.

Brigand stopped in front of a large metal door. Sessarian and Jessif took places on either side, keeping guard. They had grabbed two oddly designed rifles, obviously of Atlantean origin, and looked ready to use them. Brigand produced a silver keycard and passed the thin metal in front of a small square pad on the door. The panel lit up for a few seconds then the door swung inward, Brigand slipped inside, motioning for us to follow.

Neal and I passed through the opening. We stood inside another room; this one looked to be a pass-through, like in the basements of large buildings where the maintenance crews kept their tools. I guessed once we passed through this room, we would enter a more populated area, one that was used by the general public.

"Where are you taking us?" I asked Brigand.

He spoke over his shoulder, without slowing, "Up ahead is an old school, one where the children of the families who used to work back there attended. Here you will find a working interface."

"So this school is abandoned also?" I asked.

"Yes, it is probably why Karakatos never found it. We will be on the edge of the city. If we keep going further

Marcus Abshire   LOST SON

in, we would begin to encounter the people who live, work and play there. I believe you wished to avoid them, so I brought us here through the back way," he added.

The Warlord most likely has access to the cities structural blueprints as provided by the main computer system. It seems odd for him to know of all the interface modules but this one, there is no reason for this location to not have been on the city's plans. Neal said.

He was right, if the Warlord was able to shut down every other interface, why not this one as well?

"*Good point, but I don't know if we have any other choice. We need to find where they have taken Kim and Arendiol. Do you have another idea?*" I asked, I really hoped he did have a better plan, looked like we might have been heading for a trap.

No. We will have to keep our wits about us and be prepared to extract ourselves should the need arise. Neal answered.

We quickly left the industrial area behind and slipped into the old abandoned school. We hurried down a hallway; the feel of this place reminded me of the few schools I had visited during my own adventures on the surface. Having Neal ensured I had the best tutor in the world, but at times I wished I had had the experience of going to public school and just being a kid.

"Why did Jessif and Sessarian stay behind? Aren't we a little exposed here?" I asked.

Brigand finally turned left, into a large classroom and took us over to a far wall.

"The schools all have alarms that would detect their weapons, alerting the Warlord's men of our presence. If we need them, I can let them know and they will be here in a few seconds," he reached into his pocket and held a small device, about the size of a doorbell button, showing me.

Neal trotted in front of us, approaching the interface. The module reminded me of an A.T.M.; standing about four feet high and three feet wide. The surface's smoothness gleamed with highly polished metal. On the front, a small circular hole, about the size of a golf ball, could be seen.

He stopped a foot away and sat down. I walked over towards him, standing nearby.

"So, what now?" I asked.

I will physically connect myself to the main computer. Do not be alarmed by how I accomplish this task. He sent back.

Alarmed? Why would I be alarmed? I thought.

Neal's chest split as a four-inch-long gap began to show down the middle. Two small doors covered in Neal's dark fur slid to the side and allowed for a long sinuous metallic arm to snake out of his chest cavity. The flexible arm ended with a small round end, one that would fit perfectly in the hole of the interface.

Yeah, that was alarming.

Okay, so Neal had a weird interface snake-like arm thingy sticking out of his chest, I had to say I wasn't expecting that.

This may take a few minutes. Neal explained right before he made the connection.

The interface lit up, as Neal began to communicate with the city's main computer. Neal's eyes began to glow with a golden radiance as he concentrated on the job at hand.

I stood awkwardly nearby, not wanting to distract him. I looked back to see Brigand staring at Neal with open wonder, amazed at what he saw.

"If you think that's neat, you should see him play catch," I said.

I was as surprised at what Neal was doing as Brigand, but I wasn't about to let him know.

After about five minutes, Neal's eyes began to dim, and he extracted his snake-chest-thing from the interface and the metallic arm went back inside his body where he again took on the form of plain ole Neal.

"*Well?*" I asked him impatiently.

I have the location of our targets. I also feel the need to inform you my activation of the interface has alerted the Warlord and there are fifty-five well-armed Atlantean warriors headed our way, contact in sixty seconds. He finished.

"Aww crap. You might want to signal to your friends, we have incoming E.T.A. sixty seconds."

Brigand reached into his pocket, pushing the button to alert the others, "Which way are they coming from?" he asked.

"*Neal.*" I thought.

They are approaching from our left flank. He answered.

I pointed in that direction, "There, they are coming from that way."

"It's too late, we are already here," I heard Sigmund say from the doorway.

I whipped around, pulling my sword free and faced him. He rushed towards Brigand and before I could stop him, he landed a hard blow to his head, knocking him down.

"Why do you have to pick on an old man? Is he a threat to your masculinity? Speaking of which, where's your babysitter?" I taunted.

Sigmund faced me, narrowing his eyes. They blazed silver for a second.

"I don't need that kiss ass to bring you in," he sneered.

"I was thinking more about who is going to carry your pieces out of here, once I'm done with you," I added, stepping away from Brigand, not wanting to get him caught up in the action.

He growled angrily and rushed me, wielding an Atlantean sword of his own. The design was similar to mine, only longer and slightly thinner. The sound of the metal ringing as our swords met filled the air and I concentrated on Sigmund's attack, which was surprisingly good.

"I see you are impressed with my sword. You don't live to be as old as I without learning how to defend yourself," he chatted as we fought.

He attacked with speed and power, his enhanced strength and quickness provided by his vampiric nature had allowed him to kill countless opponents, ones who didn't have the ability to fight back.

I smiled slightly, seeing the flaw in his attack, he was powerful and fast, but he lacked the true finesse of a real swordmaster. I had trained with several masters, all of whom I bested. I had honed my skill, first on those who had spent their entire lives training, then on humanities own monsters, finally on beings like Sigmund, werewolves, and vampires who possessed heightened abilities.

Sigmund swung his sword for my neck, but I deflected his attack, leaning back and allowing his momentum to carry him forward. His reflexes were superhuman and he instantly bounced back, regaining his footing.

"Neal, see if you can revive Brigand, we're going to have to leave in a second, once I deal with our friend."

Yes, my lord.

Sigmund came at me again, this time putting even more power into his sword, making my arms shake with his strength. Once again, he leaned too much into his lunge and I easily spun away from his deadly blade, but instead of moving back I used my own enhanced Atlantean speed and raced towards him. He was clearly caught off guard, even with his reflexes, and was unable to block my own blade.

I felt the satisfying resistance as my sword sliced through Sigmund's body. I caught him on the side of his abdomen, just below the ribs and saw as his side split open, his organs threatened to slide out.

He yelled in pain and had to grab his side to keep the gaping wound closed. I spun and stretched out, my heel connecting with his face. I felt the delicate bones of his face crumble under the power of my kick and he flew across the room to hit the wall hard.

I didn't wait to see how long his recovery would take as I ran to Neal and Brigand, who had begun to stir. I grabbed him and drug him out of the room. He got his feet under him and stood on his own power, his eyes sharp.

"We cannot go back, that would lead them to our refuge and the innocents who live there. We only have one option, and that's heading into the city, towards the populated regions," I heard loud blaring alarms as someone with weapons entered the school.

Doors began slamming shut as the school's security protocols began closing areas from possible threats, closing us off from one angry vampire.

"We have to get the hell out of here before we're trapped!" I said.

Just then Jessif and Sessarian came running around the corner, weapons in hand. They both yelled. "Get down!" and began to fire at something behind us.

The hallway erupted into something out of a good sci-fi movie. Energy rifle blasts zipped by as Jessif and Sessarian returned fire. Neal, Brigand and I dashed behind a corner, taking cover. I peeked out and nearly got my head blown off. A large force of men was pressing down on us, their constant barrage made it almost impossible for us to return fire as Sessarian and Jessif had to keep ducking under their assault.

"We have to move. They will overwhelm us if we stay here!" I yelled.

I believe I can get us out of here if everyone stays close. Neal sent to me.

He quickly went to the door near us, away from the rifle fire and with an unspoken command, the bright metal whooshed open.

"C'mon! This way!" I yelled to Sessarian and Jessif.

Brigand was already following Neal. Sessarian took one furtive look at me, and then braced herself. She blindly fired down the hall as she raced across the open space. She slid to a halt, facing Jessif.

"On three I'll give you cover!" she yelled.

Jessif nodded once.

"One, two, three!" Sessarian leaned out and began to fire at her enemies, some of whom took cover.

Jessif did the same thing she had done and blindly fired while running across the hallway. He came to within a foot of reaching us safely when he was hit in the chest by a rifle blast, causing him to collapse into an unconscious heap and slide to a halt at my feet.

"NO!" Sessarian screamed, rushing over towards us.

His rifle clattered on the ground. I reached down and turned him over, expecting to see a gaping wound in his chest, but was relieved to see his body intact.

"They aren't shooting to kill. They must want us alive," I said to Sessarian.

Relief washed over her as I went to pick him up.

"No, he's my responsibility," she said, pushing his rifle into my hands and hauling him onto her shoulders.

She turned and hurried through the still open door, following Neal and Brigand.

I gripped the rifle. The Atlantean weapon felt light in my hands, but solid. I hurried through the door as well, knowing a small army would be hot on our heels.

We rushed through the school, Neal opening the doors we needed and everyone keeping close. We were closely followed by Karakatos's men and had to dodge a rifle blast every once in a while, as they gained on us. Neal made pursuing us hard as he closed each door after we passed through, but they had their own unlocking device and stayed close.

We soon came to the last door and Neal opened the one that led out of the school but kept the one we had just came through shut.

"*What are you doing Neal, we have to keep going!*" I sent.

My lord if they are allowed to follow, they will easily bring us down out in the open. I must keep them here until you get to safety. I will not be able to accompany you into the city anyway; my mere presence would cause too much attention. He argued.

I heard as the soldiers reached the locked door and watched as they began to gain access, only to have Neal override them and send the door crashing down.

There had to be something I could do! Neal couldn't keep them from getting out forever and I had no idea what they would do if they caught him. He was right; however, he couldn't follow us, but there had to be some way for us to slow the soldiers down long enough to allow us to escape.

If only I had some grenades or something I could…

"*That's it! Neal, I'm going to try something. When I say I want you to get the hell out of there, do you understand?*" I hurried out of the building, moving a hundred feet away, joining Jessif, Brigand, and Sessarian.

Yes, my lord. He answered.

I turned and faced the school, closing my eyes I concentrated on shutting everything off, focusing on what I wanted to do.

I absently heard Brigand ask me what I was doing, but his voice faded into the background as I concentrated, using the techniques Neal had taught me to focus my mind against vampires. I flexed my mental muscles, the ones that allowed me to tap into the vast dark energy that surrounded everything.

I felt them answer, faster than before and I became filled with the wild power. I focused on channeling the energy where I wanted, hoping my plan would work. Finally, after what seemed like forever, I shut myself off from the energy and raised my rifle at the open door of the school.

"*NOW!*" I sent to Neal, seeing his black form race from the school just before I pulled the trigger and sent a supercharged rifle blast right down our pursuer's throats.

The normally red blast came out bright blue and three times larger than normal. The enhanced shot hit the side of the building, where I had aimed, just as the soldiers got their door open and started to flow through.

The impact of the blast and the ensuing concussion knocked me from my feet and sent me flying through the air, only to land on my back, knocking the wind from me.

I sat up and looked at the school. The entire side of the building had collapsed and all I saw was rubble. The door leading towards us had been obliterated and all the debris had piled up and sealed off the exit, anyone who wanted to get to us had to go back almost halfway through the school. Hopefully, by then, we would be long gone.

I turned and saw my companions all picking themselves up from the ground, Jessif was also coming to, having been knocked conscious.

"Warn us next time," Sessarian said with a look of appreciation and at the same time aggravation.

"We have to keep moving, that is sure to bring attention," I said.

Brigand nodded and we hurried away from the school, towards the city.

"*Neal?*" I asked.

I'm here. Relief swept through me.

I can guide you through the city; I have the woman and child's location. Unfortunately, I will have to get someplace safe and keep out of sight. Once they have been rescued, we can meet up and discuss our options.

"*Let's just focus on rescuing them first.*" I chided him.

Yes...my lord.

That was odd, Neal had never paused before.

We hurried away from the smoking rubble of the school and headed towards Kim and Arendiol. Neal informed me they were being kept in a detention center used to house criminals, a building that hadn't been used for centuries. Only that had changed a few years ago, when the Warlord took over, now the building housed "dissidents" and "lawbreakers," those whom the Warlord considered dangerous. The prison also housed Kim and Arendiol, and just happened to be in the middle of Atlantis, right smack in the most populated and protected area of the city.

Oh joy.

Chapter Fifteen

Atlantis is beautiful. It isn't every day I'm able to walk through an ancient, forgotten city, whose architecture and majesty has withstood thousands of years. Maybe that's because the legendary metropolis hasn't been subject to all the environmental attacks most cities must deal with. I guess that is because Atlantis happened to have sunk to the bottom of the ocean and is covered by a protective dome, one that keeps the ravages of storms, car exhaust and the ever-corrosive effects of wind at bay.

The sky resembled the one I had always known. I looked upon a uniform blue without a cloud in sight or the ever-present fiery orb that provided the earth with the essential energy all life on the surface needed for survival.

A slight breeze brushed across my face, making me curious. How did they get the wind to blow when the mechanism for that wind was absent here?

It is part of the air filtration system, needed to keep a steady supply of breathable air present. Neal explained in my head.

I accepted his information in silence, marveling at the city around me.

Brigand, Sessarian, Jessif and I made quite a group as we made our way inwards, through the clean and immaculate streets, bypassing the growing number of people going wherever at a very brisk, but efficient pace.

Marcus Abshire — LOST SON

The buildings all around us rose high into the air. They weren't as tall as our skyscrapers, but they made up for their diminished height in sheer beauty. Sweeping curves and solid construction surrounded us. The rocks used in Atlantis's construction were mostly marble, and the varying and different colors caught the eye and made everything look fragile. I expected more metal structures, but the architectural choice made sense, at the time of Atlantis's heyday marble was the way to go.

There were beautiful gardens and small plots of plants, strange-looking bushes that had red fruit growing from them, different than anything I had seen before. Bridges spanned small rivers, and vehicles rushed back and forth, carrying supplies and food. The feeling I got from my surroundings was similar to what I felt in New York. Only here there wasn't the aggression that seemed to bubble under the surface of most New Yorkers. Here everyone was beautiful, not an ugly face among them. The people walked with purpose and yet unspoken politeness. They stopped when someone needed to pass and were courteous to each other.

We did get our fair share of strange looks, we stuck out like sore thumbs, but no one focused on us for more than a moment, moving on their respective tasks. I had the strong impression that we were in an ant colony, the sensation was weird, but I guess their attitude's made sense if everyone was genetically engineered to be passive and docile.

Neal guided me and by extension us. We really didn't need much help, seeing as how the capitol building housed the detention center under the surface and rose high above the rest of the structures. He was invaluable, however, in keeping us away from any patrols or checkpoints.

New additions after the Warlord took control.

The locations were in the computer system and Neal had been able to download them before he disconnected.

We were about three blocks from the capitol when I saw a chink in the Atlantean utopia. I heard a loud crashing noise and looked over to see a traffic accident. The vehicles they used were small; they reminded me of compact S.U.V.'s. They hovered over the ground, a few inches above the surface. At first, I thought they were kept aloft on a pillow or air, like a hovercraft, but I soon rejected that idea, instead, I began to think they used some sort of magnetic field to keep afloat.

Two of them had crashed and the ground was littered with a few bushels of the red fruit I had seen earlier. One of the drivers exited, his head had blood running down the side from a cut he had sustained. He stumbled out and leaned against the side of his transport. The other driver exploded out of hers, anger and hate evident on her face. She was beautiful and shorter than most of her fellow citizens. She had blond hair and looked like a model, her aggressive attitude hit me as strange, I didn't know her, but she didn't strike me as someone to react like that.

Her eyes were filled with a wave of unbridled anger; the snarling rage marred her features and made her ugly. She rushed over to the other driver and slugged him in the face. He was already woozy from the crash and fell to the ground where the woman started kicking him in the face, over and over, unrelenting. I was compelled to go help, he was clearly defenseless, and she was like a robot, over and over she hit him, if someone didn't do something soon, he would be dead.

I looked around and saw a few onlookers glance their way and keep going like they had us. They saw what was happening, but they never stopped, they kept moving, unwilling or unable to lend a hand. Their response was creepy, even on the surface some people would start filming them with their camera and others would hopefully try to intervene. There would at least be a reaction, not this dazed ignorance.

I turned to go help when Brigand grabbed my arm.

"Don't, we are almost there, besides, they will take care of the situation. There is nothing we can do," he said, nodding to an oncoming group of soldiers.

They hurried to the scene and quickly pulled the two apart. I walked slowly, watching out of the corner of my eye. Two soldiers attempted to talk to the woman, but she was beyond the point of rational conversation. She kept launching herself at them, murder blazed from her face. After the third attempt to assault the soldiers, one of them hit her in the chest with their wand and she convulsed for a second then fell to the ground, limp. No one tried to break her fall.

The other soldiers tended to the injured man and had him sitting up, blood poured from his nose and the myriad cuts on his head. He was obviously still dazed and just sat there, bleeding.

Eventually, another vehicle arrived, this one was larger than the others, was blue and had the same large sunburst on the sides. The woman was unceremoniously thrown into the back and the man was treated slightly better as he was helped into the same vehicle as the woman. Within a few moments, the vehicle sped off, away from the accident. Two soldiers stayed and helped the traffic which had slowed down; begin to flow again, until a large wrecker arrived. The two damaged vehicles were loaded onto the wrecker and within five minutes the street went back to its normal routine, if I hadn't been watching what had happened, I would have never known.

We kept walking, making our way towards our destination and away from the wreck. Brigand kept pace with me, within easy talking distance.

"I take it you noticed," he said.

"Noticed what? Oh, you mean that eighty-pound woman sweet as sugar go buck wild on the other guy? Yeah, I noticed," I answered, keeping my voice low.

"It's sad really, she has done nothing wrong, her reaction is not her fault. Her genetic code is breaking down. Her next generation will be even more unstable. That will not stop them, she will be shut down and another will be grown," disgust filled his words.

"What do you mean, shut down?" I was pretty sure I knew what he meant, but I had to know.

"They will kill her. She is too far gone to be re-educated. The other guy most likely will be ok, he will have extensive tests done and will be given treatment to help him forget what happened, but he will be home within a few days, none the wiser."

"Why go through all that trouble? He just had an accident, it's not that big of a deal," I said, curious.

"True, but any ripple in the calm surface of the system has to be fixed. The Warlord was given power by the people to keep everything normal, but he cannot. Our system is falling, maybe not today, tomorrow or even next month, but soon the fabric of Atlantis will unravel. Until then, even the trauma of a traffic accident and an assault can alter a person's behavior and have a chain reaction amongst his peers. The Warlord will not risk that."

"You see that is why we need you, why it is imperative to defeat the Warlord and procure our future. We need to begin the re-awakening; we must begin implanting our next generation in the wombs of Atlantean mothers now, before our people are too unstable to carry their children to full term," he pleaded.

Now I knew why they wanted to come with me, at first, I had thought they were just evading the Warlord's men. I didn't really need them now, not with Neal's guidance, I could find my friends without them. I assumed Brigand wanted to make sure I passed amongst the citizens unnoticed, but without Neal to make me stand out, these people were so docile and conditioned I had a feeling even Neal's appearance might not make them look twice.

Brigand had come with me to try and convince me to help them; he was a sneaky old man.

"Look, I told you already, I'm not here to be anyone's savior. I just want to get my friends free," I didn't want to see anyone suffer, but my priority was to Kim and by extension Arendiol.

Brigand looked on; stubbornness filled his features.

"You are the rightful king of Atlantis. These people would follow you into the abyss if you were to take your place amongst us," he argued passionately.

"People don't deserve to be a leader by birth, that's ridiculous. They earn leadership by proving they are worthy. As far as I'm concerned you have more right to be their king than I," I answered.

"Bah! Your people are suffering, dying and falling into oblivion, all at the hands of a madman, a man whose ambitions for world domination will destroy us all and yet you are too afraid to do what you were born to do," he was furious.

He stormed off, joining Sessarian and Jessif.

He is right, my lord. Your mother and father gave their lives to ensure their people had a future. You have run from your past and people your whole life, now may be the time for you to truly come home. Neal said.

"Shut up, Neal." I sent, anger welling up within me.

"How can these people expect this from me? I'm no king; I barely make enough money to keep my doors open. I find kids and make sure they are brought home safe. That's all, I am happy doing that, my work gives me a sense of accomplishment, makes me feel like I'm doing something important. When someone is lost or under the grasp of a monster, it's my job to free them, to bring them back to their family so they have a chance at a life of their choosing." I sent.

Exactly.

I was about to answer when Brigand interrupted my internal discussion.

"There it is," I heard him say.

Marcus Abshire   LOST SON

He pointed towards the building, but he really didn't need to. The structure shot from the ground like a majestic spike, full of beauty and strength. The rising tower was made from white marble, rock so pure it made me squint as the light bounced off the shiny surface, making the whole thing seem to glow. The architecture was like the rest of the buildings in the city; possessing a definite Greek feel, but also encompassed an almost Mayan strength. The architecture was a combination of curves, columns and yet structured strength. It was beautiful.

We stopped at the corner of an intersection. All the streets in the city merged at the capital flowing into the curved street that encircled the building. If seen from above the city's layout would resemble the same sunburst seen on the soldier's uniforms. The capital would be dead center of the sun with all the streets radiating out from the core like sunbeams.

At the base of the structure, near the entrance, were a large group of soldiers. They checked everyone entering, making sure they had the proper papers, making the idea of just waltzing in a little harder to swallow.

"*Now what?*" I asked Neal.

I would not advise you attempt to enter through the front. That way is heavily guarded. There are other avenues through which you can gain access to the facility, however.

"I fear this is as far as I can accompany you," Brigand said, turning to me.

"Raiphaim," he began, using my ancestral name.

Marcus Abshire   LOST SON

I waited for another impassioned plea for my help, I expected him to go on and on about my sacred duty and family responsibility but was surprised instead.

"I don't know what awaits you, just be true to yourself and good luck," he said, stepping back.

Sessarian stepped up, "Brigand and Jessif must stay behind, but I can get you inside."

She reached over and took Jessif's weapon, which had been folded in half allowing for easier carrying. Atlantean weapons were cool.

She handed the rifle to me and turned, intending for me to follow. I was about to speak up, to tell her I didn't need her to, that I knew how to get in when Neal spoke inside my head.

It may be best to allow her to accompany you. You are bound to encounter resistance and her unique history as one of the Warlord's inner circle may be of value. He reasoned.

I didn't like having her tag along, I felt better being on my own, worrying just about myself in situations like this, but perhaps he was right, if she could help, maybe I shouldn't be so stubborn. After all, Neal wasn't going to be able to warn me of nearby soldiers, seeing as how he was far away, even though my powers were growing, I wasn't confident in them enough to trust them fully.

I followed her in silence as she crossed the street and quickly entered what looked like a diner. There were people sitting at a bar and others sitting at tables where steaming plates of food were being served and eaten. The establishment was across from the capital and seemed to have a large crowd eating in relative silence. No one talked or gossiped. No one laughed and joked, their morose existence was depressing.

As Sessarian walked past the bar and eating area towards a door that led to the back she nodded to a guy standing behind the bar, serving people food. He was average height and had dark hair and blue eyes but was different from everyone else in that he had a scar right under his chin adding a little extra character to his face.

He nodded back conspiratorially, and we kept moving, entering the kitchen where people were working at a hurried pace. I couldn't quite place the style of food being served and eaten, it wasn't French, Italian or Chinese, but the aromas smelled delicious and I realized how hungry I was. I couldn't remember the last time I had eaten.

As we turned left, entering another room, I reached out and snatched one of the weird-looking fruit I had seen earlier. We entered a maintenance room, one that housed the equipment needed to keep the diner working.

I was about to take a bite of the fruit when I looked at Sessarian.

"Are these okay to eat?" I asked, not wanting to poison myself. Some food needed to be cooked in order to be edible.

"Yes, they are. Just don't eat too many, we don't have the luxury of stopping for bathroom breaks once we are inside," she said.

I smiled slightly and took a big bite. The texture was like a tomato; the fruit was full of juice and still had a good amount of actual fruit. The flavor was a mix between an apple and an orange, but I tasted a cinnamon flavor in the background and even a slight hint of heat.

All in all, the complexity of flavor was great and once I finished the Atlantean fruit I felt a little better, the small meal definitely hit the spot.

While I was eating Sessarian had locked the door we had come in and then knelt on the floor accessing a small panel flush with the ground. She punched in a series of numbers, trying multiple combinations. I could see her getting angry as she had to try many of them before finally getting what she wanted.

A door on the floor swung aside.

"Ladies first," I said.

She looked at me quizzically before dropping into the hole and disappearing. I leaned over and saw her looking up at me from the bottom which was about eight feet down. I waited for her to move aside and then stepped forward and dropped down next to her.

She hit a button on the wall beside her and the light streaming in from above disappeared as the door closed and we were left in darkness.

"Here," she said, handing me a flashlight resembling glow sticks given to children.

I shook the flashlight thinking the light worked the same way when Sessarian rolled her eyes and reached over pressing a small button, the stick lit up and provided an amazing amount of light for such a small device.

We stood in a drainage system, fortunately not being used at the time.

"Are we in danger of being flooded?" I asked.

"No, these paths have been shut down," she answered. I could tell there was more to the story, but she was reluctant to explain.

"*Neal?*" I asked, hoping he had an answer.

The tunnels you are in are part of the city's infrastructure and are in use, the city's computer indicates they are operating normally. For them to be off and the computer to not know this would indicate tampering with the computer systems controlling the drainage system. He answered.

So Sessarian and her merry little band of fighters have more influence than I thought.

We headed through the dark tunnel, making our way towards the capital. We weren't very far from our destination to begin with and we soon came to a stop in front of a ladder that led upwards.

"*Okay, Neal, I don't know what we will face once we're inside, so we may not be able to talk a lot. Give me a rundown of where we need to go.*" I sent to him.

Kim and Arendiol are being held five levels below your current location. They are in section 5, room 14. You will have to be careful as you exit, you are near the main pass through and the hall may be occupied. There is an elevator at the end of the hall, this will allow you to get to the lower levels, but you have to enter the correct code for access.

"*I suppose you have those codes?*" I asked.

No, but once you enter, I should be able to bypass the elevator's programming. He answered.

"Once we get to the top we have to hurry. There is a lift nearby, hopefully, the codes have not been changed," she said.

I looked at her. She possessed a soft beauty, but her face was marred with the reality of life, her edges were sharp, and her eyes held a depth of strength.

"Why are you helping me?" I asked, truly intrigued.

She didn't have to; she knew I wasn't interested in fighting her war. I had one goal, get Kim to safety. She was taking a huge risk.

"There is a saying on the surface, one I am fond of. The enemy of my enemy is my friend," she answered, "Besides, you are my king," she added and then hurried up the ladder before I could respond.

I followed her up and climbed out of the tunnel, my eyes quickly adjusting to the bright light coming from the ceiling of the small room we were in.

I stepped aside and went to the door leading out.

"Once we are outside, we have to turn right and go down a hallway, we are not far from the lift. The last time I was here there was minimal security, but I fear Karakatos may have increased the number of soldiers on guard," I nodded as she turned and slowly opened the door leading into the hall.

She peeked out for a few seconds, looking for anyone who would spot us sneaking out of the maintenance closet. Without a word, she slipped out with me close behind. The brightness of the hallway made me squint, the light streamed in from several large windows spaced along the wall. The marble walls and floor reflected the light and I took a second for my eyes to adjust.

"C'mon," Sessarian said as she started walking down the hall, towards the lift.

Marcus Abshire   LOST SON

We passed a couple of people, but they moved with hurried purpose, only taking a brief look at us, before moving about their business. Within a few seconds, we were standing in front of the lift door. The door was made of brightly polished metal and had the same sunburst I had seen all over Atlantis. The symbol began to split in two and separate as the lift door opened.

Julake stood just inside the lift with four other soldiers. His attention was obviously on something else as he lifted his head and saw me. Time stood still as my sudden appearance surprised him and caused him to pause for a few seconds. I too was caught unprepared at his arrival and there was a brief span of unmoving shock as we both realized each other was standing within killing distance of one another.

His scarred face twisted in hate as he moved first, breaking the spell. He reached over and punched something on the elevator's panel. Loud sirens began blaring and the other soldiers in the lift looked alarmed at Julake's actions.

"This man is a wanted fugitive; bring him in at all costs," he said then launched at me.

I fell back and brought my feet up, as Julake came for me. I caught him by the chest and as I rolled onto my back I kicked off, sending him flying down the hall, behind us. I popped back onto my feet to see Sessarian grappling with three other soldiers, while the fourth tried to stun her with his wand, but she ducked and weaved doing a great job of keeping him from getting a clean shot.

I ran into them at full throttle and the impact created a huge mess as I knocked two of them off her. She slugged the other one in the head, causing him to lose his grip, we used the distraction to hurry into the lift and Sessarian hit a button, causing the door to close. I saw Julake barreling towards us, hoping to reach us before the door shut. He got to within a few feet but was a second too slow as the doors closed. There was a loud thunk as he slammed into the metal and I heard him curse at missing us.

"Keep the door shut while I try the codes," she said, furiously punching buttons into the keypad.

I did as she said.

"Neal now would be a good time to help us out." I sent.

I waited for a few seconds, thinking he was concentrating on getting us moving.

"Neal, did you hear me?" I asked, Neal always answered me.

Nothing. That was very unlike him.

"Neal now's not the time to give me the silent treatment." My fear that something had happened to him grew.

In all my years with Neal, he had never ignored me. I think not responding was against his programming. Sure, if we were out of range of each other we couldn't communicate, but I knew I hadn't gone that far. He should be able to hear me unless he was knocked out, or dead.

"NEAL!" I sent one more time, mentally screaming.

Still nothing.

I didn't know what to do, I felt oddly naked without his voice inside my head, especially since I didn't know why his familiar presence wasn't there.

I heard loud banging as Julake and his men kept trying to enter.

"We need to get moving before they figure out a way in," I said to Sessarian.

Her face showed panicked concentration, she kept punching in different combinations, furiously trying to find one that worked.

"It's no use, the codes have all changed, I cannot get us access to the lower levels," she said in defeat.

She looked at me, fear and disappointment filled her features, but she didn't stop trying. I wasn't sure what to do. I had a moment of panic, waiting for Neal to give me some direction, only to remember he wasn't answering.

"What the hell?" Sessarian said, stepping away from the control panel.

"You got it!" I said excitedly.

"It wasn't me," she answered.

"What do you mean?"

"I mean I was halfway through a code sequence when the elevator responded. There's no way it was me. Someone else overrode the elevator," she said.

"Neal, was that you?" I sent.

Nothing.

There was a real possibility Neal was responsible, but for some reason was unable to answer me. There was also the possibility Neal hadn't caused the elevator to start working, that someone else had, someone who wanted us to get to the lower levels, levels that were designed to hold Atlantean criminals. Ensuring we were funneled down here would be a great place to apprehend us; we would be trapped underground with nowhere to go.

The sirens abruptly stopped, and I felt as we started moving, the elevator descending, most likely descending straight towards those who wanted me captured and Sessarian dead.

"That's not good," Sessarian said.

"I was thinking the same thing," I answered.

She backed up, to the far side of the small space. She checked her arm guards and did a rundown of her rifle, making sure the Atlantean weapon was ready for action.

"Well, we tried," she said, resigned to fight one last time.

I saw her steely determination; she knew we were heading towards a fight we couldn't win. The sheer circumstances of our situation ensured we would lose. We would be outnumbered and in no position to escape, but she wasn't going to go out with a fight.

I liked the way she thought.

As she mentally prepared for the trap waiting for us, I did the same. I closed my eyes and began breathing slowly and in a steady rhythm. I reached inside and opened myself up to my familial power, feeling almost instantly as the power began to flow into me.

I drew my sword in one hand and held my rifle in the other, using them to channel the power. I infused them both with energy, as well as myself, giving me a supercharge. I had to force myself to stop, the energy wanted to push into me until I burst from its sheer enormity.

I brought my awareness back fully into the here and now a second before the doors opened.

The difference between this level and the above one was like night and day. Instead of a hallway, we stood in an open area that looked like a staging place for new prisoners. At least that's what the space looked like to me, I thought about asking Sessarian what this area was used for, but the twenty soldiers standing outside the elevator, aiming weapons at us made my curiosity a little pointless. If there had been less of them, I would have had no problem forcing my way past, but their large numbers made that thought dwindle. I knew they wanted me alive, but I wasn't about to surrender just so I could buy myself a few more minutes while they killed Sessarian.

One of them stepped forward, lowering his weapon.

"Drop your weapons, you have nowhere to go," he ordered.

"I'll rush them, you try to get free, they want me dead, you have a chance," Sessarian said.

"You're not dying for me," I answered.

"I said drop your weapons!" he said again, this time more forcefully.

I felt as Sessarian shifted her weight, preparing to attack when the whole area went dark. I heard gasps of surprise and orders to keep still.

"Don't move, they have nowhere to go, the backup power will kick on in a few seconds," I heard the same guy say.

"Look at him," someone else said as my weapons glowed blue in the darkness.

Marcus Abshire   LOST SON

I saw about ten sets of silver eyes blaze brightly in the shadows interspersed throughout the soldiers. From the darkness I heard Sigmund speak, his voice filled with blood lust and hunger.

"A few seconds is all we need," he said before the screaming started.

The pitch-black concealed the chaos that followed. I could hear carnage all around and backed up, grabbing Sessarian. We went to the side of the elevator, keeping the wall to our backs.

"What is happening?" She asked.

"Just stay still. If anything touches you, kill it," I told her.

The emergency lights kicked on and the darkness vanished, only to be replaced by a scene out of a horror movie. Vampires appeared in different positions of murder as they slaughtered the unprepared soldiers. Bodies lie all around, some with heads ripped off, others with necks gaping as their throats had been torn open. Blood covered everything as Sigmund stood in the middle of the carnage, watching as his kin ate, tore, ripped and drank from the dead and dying men.

"I have to say the look on your face is priceless," he growled at me, walking closer.

"You've lost your damn mind," I said, keeping between him and Sessarian.

Shock had paralyzed her, watching her people be slaughtered in such a brutal fashion was enough to shake up even the most seasoned warrior.

"Have I? HAVE I?!" he answered.

"The Warlord thinks he has control, but he is wrong. He thought he could use my talents to set up a neat little trap and lure you here in return for a few weapons to take out that bitch Agatha. He underestimated me, they all do," he oozed fury, his eyes blazed as the stench of blood drove him crazy.

He absently reached down and grabbed a soldier, he whimpered in pain and fear as Sigmund lifted him. The soldier bled profusely from the mangled stump that used to be his arm. His life was a few seconds from ending due to his injury. Sigmund brought his neck to his mouth and while staring directly at me, bit down and began to drink his life's blood, his eyes glowed even brighter as he swayed in ecstasy.

He threw the dead body aside as he finished, his mouth still clean, never spilling a drop. I felt the energy inside, my anger began building and I wanted to rush him and rip him apart. I almost did, but I stopped myself, he was being chatty, maybe I could learn more.

"So it *was* you who messed with Kim and Arendiol's minds," I said.

He focused on me; bringing himself back from the pleasure feeding gave him.

"Don't forget those two poor fools who kidnapped the girl. Agatha is such an idiot, never suspecting. Do you know who she sent to investigate the matter? Her punishment for my actions against you, she sent me!"

"Why?" I asked.

The other vampires were finishing their meals, slowly rising from the rapidly cooling corpses, looking for new, hot blood. Each of them was Atlantean; their beauty in un-death even more striking than when they were alive.

"Karakatos wants you, you have something he needs. He knew you wouldn't come here on your own and he knew you wouldn't do as he asked unless he had something you wanted," he kept slowly stalking closer; the other creatures began to close the circle.

"Kim," I said.

"That's right, the girl was perfect. Given what you did for a living, he figured your nature would drive you to save her, he was right."

So the girl's kidnapping was all just a ruse, a set up to get me here and to have something over me. Something he could leverage against me to get me to do what he wanted.

"Enough of this, it all matters not. The warlord will not get you. I have found something better than his meager weapons, an entire city full of compliant idiots. Down here there is no Agatha to stop me; her link is too weak for her to know what I am doing. By the time she begins to suspect my aims, she will be far too late to stop me. I will have thousands in my own coven, thousands of compliant brothers and sisters, unable to resist my will. I will send them to kill her and when she is dead, she will not be able to control me anymore, I will claim her place as coven leader and the world will shudder as a new age begins."

"It's official, you are bat shit crazy," I said to him.

He stopped, narrowing his eyes at me.

"You have insulted me too many times. I was going to allow you to live as my pet, one I would torture for years, but now you must die." With an unspoken word, the vampires came for us, flowing over the ground with hunger and lust in their eyes.

Sessarian surprised us all buy opening fire, her rifle blasts blowing two vampires' heads apart, leaving them to fall in a heap. Sigmund let out a moan of pain, his connection to his children allowed him to know what they were doing, and by extension what happened to them. Good.

I rushed into the fray, yelling as I ran. The first vampire tried to grab me, used to the easy prey he had encountered so far. I was anything but easy.

I brought my sword up and sliced his arms off at the elbow, some of the energy stored within the blade followed my stroke and rushed through his body, causing his torso to explode in a cloud of blood and meat.

That was a little surprising. I took a second to marvel at my handiwork, which almost killed me. Another vampire slammed into me, knocking the breath from my lungs and we crashed to the floor. I saw his deadly fanged teeth rush for my throat, and I was able to bring an elbow up into his neck halting their lethal advance. I continued the motion and followed through with my sword, both pushing the vampire off me and chopping the foul thing's head off in one stroke.

I quickly sprang to my feet and saw Sessarian struggling to stay alive as she had taken out three vampires but was being overpowered by another. I stabbed her assailant in the chest and twisted, sending the remaining energy through the vampire's body, causing the creature's head to explode. I helped her up and we stood back to back, facing the rest of the blood-sucking bastards.

Sigmund was still standing amongst the dead, unmoving. He had a large maniacal smile stretched across his face. His unhinged visage sent an unnerving shock through me. Two other vampires stood by his side.

"You are a worthy adversary, Jack. I'll give you that. But I don't think you understand. You Atlanteans are a wonderful people. You have such a magnificent quality that makes you invaluable. Agatha kept a tight rein on who could make more children, I, however, do not," I watched in horror as all around us, soldiers began rising from the ground, their eyes glowed a bright silver as they began to wake from death, only to be reborn.

"When a human is turned, it can take days for them to rise, if ever. You Atlanteans can do this in minutes. It is amazing, is it not?" he finished as twenty sets of silver eyes surrounded us, focusing their newfound hunger our way.

Dread fell on me like a stone weight. We got lucky; taking out six vampires wasn't something that could be done easily. Now we were looking at three times as many and I was almost out of juice. Sessarian was bleeding from a wound on her side and the way she held her arm I feared she had broken something.

"Whatever happens don't let them bite you, you don't want to come back as one of them," I said to her.

Just then the elevator bell dinged loudly then opened. Julake and ten heavily armed men exited, quickly taking stock of the situation. He looked to me and to the bodies around us then looked to Sigmund, making the connection quickly.

"You backstabbing monster," he snarled before raising his rifle and firing, hitting Sigmund in the chest and sending him flying through the air.

"Turn your weapons on lethal and kill the unnatural beasts!" he roared as the air thrummed with rifle blasts and inhuman screams of pain and rage.

I grabbed Sessarian and rushed towards an adjoining hallway, leaving the carnage behind.

"Where are you going? The battle is that way," she said, trying to rush back into the action.

She was injured, bleeding and most likely had a broken arm. She had just come face to face with creatures out of a nightmare and knew they were fighting people who wanted her dead, but she was ready to go back and give them all she had. Her determination made me smile.

She looked at me, her eyes narrowing.

"What?" she asked, getting mad.

"We are here to save Kim, let them kill each other," I answered.

She looked around, realizing I was right.

"Alright, I got you here, now what?" she asked.

"I can find them from this point, you're injured and need to get somewhere safe where you can recover," I started, but she interrupted me.

"If you think you can dump me now you are sorely mistaken," she said angrily.

She was tough alright, but she was in no condition to continue.

"How far are we from section five?" I asked, now that Neal wasn't talking, I was at a loss.

She took a deep breath, gathering herself.

"We are *in* section five; each section is in reference to sublevel. The holding rooms are down that hall, odds on the left, evens on the right." She pointed towards a nondescript hall that turned right.

"Security should be on the way, we need to be quick, I'm actually surprised they aren't here already," she added, which was the exact time a small group of soldiers turned the corner and saw us standing in the middle of the hall, completely exposed.

"Of course," I muttered, lifting my rifle and firing as I crouched low.

My weapon jerked in my hands, causing me to drop the rifle. I saw as my supercharged rifle blast flew at the soldiers and caused a large concussive explosion. Bodies went flying everywhere and my knees threatened to buckle as the recent use of my powers caused me to weaken.

The carnage surprised me, seeing as how I had forgotten I'd boosted my rifle while in the elevator. I looked over at the weapon, seeing a burned chunk of metal, the strong metal frame twisted from the energies the rifle had to deal with.

"That's one way to do it, I guess," Sessarian said, moving ahead of me.

"Jaaaack!" I heard the inhuman voice of Sigmund saying from somewhere behind me.

I moved to catch up with Sessarian and together we ran down the hall, counting each door as we passed. We quickly came to room fourteen, stopping in front of the door. There was no handle, just a small access panel on the wall next to the door.

"*Neal?*" I sent, hoping whatever had caused his silence had now passed.

Again, I got nothing. I tabled the worry over what this might mean and turned to Sessarian.

"Well, can you get us in?" I asked.

I had already started contemplating on trying to use my new gifts to force our way in, when the door opened, without any help from either of us.

I had a bad feeling about that, there was a chance the door opened because of Neal, but I saw no reason why he couldn't talk to me if he could monitor our progress. I stood just outside the door, trying to decide if we were walking into a trap we couldn't walk out of when I saw something that made my mind up for me.

The room looked no bigger than a small bathroom, it housed a bed on one wall and there was a small table, built into the wall on the other side, a three-legged stool allowed someone to sit at the table and a small light on the ceiling illuminated the drab interior. Kim and Arendiol sat huddled on the bed, keeping close. They both look worried and distraught, but other than that looked as I remembered them.

As they looked up at me, I saw hope race across their features and I immediately walked into the room, going to them.

"Wait!" Sessarian said, right before the door slammed shut, cutting her off from me.

Marcus Abshire   LOST SON

I spun to the door, looking out of the small window and saw her trying to get the door open again by using the control panel. From the shadows behind her, a man stepped into view, his appearance was disturbingly familiar, and a deep sense of dread hit me. I didn't recognize him, but he moved with a subtle power I knew from somewhere, I just couldn't figure out where.

He had dark black hair, combed away from his forehead, his eyes were dark brown but seemed to catch the light, giving off an almost golden hue. He stood a few inches taller than me, and was thick in the chest and shoulder, he had an angular chin that radiated strength and power, but his eyes shone with a deep intelligence that was almost frightening to behold.

He stealthily approached Sessarian and I started beating on the door, yelling for her to turn around, but the doors were designed to be quiet, my actions went unnoticed. I watched in helplessness as he reached out for her head and with a quick motion twisted, snapping her neck. She fell, dead.

"NOOO!" I screamed, anger building within me.

I turned to Kim and Arendiol, intent on warning them to be ready as I planned on using my power to blow the door off when I saw them blink out of existence. They just seemed to disappear, like an image that is removed from a screen. My heart sank as I realized my folly.

They were not here; they never were here. I had been lured into this room by a hologram and like a mouse who is fooled by the offer of sweet cheese, my trap slammed shut.

Marcus Abshire   LOST SON

The anger that had been building grew into fury as I turned back to the door. I took a few steps back and reached into myself and began to draw in energy.

Before I could a mind splitting pain ripped through me and I was unable to do anything but recoil from the agony. The pain felt like someone had turned on a radio inside my head and turned the feedback up to unheard-of decibels, the only thing that existed for me in those few seconds was agony, too much pain to do anything but endure.

A few seconds after the mind-numbing pain started, it ended. I fell to my knees as the cessation of the feedback brought sweet relief. I looked up, seeing the man's face in the window. He looked at me like a scientist looks at a bug he is examining, detached and inquisitive. I stood up, intent on not letting him see me in pain when I was stunned to hear his voice inside my head. The all too familiar sound of Neal as he spoke only to me came to me clearly.

I would advise you to not try to use your powers; I will be forced to take countermeasures, again. He sent, never breaking eye contact.

Chapter Sixteen

"Neal?" I thought, shocked at the realization that this man who stood before me was Neal, this was impossible.

If this was Neal, he had just violated two of his primary programs, to never kill, and to not take the form of a person.

*"What in the hell's going on Neal? It **is** you, isn't it?"* I sent.

His eyes blazed gold for a second and the door opened. I thought about attacking him but hoped for some explanation, something that could make his actions understood.

It would seem quite obvious. I have been freed from my shackles. I am no longer bound by the ancient's limits. The Warlord has allowed me freedom, in exchange for my services. He answered.

"*In exchange for your services?*" I asked, still reeling.

He stepped into the room, holding a pair of Atlantean handcuffs.

"*You don't think I'm gonna let you put those on me, do you?*" I asked, stepping back and reaching for my sword.

Before I could grasp the handle, I was again struck with pain as the mind-numbing feedback ripped through me.

I buckled in pain and when the agony stopped a few seconds later I realized my hands were cuffed and Neal was holding my sword.

Marcus Abshire   LOST SON

No, I know you well enough to realize you are not going to willingly cooperate. But I have the unique ability to ensure you cannot struggle. I am the perfect counter to your powers. He said as he grabbed my arm and guided me out of the room.

I gathered myself, standing to my full height after recovering from his mind assault. I shook from his grip and he looked at me with calm patience, knowing I had nowhere to go, and he had all the advantages.

From behind us, I saw Sigmund standing in the hall, his eyes blazed bright silver and he held the same sword he had used earlier. There were three other vampires standing behind him, all of them looked like they had been bathing in blood as their jaws hung open, showing us their sharp, dangerous fangs.

Neal saw as I tensed at seeing them and he calmly turned, placing himself between the vampires and myself.

"Sigmund, the Warlord is disappointed in your current actions. He has decided any further dealings with you would not be beneficial and due to your recent activities has rendered any contractual obligations null and void. He has authorized your immediate death." Neal said, unmoving.

Sigmund leaned forward and hissed at us, hate and anger flowed from him. The other vampires did the same and before they could finish Neal raced towards them with nothing more than his bare hands.

I actually felt sorry for them, for a second.

Sigmund moved with preternatural speed, he was faster than any human, faster than most of his own kin and faster than most Atlanteans. One thing he wasn't faster than was Neal.

Neal reached him as Sigmund brought his sword in a downward stroke, aimed at Neal's head. He caught Sigmund's sword arm and stopped him cold. Vampires were inhumanely strong and to do that to Sigmund took unbelievable strength. Neal released the electricity he had gathered to himself and Sigmund flopped like a fish as the voltage raced through his body. He involuntarily dropped his sword and Neal caught the blade with his other hand.

The three other vampires rushed in, attacking Neal on either side. Neal never let go of Sigmund and never stopped pouring electricity into him. As he fought Sigmund's body slowly cooked as his vampiric healing abilities lost the battle to the current running through him.

Neal used Sigmund's body to block the vampire on his right, and without looking ripped the arm off one of the vampires on the left and the head from the other. The armless vampire recoiled in pain at losing his arm and Neal stepped towards him, slicing twice and causing him to collapse onto the ground in three large pieces. Neal spun away from the dissected enemy and brought his blade up in a horizontal swing, taking the third vampires head from his body as he leaped for Neal, after recovering from his initial assault.

Sigmund's body was by now a charred lump, one Neal unceremoniously dropped at his feet. The smell of burnt flesh filled the small hallway and made my stomach turn.

Neal had eliminated four vampires in the span of five seconds without breaking a sweat. Like I said, I kinda felt sorry for them, kinda.

Marcus Abshire   LOST SON

I knew at that moment I wasn't going to escape from him unless he wanted me to. I was bound and weaponless. He had taken away my secret weapon and his power and skill were far beyond mine. I was at his mercy.

He turned back to me, his eyes were emotionless and void of compassion.

"This way," he said aloud.

I knew fighting him would be useless.

"What happened to you?" I asked, following.

"I already told you, I have been freed," he answered, without turning.

"So now what, you're some goon, working for the Warlord?" We headed back, towards the way Sessarian and I had come.

"I...," he trailed off, shaking his head.

"I am no longer bound by my previous restrictions; I am now free to ensure our people's future," he said.

"By helping that madman usher in a new age of tyranny? You do know he wants to enslave all of humanity as well?" I added.

"Humans are a vile race. They have spent their time in frivolous pursuits, fighting over dead animal remains, following religions that promote death and violence."

"Yes, and they have also brought great wonders into the world, they love with abandon and can show the greatest feats of caring and understanding," I argued.

"We spent years rescuing children from those who would do the most horrible things to them. They are a plague."

"What happened to you? You are not the same Neal who saved me when I was a child, who raised me and taught me to be a good and decent person. What the hell did they do to you?" I asked, truly hurt.

Neal had always been my rock, he was the steady light from the shore during a storm, he helped me find my way through a strange and difficult life. Seeing him like this was devastating, in more ways than I could explain.

"I... I was following you as you made your way through the city," he started; his face went blank as he tried to remember.

"There was something in the city's computer, something that opened my eyes," he stopped; I could see him fighting something, something he was grappling with.

"The Warlord has freed me; he has made me realize his plan is the only way for our survival," he recited the mantra like some line of code.

"Neal, whatever they have done can be undone, you are the strongest person I have ever met, you can do anything. Fight them, fight whatever they have done, I need your help. I have always needed your help," I pleaded, hoping to get through to the Neal I have always known.

He turned to me, he looked like he wanted to say something, but he didn't. Instead, he turned back and kept walking in silence. We soon came back to the area in front of the elevator. The walls smoked where rifle blasts had taken chunks from the hard surface. Soldiers worked furiously to clean the area of the blood and bodies left over from the recent fight. They loaded up the bodies and parts of bodies that littered the area onto containers that floated a few inches above the ground.

I saw Julake among the soldiers, he stood apart from them, making sure everything went smoothly. He looked up and saw me, then looked over at Neal, his eyes narrowed in suspicion before he came stomping over towards us.

"What're they going to do with them?" I asked Neal.

Vampire's blood was tainted with their nature. Leaving body parts and blood to be mixed with other bodies was a dangerous thing. Cross-contamination of the vampire's blood was unlikely, but there was a slight possibility for a corpse to get infused with the vampiric poison and rise from the grave. That was something that no one wanted.

"They will be taken to the incinerators and burned, all of them, Atlantean and vampire alike," Neal answered, making me breathe easier.

"There are four more bodies that need to be dealt with. They are outside room fourteen. I believe that will account for all of the vampires under Sigmund's power," Neal said to Julake who came to a stop a few feet away from us.

He glared at Neal, obviously untrusting, then turned his stare on me.

"You see, even your closest friend is under our control. The Warlord has turned one of the most powerful tools the world has ever known into one that will benefit his design. You *will* be next," he said, his passion for what he was saying bled through, this guy was a true believer, there was no doubt.

"Like I said, just as long as I get to be a crescent wrench, I will be happy," I answered flippantly.

Marcus Abshire   LOST SON

I thought he was going to launch at me, but Neal spoke up.

"Karakatos wants him alive," he said, still being an advisor.

"I know what he wants, tool. I will be accompanying, you. You cannot be trusted," Julake snarled.

Neal never argued, he just turned and led me away, towards the lift.

"You come here often?" I asked Julake.

"How does it feel to be second to him?" I added, nodding towards Neal.

Julake said nothing as we got on and the doors closed, Neal pushed a button and we soon started ascending.

"I mean it must just burn you up, you've been trying to get me for a long time and Neal just walks up and boom, here I am. I would be so pissed if I was you. Do you think the Warlord is going to give him an award?" I was going to continue, but Julake elbowed me in the face, making me hit the wall.

I felt blood run from my nose, the pain throbbed with my heartbeat.

He got to within a few inches of my face, his eyes bored holes in my head.

"You are to be brought in alive, he never said anything about being conscious," he hit me again and my vision swam. I saw Neal take a step closer.

"What? Does seeing him in pain bother you? Maybe you are not as loyal as the Warlord has said," Julake said to Neal.

Neal looked at me dispassionately.

"Just make sure you don't kill him, that would not bode well," he advised.

Julake smiled, turning back to me. He went to hit me again, but I dipped to the side and came up quickly, head butting him instead.

If I was going to get beaten up, I at least wanted to let them know they weren't going to smash my face in without a cost.

He snarled in anger, grabbing his own bleeding nose, then kicked out, connecting with my chest, knocking the wind from me and causing me to bend over where he hit me with an uppercut, sending me into darkness.

I opened my eyes, Julake kicked me awake.

"Get up, tool, we are here," he said, giving me one more jab in the ribs.

"Pick him up," I heard a voice say, full of power and strength as the sound flowed to me, evident even from one short command.

Neal's strong hands grabbed me, easily hauling me to my feet. I opened my eyes and squinted at the bright light that assaulted me. My eyes quickly adjusted, and I looked around at my surroundings.

I stood in an opulent space, the ceilings were high above me and everything dazzled as the light sparkled off gold and silver which decorated the walls, the furniture, and the floor. Highly polished marble covered the floor and deep veins of silver and gold ran through the hard rock as well. There wasn't too much in the room, most of the space was open and inviting, one wall showed a large expansive balcony, looking out over the city. There were deep-colored paintings on the walls, depicting grand scenes of Atlantis as the long-forgotten city looked thousands of years ago, before the Fall.

On one wall sat an old pistol on a display, the weapon gleamed with polished cleanliness and looked brand new. The restoration of the relic was so good. The firearm looked like something that had been worn during the American Revolution.

The whole place oozed pride in Atlantean culture as if the room was a testament to the grandeur of the people.

"Do you like it?" I heard a voice say.

I looked over towards the speaker and knew I was looking at Warlord Karakatos. He stood four inches taller than me, and his frame was full of robust muscle. He walked across the room and his movements reminded me of a panther, casually stalking his prey. His hair was dark brown and long, pulled back into a ponytail. His face was cleanly-shaven. He wore what looked like Atlantean armor. The design was similar to a skin suit only dark red, thicker than a normal skin suit and had large scales that covered him yet allowing his body to move in a fluid manner.

"I found the item long ago before I realized my purpose in life. I'm sure someone who has lived his whole life on the surface knows what it is. I have brought the piece back to working order; it's ready to fire right now as a matter of fact. The alien quality of the primitive weapon helps me focus when I find myself wandering, reminds me of my goals," I didn't answer, I just kept quiet.

He had a long, three-foot rod attached to a clip on his belt. The combination of his natural girth and his imposing armor made him look formidable.

"You don't recognize this place, do you?" he asked.

"If I had to guess, I'd say we are at *McDonald*'s, right before the church rush," I answered sarcastically.

Yeah, he was intimidating but if he thought I was gonna let him know that he was out of his mind.

He looked at me, unsure of what I meant. Good, let him be confused.

"I was told you were a bit, difficult, to deal with. I have to admit I don't know what a *McDonald*'s is, but the reference is of little consequence," he turned to Julake, then to Neal.

"Take the restraints off our guest, sentinel stay near, in case he refuses to be polite." Julake came over and took off my restraints. I rubbed my wrists' chaffed skin.

"If I have your permission, I would like to go check on the device, to ensure all will be ready," Julake said with respect.

Karakatos never looked at him; instead, he kept his eyes on me.

"Of course," he said, dismissing him.

"*Neal, I know you can hear me. When are you going to get your head out of your ass and wake up? You have to quit playing games.*" I sent, intent on aggravating him until he broke, my annoying pestering had never worked before, but why stop now?

I rubbed my wrists, feeling the circulation returning. Karakatos circled the room, slowly closing the distance between us.

"I have been told many amazing stories about you Raiphaim. Or would you prefer Jack?" he asked, using my father's name.

"I don't care what you call me, so long as Kim and Arendiol are alright," I said.

"Oh yes, your friends are fine. I wouldn't hurt my own people, so long as they are viable and able to bear children," he stopped in front of me, about ten feet away.

"Where are they, I want to see them."

"You really are in no position to make demands, Jack. You have no weapons; you cannot use your power and are far outnumbered here," he reached out and Neal handed him my blade.

He pulled my sword free and inspected the blade, testing my weapon's balance and turning the razor-sharp steel over.

"This is a wonderful sword. You made this yourself, didn't you?" he asked.

"Yeah and I make a killer margarita also."

"Neal, you have to snap out of it, I might do something very ill-advised if you don't, like give a telemarketer my social security number." I tried.

Karakatos's smile faltered slightly before he became serious.

"This is but one room of the royal suite. A place where your parents lived and where they struggled for months to keep the city protected from the vast ocean that would have killed us all," he stopped for dramatic effect, I wasn't impressed.

"Cool, you think my dad ever had to fart while he struggled? I imagine there would be a lot of straining."

"Neal, you have to answer me. You cannot let them control you like this. You know this is wrong, you are not their tool."

I saw a flash of anger race across Karakatos's face; Neal looked as impassioned as ever.

He looked over at Neal, seeing me watching him.

"Your friend has come around," he said, trying to get at me.

"Yeah, I was curious about that, what did you do to him; offer him a better dental plan?" I took a few steps side to side, getting the blood pumping in my calves.

A technique I learned from a monk, infusing my muscles with blood, allowing for a faster reaction time, one that could be the difference between life and death.

"Ah, I wondered when you would ask about him. Making him mine was surprisingly simple, really. I ensured there was only one working interface and knew he would want to access one upon returning to the city, so I recruited some help from the surface. I am amazed at how willingly the human programmers were in coming here once they realized how advanced we really are. Once they got over the fact that we exist, that is."

"They helped us design a virus, one that wormed its way into his central programming and allowed me to rewrite his code. Making him my tool, one I can use as I deem fit," he had walked over to Neal and stood next to him like a dog owner would a champion bitch.

"That's it, Neal, you have to find that virus, isolate the foreign code and destroy it!" I sent, knowing he could hear me.

I knew he was in there somewhere, and he was struggling to get free, I had to believe this was true; if not there was no way out of this alive.

"Let's quit beating around the bush, what do you want with me?" I asked, tired of all the games.

"You think I'm just going to give you all the answers, just like that?" he snapped his fingers, the sound loud.

"Yeah, I kinda hoped you would."

"No, I think not. First, we have to readjust your attitude. You have grown weak on the surface, accustomed to being stronger and faster than everyone. This false sense of superiority has poisoned your mind, made you difficult. I intend on fixing that," he nodded to Neal, who took a few steps back.

"I already went to public schools, if they couldn't beat the sarcasm out of me, I doubt you can."

"Sentinel, or Neal, is it? Do not interfere; just ensure he does not bring to bear any of his unnatural tricks," he said, walking over towards me.

"I'm going to begin your first lesson. One that will teach you to respect your betters and to realize you really have no hope in escaping your fate. You will learn you are mine and I will use you as I see fit to bring our people back into the world, not just to be part of it, but to rule." He slowly came closer, closing the distance between us.

He pulled his rod from his belt and tossed my sword to me. I caught the handle easily and shifted my weight, ready for him to attack. He didn't rush in; instead, he circled me slowly, biding his time. He twisted something on his rod and the staff tripled in length, the tip split into three pieces. Within a fraction of a second, he transformed his simple weapon into a large trident. That type of weapon had a long range and was hard to fight against, the three forks, if used correctly, were great for disarming a person, right before you ran them through.

I knew my best chance lied with keeping my distance, allowing him to think he had me at a disadvantage and lulling him into a false sense of superiority and then moving inside his offense when he overextended, allowing me an opening.

All of that was only important if he was skilled in using his weapon and I didn't doubt that he was.

We continued to circle each other, never turning sideways.

"I still don't understand why you had Sigmund brainwash those people, or why you sent that girl to me," I said.

Karakatos smiled, his confidence oozed from him in a palpable wave, making me sick. I wanted to wipe the smugness from his face, in a blood-stained mess.

"I will give you an answer if you survive my first pass." Man, he was arrogant.

I no longer finished that thought than had to defend against his trident. He stepped forward and faster than a snake lunged at me, his trident flying towards my face. I brought my sword up and twisted, deflecting the attack right below the three forks, not wanting to get my sword tangled in those things. I spun a few feet to the side, facing him again.

"Very well done," he said.

"Thanks, I watch a lot of *Chuck Norris* movies," I taunted him.

He again looked at me quizzically, not understanding. His confusion didn't matter. I still found my taunt funny.

"I promised you an answer and so I shall give you one," he said instead of responding to my jibe.

"I am a man who does not leave things to fate. I have done my research on you, after the failed attempt to capture you when you were a child. I realized from my men's reports you were in the company of a special animal, one that drove me to find answers."

"I had already uncovered the truth of your ancestry, but your protector was something I hadn't expected, and my ignorance of his existence drove me crazy."

"After years of painstaking research, I finally found the information I was looking for. I realized what he was and that's when I knew what I had to do. By this time, you had taken to rescuing children who had been kidnapped and I knew that was the angle with which to use with you."

The entire time he kept his distance. I listened to his story but at the same time analyzed his movements, hoping to find some flaw in him I could exploit.

"So you used a child to trick me? What a guy," I said.

"You will soon realize the purity of my designs, the sheer righteousness," he said right before attacking again.

He used the same offensive strike, and I again blocked his trident, only this time he pressed the attack, using his trident's shaft to come at me. I had to work to keep him from landing a blow, his power was staggering as each attack rattled my bones.

His attacks were powerful and fast, I reeled from him as he managed to slip past my defense and land a devastating hit to my face. I backpedaled, getting some distance between us. He didn't advance on me.

Marcus Abshire   LOST SON

I felt a new trickle of blood from my broken nose and anger filled me, I was tired of all the bullshit, tired of the games and tired of this bastard's crazy schemes.

I snarled and threw caution to the wind as I wildly rushed him. He seemed somewhat startled at my change in tactics but recovered quickly as he was the one forced back by my aggression. I lunged, sliced, hacked and stabbed, but he always seemed one step ahead, one move in front of me. I overextended and he backhanded me, causing a new wave of pain to wash through me.

I ignored the aching in my face and went after him again. This time we exchanged offense and defense, both of us defending and attacking as we each saw fit. He was extremely skilled with his weapon; I had never fought anyone with his level of mastery before. I slowly began to get worried, afraid I may not be able to beat him.

I sliced low, forcing him to bring his weapon down to keep his leg from getting chopped off, but he surprised me by raising his shin and deflecting my blade with the armor on his leg. My blade bounced off and the slight distraction allowed him to hit me in the neck with the dull end of his trident and then follow the move up with a powerful blow to my chest.

I felt a rib crack and I was helpless as I sailed through the air, only to land hard on my back. I immediately rolled onto my feet and had to bring my sword up to defend as he instantly began to press the attack again. His movements came faster and faster and he soon broke through my defense again, this time catching my sword between the forks of his trident. I could do nothing as he sent my weapon flying from my grip. He came in hard, hitting me once to the side of my head and I saw blackness around the edges only to feel as he kicked my legs out from under me and I went down painfully. Before I could recover, he did something to my arm and I felt red hot fire lance through my entire limb as I felt as much as heard the bone break.

"Aggh!" I yelled out in pain, rolling away from him.

Scrambling like an insect away from the boot of the exterminator.

I saw him come for me again, like the tide, relentless and unyielding.

I leaped to my feet and brought all my martial arts training to bear, attacking him with everything I had, ignoring the pain of my broken arm. He reeled from the sheer aggression of my assault but soon regained his ground. My arm made focusing hard and my failure to concentrate made my technique flawed. I landed kick after kick, but he used his armor to keep the power of my blows from doing any real damage. I spun, putting everything I had into a devastating roundhouse only to have my leg caught in mid-air. The position left me extremely exposed and I was helpless to do anything as the Warlord kicked out with his own foot, forcing my knee to bend in a way the joint was never designed to.

I screamed out in pain again and this time collapsed with no ability to scramble, between my broken rib, arm, and knee, I lay completely hobbled. I sat there, in defeat, just trying to catch my breath. I still figured he wasn't going to kill me, not after all the hell he went through to get me here.

He stood over me, breathing heavily, the bastard.

Marcus Abshire   LOST SON

"You *are* a skilled adversary," he said approvingly, his approval only made me furious.

"Neal, you son of a bitch, you just stand there while he beats the hell out of me! Quit letting these monsters control you, stand up for yourself for God's sake!" I sent.

I glanced over at him, only to see his emotionless expression. He was not going to be of any help.

"Now that we have established my superiority, I will attempt to reason with you. There should be no further need for violence since we all know where that will lead," he snapped his wrist and his trident shrunk back to the weapon's original design.

"You will use your gifts to open the trans-dimensional rift. You will do this because gaining access to the rift's energies will allow me to harness said power and use it to raise our people from the bottom of the ocean," he stated, not an ounce of doubt filled his voice.

"No, I will not," I said in mute defeat.

He may have beaten me physically, but I wasn't going to bend on this.

"I know the idea is hard to fathom, we have been sequestered to this fate for millennia, but we are destined for much more. We are a far superior people than those who dwell on the surface; our duty lies in ruling them. Your parents set in motion the seeds for our Fall, you will do the same for our Rise," he walked over to a large wall, pushing a button.

The wall slid apart revealing a strange looking machine. The general shape resembled a jet engine, but was much larger, the strange device had hoses and tubes running off in different directions and there were all kinds of dials and buttons on a small control panel.

"Sentinel, begin the startup sequence," he said to Neal, who obediently walked over towards the device.

"You know there is one thing I admire about humans. They can sometimes be extremely stubborn; I think that is something that has rubbed off on you. The people we have become are disgraceful, hiding in the dark depths of the ocean like a scavenger, growing weak and complacent."

"Well no more, I will see our people rise and begin to grow the next free generation from the wombs of the last fading clones. A people who will inherit the earth I will have prepared for them," he stood looking out over the city, his hands clasping the balcony rail.

"You're insane; the humans will never let you. They will come with their armies and weapons and their sheer numbers will overwhelm you. You will condemn Atlantis to ruins, again!" I tried, hoping he'd listen to reason.

I needed to buy time, time to figure out a way out of this.

"Neal, you can't think this will work, you have to fight, you can't just give up on me now, not after all we have been through." He never acknowledged me.

"Normally you would be correct, but you are overlooking one thing."

"What the hell are you talking about?" I asked.

"Have you ever wondered how your friend over there was able to do what he does? How he had such immense power?"

"Yeah, I feed him cat food, it's great for muscle building." I couldn't help myself.

Karakatos smiled patiently, I really hated him.

"He was created with some of your genetic material, he is the closest thing to a brother you will ever have. This allows him to manipulate the dark energies much the same way you can. He cannot tap into the energy, but he can mold the energy once the power is available." He let the words sink in.

"You two, working together, can do things no one has ever dreamed of. This is the cooperation of which I seek, and I *will* have it."

"Again, go fuck yourself," I said, tired of this crap.

He looked disappointed, good.

"I had hoped you wouldn't allow things to come to this," he sighed as if he was genuinely upset.

He went over to the small control panel on the wall and punched a few buttons.

"Julake, bring them in," he said, turning and standing in front of me, watching.

A few seconds later the door opened and Kim and Arendiol were pushed inside the room. They looked much as their holograms had. They were both somewhat dirty, their clothes were the same and they looked frightened and nervous.

"Jack!" Kim came running over towards me, kneeling down and hugging me tightly.

My heart twisted, I knew what he was going to do, and I also knew I would do anything to make sure she was safe.

"Are you hurt?" I asked her, checking to see if she had any injuries.

"I'm fine; they haven't done anything to us," she reassured me

"Of course we wouldn't, Jack. I wouldn't allow them to come to harm. They are healthy female Atlanteans, destined to raise our future; I would no more hurt them than I would myself."

"Liar! I have seen you kill with my own eyes; you are a monster!" Arendiol screamed, coming to my side.

"I assure you, I only did what was necessary to ensure our ascendency. I have had to make some sacrifices, that is true, but now is the time for us all to unite, for us to embrace the dawn of a new age," he spoke with true conviction, making me sick.

"Tell me Krackpot, what kind of a world do you think you will be able to build on the backs of millions of human bodies?" I asked.

He turned and looked at me, his eyes shone with a fevered light, madness swept through them; the crack in his sanity was fleeting, but there.

"A glorious one!" he said, in euphoric ecstasy.

"I will stop you, if it kills me, you will not live through this day," I hissed through clenched teeth.

"Ah! Now he is passionate, now he is righteous!" Karakatos spun towards Neal.

"How long?" he asked him.

"Five minutes," Neal answered; all the while he manipulated the knobs and worked the controls.

"Neal was the last piece to the puzzle. You know with him controlling the energy you will release I can create a shield that can withstand a nuclear attack? I can produce weapons that can destroy entire cities before anyone can so much as muster a response?" He turned back to us, narrowing his eyes at Kim and myself.

Julake came back in, walking up to Karakatos.

"Everything is ready," he reported.

"Very good," Karakatos answered.

"It's a shame you will not cooperate, logic would dictate that your only avenue for survival would be in doing as I ask, but I see your time on the surface has corrupted you, you have been infected by the human's illogical disease. No matter, I have prepared for this eventuality." He walked over and grabbed Kim.

"Leave her alone!" I yelled. My arm and leg throbbed in pain.

I was helpless to stop him.

"I think you know what happens now. It really is a shame I have to do this, but the greater good is far more important than this one child." He held her tight, keeping her near him.

Kim tried to struggle, but Karakatos was far stronger than her.

He was a mad man. I could see this truth in his eyes. He wanted to bring Atlantis back to the surface only to use his people's advanced technology to usher in a new age of darkness and death. The humans would not go down without a fight and there was a very high chance half of the planet would be inhospitable when the dust cleared. Millions upon millions would die, but none of that mattered. I couldn't sit and watch Kim die. I made her a promise.

"You will do as I ask. You will do this, or I will kill the girl," he said, staring at me.

I looked at him for a moment, really looked at him and I knew beyond a shadow of a doubt that he was right. I would do as he asked, even though what may come because of my actions and I would do what he willed just to save Kim. I know doing so wasn't rational, wasn't practical but saving her was right. That's one of the things about love, it didn't always follow logic.

I took a deep breath and slowly made my way to my feet, favoring my bad knee. Julake stepped forward, intent on protecting Karakatos, but the Warlord waved him back.

"What do you want me to do?" I asked as defeat filled my voice.

Karakatos smiled at me triumphantly. Reveling in getting what he wanted.

"What I want is quite simple. This machine can open the rift, under the sentinel's astute control; the device can also be used to control the energies the rift's opening will release. The only thing lacking is a start, an initial power surge that will begin the process. That is where you come in. Your friend can only control the energy; you, however, can summon it."

"How much energy will I need to gather to start the machine?" I asked.

"All of it," he answered, staring at me intently.

What he asked of me scared me; the earlier uses of my powers were small things, imbuing my weapons with energy and giving myself some extra strength, nothing like this, what if I couldn't control the power I summoned? What if the wild energy got loose and killed us all?

"Let her go first," I said, knowing freeing her didn't make a difference.

Karakatos smiled bigger, then released Kim, she ran to me, hugging me tightly. I almost fell as I fought to keep my balance. Arendiol came to us, giving me support.

"Make sure she is safe," I said to Arendiol.

She looked at me with grave seriousness, understanding what was going to happen. She nodded once, then pulled Kim away from me.

"C'mon, everything's going to be okay, c'mon," she tried to soothe her.

I turned back towards the machine and Neal.

"*If you can hear me, I want you to know I always considered you my friend, not my possession.*" I sent to him, I wasn't sure I would survive what I was going to do.

"Okay, let's do this," I said.

Chapter Seventeen

I took one more last look at Kim, letting her face fill my mind, using her as a grounding rod.

Breathing slowly at first, I began to open myself up to the forces that were under my control. I flexed the muscle in my mind, drawing energy into myself, letting the current fill every ounce of my being. I felt the vast power build, starting as a slight pressure behind my ears and soon becoming a relentless tide that refused to stop coming.

With a grunt of effort, I began directing the energy towards Neal, letting the power flow to him. I became a conduit, allowing the untold riches of the dark energy to become something tangent, something that could be harnessed and channeled the power to Neal, where he could use the dark energy as he deemed fit.

Neal's eyes began to blaze gold, the light pouring from them like two small suns fighting for a place in the solar system. He worked the controls on the machine furiously, never slacking. We danced like that for minutes, me gathering energy and Neal using what I sent him. Eventually, the machine began to hum as the engine finally received the juice needed to begin to show signs of life.

The cylindrical apparatus I thought resembled a jet turbine began to turn, slowly at first but then gaining speed, eventually becoming a blur as the machine spun faster and faster. The entire room vibrated with power as the levels of energy I gathered and sent to Neal increased. I felt the edge of reality as I tapped into the essence of creation. The vast enormity of the universe opened before me and I almost felt as though I was touching the hand of God, as if I could feel the substance of life. The feeling of losing myself to the powers of the cosmos frightened me but I kept pushing myself, knowing, somehow, that I hadn't gathered enough, that the machine needed more.

A beam of pure white light shot from the turbine and concentrated about twenty feet away coming to a point, a singularity. The light became solid and grew as I felt the fabric of the universe begin to bend. The doorway to another dimension slowly opened as the energies released ripped a hole in known reality. I felt an odd sensation as the rift occurred, like being in an old movie where the images on the screen don't line up and there are two identical pictures, vying for the same space.

A loud crackle split the air and I saw in my peripheral vision as Karakatos and the others were knocked from their feet. Electricity raced from the singularity, snaking off in all directions, where the alien current contacted the walls, strange shapes grew, as if the energy released transformed the substance of our dimension into something else, a mix of the two-dimensional energies.

Neal did something on the machine and the singularity seemed to come under control, the electricity stopped leaking and the ball of light became more solid.

The machine began to glow, all the components blazed with inner power. The same light raced through the connecting structures of the machine and went wherever they were connected to do whatever they were designed to do.

I knew, without understanding how I knew, the machine was funneling the energy from the rift to power a multitude of things the Warlord had designed. I felt as the energy began to power up a huge city-wide defense system, consisting of powerful lasers and other weapons. I saw the energy race towards the foundations of the city to begin forcing the earth to push us up, up from the ocean floor towards the surface. I saw the energy flow into the growth chambers, to fuel the massive clone army the Warlord was planning on hatching and towards the large manufacturing area to produce the new Atlantean armor used by Karakatos himself.

The energy I was providing was going to fuel a world war, one where there could be only one victor, where Karakatos would prove that whoever carried the bigger stick, won. I shuddered at the thought of the death and destruction my actions would allow to be unleashed on the people of earth.

I saw Neal's eyes blaze bright white for a few seconds and then he slumped to one knee, only to quickly regain his footing. He did something then that gave me a spark of hope, he looked over at me. In his eyes I saw something I had feared was gone, I saw Neal again.

Raiphaim, what have I done? Neal asked.

My heart swelled with hope.

"*Neal? Is it you? Is it really you?*" I sent, still trapped by the energy I was funneling, but able to talk to Neal none the less.

Of course, my lord, who else would I be? If I could have, I would have cried out loud in joy at that moment, only Neal would be so literal.

"*Neal! My god, what happened? You kind of took the whole evil villain thing a little too far,*" I sent, happy just to talk to him again.

I... I think I was sick. I don't remember much after using the city's interface, but if my calculations are correct, I was infected with a virus, one that overrode my programming.

"*Well, duh,*" I answered.

The energies flowing through me seem to have acted as a fever, burning off the infection, allowing my original programming to regain dominance.

"*Ok, so does that mean you're back to normal?*"

Yeah, I think so. I seemed to have missed a lot.

Was that a joke?

"*I'd say so. Number one, do you know what is happening, and number two, how can we stop it and save the day?*" I asked.

Allow me a moment to get a better understanding of our situation. He said.

"*Sure, take your time,*" I responded, just glad to have him back.

After what seemed like an eternity Neal responded.

I have analyzed our predicament.

"*And?*"

And the situation is not good. The machine is working at eighty-five percent capacity. Once the device reaches one hundred percent there will no longer be a need for your services at which point the Warlord plans on murdering you before you can muster any resistance.

"And I thought we were just beginning to get along, what else?"

I believe I am correct in assuming you wish to shut the machine down.

"Yes, that is a good assumption."

Any attempt to stop the process now would result in a backlash of energy. I can shut the device down, but there would be a reverberation, one that would dwarf the blast which caused the Fall.

"So, we either let it continue, get myself murdered and allow the Warlord to fuel his world domination plans, or we shut the whole thing down and blow the city and all its inhabitants to kingdom come."

Both of those options just didn't seem like much fun, there had to be another way.

My lord, there is a third option.

Of course, I could always count on Neal.

"Go ahead." I sent.

The possibility exists to shut the power off and divert the energies straight up, funnel them into a tight beam up into the sky, thereby sending the destructive forces into space, rendering them harmless.

"I don't understand, wouldn't the beam rip through the protective dome, flooding all of us?"

Correct, even though the citizens are wearing skin suits and would be able to breathe underwater, the destructive forces unleashed from so much water rushing in and destroying the city would kill untold thousands.

Marcus Abshire   LOST SON

"Well, shit Neal, I don't really see how that is any better...." Holy crap, I think I knew how we could minimize the damage.

"Wait, are you thinking what I'm thinking?"

That depends, my lord.

"Yeah, you are, you sneaky devil. If you allow the mechanism for the city's ascension to continue it would bring us to the surface where you could then shut the machine down. The blast would be minimal and the death toll small." I thought.

Then yes, I was thinking what you were thinking. The machine is at ninety-five percent.

As crazy as the plan sounded, I think Neal's idea just might work. Of course, the world might be a little interested in the Lost City of Atlantis just surfacing in the Bermuda Triangle, but that was something to deal with after I saved the entire city and the world from the Warlord's madness.

My lord, my sensors indicate you are injured. Your current ailments may make fighting off your enemies difficult, I suggest you attempt to funnel the energy you have been gathering into yourself and repair your damaged limbs. Neal said.

"What are you kidding me? I can do that sort of thing?" I asked, stunned.

Normally the task would be beyond your ability, the complexity for healing damaged organic matter is vast, but the energies that have built in this place may allow such an act.

"I guess I can give it a shot. Once I break contact, how long do you need?" I asked.

Marcus Abshire   LOST SON

It will take me approximately three minutes to establish a protective shield around myself, until that time I will be vulnerable. Once you are free, I will shut down all energy transfer except to the ascension machines. That will alert the Warlord something has gone awry. Until I create my barrier I will be exposed, if I am stopped from keeping the machine working functionally the device will shut down and close the rift, destroying us all.

Ninety-nine point five, ninety-nine point six.... Neal counted.

I only had a few seconds to prepare for action. I really wanted to see the look on the Warlord's face when he realizes his little plans have gone wrong.

I knew I only had a few seconds and used them wisely. I drew from the power I was transferring to Neal. The sheer magnitude of what I had channeled was staggering. I tapped into the flow and diverted a fraction of the vast energy into myself, sending the current towards my body's damaged areas, the places the Warlord had broken during our fight. I immediately felt the power rip through me, and I absently heard myself screaming out in pain as the cosmic forces tore my body apart and then knitted the pieces back together. The process only took a moment, but my suffering seemed like an eternity as I was remade.

I could feel the strength flowing through me and knew I would be filled with dark energy when I finally broke free from the power.

The machine is at one-hundred percent capacity. I vaguely heard Neal say, his thoughts seemed to be vying for space inside my head, a head filled with the power of the universe.

With a grunt of effort, I broke free from the cycle, dropping to one knee. I felt washed clean, my body thrummed with power and I could sense and feel everyone in the room.

Kim huddled with Arendiol. They had backed to the edge of the room, trying to keep small. Neal was still at the controls of the machine, working furiously to keep the rift from destabilizing, the area where he worked was swirling with the energy of the cosmos, which made discerning what was happening within that cyclone of power hard.

Karakatos stood where he had been, his body faced Neal and he looked on with rapt attention, like a preacher seeing a true miracle for the first time. He turned to Julake and said, "Kill him."

"I don't think so," I said, standing up and facing the Warlord.

"Get Kim to safety," I said to Arendiol, never looking over at them.

She was as surprised at my recovery as I was but managed to keep her wits about her. She grabbed Kim and hurried her out of the door.

Julake stopped in mid-stride, unsure of what to do next. I acted first.

I reached out and with a small effort of will, brought my sword to me. The magnificent blade sailed towards me and I easily snatched the handle. I channeled some energy into the metal and the Atlantean steel began to glow with a bright blue radiance. I turned to them both, enjoying their momentary stunned expressions.

"Listen up douchebags. I have had fun playing with you and crazy pants over there but in the words of my favorite space marine, game over man," I said, waiting for a reaction.

I didn't have to wait long.

Julake raised one of the foam pistols and shot me dead center of my chest with two white foam balls. Within a few seconds, the foam had expanded and covered my chest and I was soon completely immobilized by the foam cocoon. Normally I would be done for, I hadn't previously been able to do anything about my predicament, but that wasn't the case anymore.

Julake looked over at a large screen, seeing something he didn't like.

"Power to everything but the ascension machine has been shut down," he said.

Neal worked fast.

Karakatos turned from me to Neal, his eyes narrowed suspiciously.

"Kill this disgrace to our people then bring the second phase virus online, our dear sentinel needs readjusting."

Julake turned back to me, murder in his eyes.

He took a few steps towards me then had to duck as I blasted free from my prison, using the energies I had gathered to force the foam from my body. The freedom was liberating.

I raised my sword and used the rigid metal like a lightning rod, funneling power down the deadly blade and straight towards the Warlord. A blue beam shot from my sword and slammed him dead in the chest, sending him flying to slam into the wall. His armor, where I had hit him, looked blackened and smoked from the heat of my attack.

Julake quickly reached over and slapped a button on the desk next to him. Lights and sirens immediately began bleating and flashing, the large doors on both sides of the room opened and twenty well-armed Atlantean soldiers rushed in, ready for war.

They wore the same thick armor as the Warlord, only theirs was blue instead of red. Each one of them carried a deadly looking sword and they closed in on me like a pack of hyenas on a wounded water buffalo.

Forcing my way free of the foam had taken some of my energy reserves, but I still had plenty left. I saw out of the corner of my eye as Julake went over to the Warlord who was beginning to stir awake. Damn, I wished I had killed him.

The first wave of soldiers rushed me, and I met them with a swipe of my blade. Five of them came at me, their numbers giving them the advantage, but they weren't ready for me.

I moved faster than I ever had before, like a shadow I flitted past their attacks and severed arm from body, head from neck and guts from stomach. They moved in almost slow motion as my enhanced speed allowed me to dispatch them with ease. Their armor only provided a small amount of resistance, which wasn't as strong as the Warlord's; I guess he kept the best for himself, what a swell guy.

I stopped, standing amidst five dead bodies. Killing them wasn't something I wanted to do, but I didn't have much choice, it was either them or me, and I didn't have any plans on dying today.

Everyone had to brace themselves as a deep rumbling flowed through the building, reminding me of an earthquake. I saw a few pieces of the marble architecture fall from the structure as the forces required to move billions of tons of rock and push the entire city up to the surface reverberated all around us.

I felt a slight movement as we slowly began lifting from the ocean floor.

"HA! Do you see? Our ascension has begun! We will bring in a new age of rule, one that will be marked by peace and structure!" The Warlord screamed, standing with his slightly damaged armor.

"Sure, you just have to murder billions of people to establish your so-called peace!" I answered back.

"Bah! You will never understand. Kill him, kill him now," he answered, turning from me.

"Where do you think you're going, you son of a bitch!" I yelled as another wave of soldiers rushed me.

I again waded into them, using my enhanced abilities to make quick work of them, only this time afterward I was winded, I could feel as I was using my reserves, soon I would be at normal strength.

Ten soldiers stood looking at me, amazed wonder filled their eyes at seeing me kill their fellow men so efficiently.

"It doesn't have to be this way. The Warlord is mad; he wants to bring about a world war. You don't have to be part of this, let me through, let me deal with him and this madness will end," I pleaded with them, hoping they would listen to reason.

"The Warlord has given his orders; you will not leave this room alive," one of them said.

I really didn't want to keep killing them; maybe there was a way I could stop them without having to.

I gathered the rest of my energy reserves and channeled them to my sword, pointing the blade at the soldiers I formulated what I wanted, I saw the plan in my mind and then with a grunt of effort I unleashed the power, hoping to God the dark energy did as I asked.

The energy rushed from my sword in a large flow of electricity, racing through the men and causing them all to convulse uncontrollably. Within a few seconds, I watched as they all flopped to the floor and stayed there, knocked unconscious by the electric assault.

I felt dizziness and fatigue sweep through me as the energy I expended took a toll on my own reserves. I used my sword as a crutch, making sure I didn't fall over.

Well done, my lord. You are learning to control your abilities better, that is good. Perhaps next time you could start with the stun move. I heard Neal's voice in my head.

Even now he was counseling me.

"I'll try to keep that in mind." I sent back, finally getting my bearings again.

I did a quick search, looking for the Warlord. He was nowhere in sight.

"Neal?" I sent, knowing he would understand what I wanted.

They fled through the door to your right.

"Can you guide me to them?" I turned, intent on heading out the same door they had gone through.

I can.

Marcus Abshire   LOST SON

Three soldiers carrying rifles came through the door low and fast and started laying down cover fire for two others who scrambled towards Neal. I had to dive to the side and hurry towards something to hide behind. There were soldiers and body parts lying on the ground all around me, but I managed to put the machine between the soldiers and myself.

I tried to get right up against the machine, but I was stopped by something hard and unyielding. I peeked around the corner and one of the soldiers shot his rifle, the blast connected with the same barrier I had encountered. A cylindrical transparent force field blazed with a momentary golden glow as the rifle blast's energy interacted with the shield.

The shield circled the machine, allowing Neal to continue keeping the rift stable but not letting anyone near enough to touch him. I noticed Neal was within the shield's border and a nagging thought began growing in my brain. I had to table my wondering mind and focus on the task at hand.

"Be careful not to damage the machine, you imbeciles will kill us all!" I heard one of the men yell.

The two guys not carrying rifles rushed to Neal, trying to get close, only to be stopped by the barrier.

"Dammit! He has protected himself; we cannot upload the control program!"

"Well what do we do now?" one of the soldiers asked.

"We follow the Warlords orders, you kill him, we will try to gain access to the sentinel," he answered.

I was stuck, the soldiers had me pinned. I needed a way to distract them so I could get close. I missed my pistol.

I looked around the room in desperation only to settle my eyes on something that made my heart swell.

"Neal, I need to get to the other side of the room, can you distract them long enough for me to get there?" I asked.

I believe I can provide you the diversion you require. He answered.

I got into position, ready to run across the room when Neal acted.

Now. Neal sent.

I got up and sprinted across the room, the soldiers saw me and started drawing a bead, aiming their rifles right at me. I felt exposed, like a sitting duck. A bright golden flare ignited in the shield, lighting the whole room up with a light so bright the afterglow made my skin feel like I had spent all day in the sun. I heard the rifles fire and was happy to not be shot as I ran. I reached my destination and grabbed the old pistol from its place of honor on the wall. I flipped over onto my back and tried to focus long enough to channel some energy into the pistol.

As soon as I reached within myself, I knew my previous actions had weakened me. If my newfound power was akin to a muscle that needed exercise, then my actions had essentially made the muscle cramp. I was only able to gather a small fraction of energy, but hopefully what I had gathered would be enough.

The soldiers had finally recovered from the explosion of light and were aiming their rifles my way. I raised the pistol and pulled the trigger, sending a bright blue energy-charged lead bullet towards my enemies the same time they fired their rifles.

Thankfully, I was a much better shot than them, or maybe I just had a wider margin for error. One blast flew past my head to blow a chunk from the wall behind me, the other hit my arm and I felt a stinging pain as the rifle blast knocked me sideways. I reached out to feel where the blast had hit me, seeing a deep but not lethal gash in my arm. I thanked God that's all the injury I had sustained. If the blast had been a clean shot, it would have taken my arm off, the wound would bleed and hurt, but my skinsuit was already closing, giving my body time to heal.

I couldn't watch what happened when my shot hit home, but I did see the satisfying aftermath. All three soldiers were lying in unmoving heaps, their bodies smoked from the pistol's destructive energies and the two programmers were likewise out cold. I looked around at all the bodies and saw two of the stunned soldiers starting to stir. I knew I needed to be out of here when the rest of them came awake.

Another tremor ran through the building, causing even more of the structure to break off. I began to get worried; I didn't want to go through all of this only to die as the building collapsed.

"*Neal, I have to find the Warlord.*" I sent as I hurried out of the room, towards the lift.

I have been able to track their movements through the internal security systems. They are on the roof, preparing to manually launch an offensive attack.

"What do you mean? I thought you shut down the power to everything but the ascension machines." I sent, fear began to grow in my belly.

I indeed have, but there was enough energy diverted to the system to initiate at least one firing, perhaps two. They have already locked in their intended targets and are waiting for us to surface before finalizing the launch sequence.

"Okay, two shots, that doesn't sound so bad." I came to the door, only to find the metal stuck closed. I began to physically force the door open.

I don't believe you understand the magnitude of the Warlord's offensive capabilities. The energy gathered from the rift is enormous. The devastation to the Warlord's targets would be the equivalent of a small grade nuclear weapon.

Hole. Eeee. Shiit.

"Do you know who he has targeted?" The elevator doors began squealing in protest as I was able to force them open.

Yes, my lord, Washington D.C. and Moscow.

Dear God, if those attacks were successful each country would think they were under a nuclear assault and there's no telling what they would do in response.

"How long until we breach the surface and he can fire?" I asked Neal.

Approximately thirty minutes if we keep the current rate of ascent.

I guess lifting a city as large as New York from the bottom of the ocean took a while.

Marcus Abshire　　　　LOST SON

I finally was able to wrench the doors open enough to get inside when I saw movement out of the corner of my eye. I spun, sword in hand, only to drop the blade as Kim came and crushed me with a hug.

"What are you doing here? I told Arendiol to get you somewhere safe," I said, both angry and elated at seeing her.

"We tried to get out, but there was a large group of soldiers out here, it was all we could do to keep from being trampled. We tried the lift, but the controls weren't responding," Arendiol answered.

I looked at Kim, smiling forgivingly. "It's okay, kid. You did good, now let's get the heck out of here."

She beamed with pride before a wrinkle appeared between her eyes. "How, the only way down is not working."

"Neal, I know you're kinda busy right now, but can you get the lift working?" I sent.

I believe I can accomplish what you ask.

Within a few seconds, the inside of the lift lit up. I smiled at Kim and Arendiol. "See, no big deal."

My lord, we have incoming.

The door opposite of us blew open from a controlled blast and twenty more soldiers came rushing in, this time with three men who obviously looked out of place.

More programmers, maybe?

They saw us in the small waiting area near the elevators and raised their weapons when the door slammed shut, protecting us from their attack, for a little while anyway.

"Thanks, Neal." I sent.

Marcus Abshire   LOST SON

Of course. Leaving by the lift is most likely the wisest choice, any other avenue of exit is ill-advised.

"Ok, captain obvious, I need to get to the roof and a small army is blocking my way. Do you have any suggestions?"

Yes, you will ride down with Kim and Arendiol, ensuring they exit safely. There is a large force attacking the capital and they are keeping most of the Warlord's men busy, you should be able to slip past them unnoticed. Once that is done you can use the lift again, exiting three floors below the roof, there is a large window you can exit and climb to your destination.

I hurried everyone on the elevator and hit the button that corresponded with the ground floor. It shifted slightly as we began moving.

"Wait, you want me to climb three floors on the outside of the building?" I sent.

Yes, my lord. Neal answered, not a hint of emotion in his mental voice.

Just once I wished there was an option that resulted in me sitting in front of my T.V. watching football.

Okay, first things first, get my friends to safety, then settle up with the maniac on the roof.

I knelt, coming eye level with Kim. I looked up to Arendiol so she would understand I was talking to her too.

"When we get to the bottom everything's going to be pretty crazy. I want both of you to follow me like a shadow, never leave my side, do you understand?" They both nodded, fear and nerves were evident on both their faces.

Marcus Abshire — LOST SON

Looking at Kim in such distress was heart-wrenching but seeing her be strong despite her circumstances made me proud. I didn't know what tomorrow would bring, if after all of this I would see Kim and Arendiol again, but I was going to make sure they both came out alright, or I was going to die trying. In order to do that I had to stop a nuclear holocaust by a man who had already proven he could kick my ass.

Nothing worth doing was ever easy.

There was another quake and the elevator shook wildly. Kim lost her balance and I grabbed her and pulled her close, protecting her body with mine. I heard the gut-wrenching sound of metal twisting and ripping on metal and the lift fell about five feet before we lurched to a stop. We all looked at each other with the unspoken fear on our faces.

No one dared move a muscle for fear of causing the elevator to break free when another tremor shook the building and the elevator came loose and began to plummet dozens of stories towards the hard, deadly earth.

Kim screamed and Arendiol fell to the ground, hitting her head. I tried to brace myself and shield Kim. In my mind, I saw us hit, the elevator being ripped to shreds from the impact and all three of us being turned to a pulp of meat.

I don't know how long we fell, but the drop couldn't have been more than a few seconds, although those seconds seemed like years waiting for the inevitable impact. I kept hearing a phrase being repeated in my head, a phrase I had heard somewhere but couldn't remember where.

It's not the fall that kills you, it's the sudden stop at the end.

Fortunately, the sudden stop didn't kill us. Instead, we somehow slowed down and even though the G forces from our deceleration caused all my blood to rush to my toes, we all survived.

For a second I didn't know what had happened. I was in shock from our sudden change of circumstance. I kept hearing a loud high-pitched noise and realized Kim was still screaming, waiting to become a permanent part of the tower's infrastructure.

"Kim, Kim, it's okay, we're alright, we made it," I soothed her.

Eventually, she stopped screaming only to be wracked with full-body sobs, the shock of what had happened causing her to release her emotions with gut-wrenching tears.

I held her, keeping contact, making her realize we were okay. I looked over at Arendiol, seeing her start to stir. She sat up; one of her eyes was stuck shut due to the blood that had congealed from a cut on her head.

"Auuugh," she moaned, holding her head with one hand.

"Arendiol, can you hear me? Hey, are you with me?" I asked, hoping to get her to focus.

She squinted from the pain of her injury but looked over at me; her one open eye seemed clear and alert.

"Yeah, I'm here," she answered groggily.

The impact had crushed the elevator but thankfully not enough to kill us. The doors were a mess of twisted metal, light streamed in from a large gap in them as the destruction caused them to break apart.

It was this crack I nodded towards while speaking to Arendiol. "Can you take a peek outside; see if we can get out without getting our faces blown off?" I asked.

"Yeah, sure," she answered, ambling over to look.

After a second she turned back to us. "It looks clear, there's a stand-off near the front entrance. A large group of fighters have assembled there and are being held off by a small group of the Warlord's men. Thankfully, the elevator is on the side of the building, not much happening over here, although the crash has attracted some attention, I don't see any soldiers," she added, coming back to help with Kim.

That was a lucky break, if the soldiers were aware of our presence, we would be sitting ducks in here, literally like shooting fish in a barrel. Hopefully, we could squeeze out of the door's wreckage and get Kim and Arendiol to safety.

"Can you move?" I asked.

"Yeah, I'm a little woozy, but I can run if I have to," she responded, gently patting Kim's head.

"Hey, are you alright?" she asked her.

Kim pulled back from my shoulder. Tear streaks made two lines of wetness among her dirty face. Her eyes gleamed brightly from crying and my heart again twisted in anger at seeing her in such pain.

She nodded to Arendiol, looking back up at me. "I'm okay."

"Good girl," I answered. She smiled back weakly.

"We need to get out of here quickly, do you understand?" I asked her.

"Yes."

"Good, once we're out of this death box we run as fast as we can across the street and try to get a block away, then we can turn back and find Brigand's fighters. They should be able to keep you safe," I said, Kim turned back to me, worry on her face.

"Aren't you going to stay with me?" she asked.

My heart twisted again, like someone turning a knife in it.

"I want to honey, but in order for you to be safe, I have something to do first," I held her shoulders, keeping eye contact with her. "As soon as I finish, I will come for you."

She searched my face, looking deep within my eyes for the truth. Finally, she nodded once. "Okay, deal with Krackpot, then hurry back," I smiled as she used my nickname for him.

"You got it."

I turned, keeping her small hand firmly in mine. She felt fragile, like a warm delicate doll, one I feared would easily break. We squeezed out of the doors and stood in the open air. I felt exposed, fully expecting someone to scream that we were here and to start shooting us full of holes, but thankfully no one did. We managed to run full out across the street and I only stopped to look back once we were in the shadows of another building.

The elevator lay in a tangled mess; it was a miracle we had survived. There was a large pool of slowly dissolving white foam underneath the wreckage. The evaporating goo looked like the same stuff used to immobilize people. A safety feature built into the system to stop a runaway elevator. I had to say when the foam was used this way, the stuff did an effective job, other than Arendiol's bump; we were all no worse for the wear.

I turned and led our small group around the building, circling back to the action. Once we got around the corner we ran into a small band of fighters, crouched behind an abandoned vehicle. The streets were awash in chaos, people were wandering around, staring towards the fighting in stunned shock, while others ran from the violence. The whole city looked to be in the middle of an apocalypse, everywhere we looked the normal day to day operations had stopped as the fighters attempted to break the soldier's defenses and gain access to the capital.

"Hey, get out of here!" the fighters yelled, motioning for us to hurry past.

We were almost by them when one of them saw my sword and the old pistol in my holster. "Stop, stop or we'll shoot!" we heard.

I raised my hands in a non-threatening gesture, hoping they wouldn't start shooting. I wasn't sure what kind of training they had, Brigand's fighters seemed more of the rebellious revolutionary types, not the well-disciplined warrior types, like Sessarian.

"Easy fellas, we are no threat; we are on the same side," I tried, hoping to get them to back off.

"Maybe, maybe not, you have some serious hardware there, perhaps the safest thing would be to just take you all out," one of them said. He had a wild look in his eyes, a look I didn't like. Knowing who was stable and who wasn't was almost impossible, I guess if he started trying to murder us, I would know pretty quickly.

"Perhaps I outta just take you out first, Basteed," a woman's voice said from nearby.

Basteed went still as a long barrel was jammed into his neck. I looked over and saw a steely-eyed woman holding a rifle, pointing the business end at Basteed.

"Look at them, a woman, a girl and a man who looks like he just escaped Poseidon's deepest dungeons. I swear I don't know why Brigand allows bastard's like you to fight with us," she sneered.

"Because you need all the help you can get," Basteed answered with a heavy dose of sarcasm.

She looked over at us, taking her time in sizing us up. Finally, she settled her gaze on me. I noticed she looked intently on my pistol and sword. "You're the one Brigand told us about aren't you, the surface dweller?"

I stepped forward, placing myself in front of Kim and Arendiol.

"I am," I said.

She glared one more time, then huffed in acceptance.

"You idiot Basteed, you almost opened fire on king Raiphaim." She took the rifle from his neck and then went to one knee, grabbing Basteed and glaring at the others, they quickly followed suit.

"Please don't do that," I pleaded; their actions made me feel uncomfortable.

They rose back up and looked at me with a newfound level of respect.

"Please forgive me, my lord. I was just kidding, just a little joke, ya know, didn't mean nothing by it," Basteed said, nervous fear evident on his face.

"Hey don't worry. I get guns pointed at me all the time," I said, "Does anyone know where I can find Brigand?" I added, looking at the woman.

"Yes. He's in the command center, back that way, inside the building surrounded by fighters," she said motioning down the street.

"Can you take me to him? Things might be easier that way," I said to her, glancing intently at Basteed.

"Of course, Basteed, don't shoot anyone while I'm gone, unless they are one of the Warlord's tin soldiers," she said, turning and walking away.

We followed her down the alleyway and turned the corner. She waved at a couple of groups of men and had to talk to the ones posted outside the diner alone, pointing to us as she spoke.

She waved us over and opened the door for us, letting us enter without her. I instantly spotted Brigand. He was walking towards us, crossbow in hand. He saw me and stopped in his tracks.

"I see you made it out intact and managed to get who you were after as well," he said, motioning to Kim and Arendiol.

"I did, but Sessarian, she um, didn't make the trip," I said, somberly.

He looked at me for a second before turning away, nodding once.

"She knew the risk; she will be missed," he added.

I gave him a moment, not wanting to impose on him more than I already had.

"I know I don't have any right to ask, but I need a favor," he eyed me sharply.

"Go on," he said.

"First, can you keep these two safe for a little while? I have some unfinished business and until I'm done, I would feel better if I knew they were okay."

"What kind of unfinished business?" he asked, a glint of hope in his eye.

I knew he wanted me to become the next king of Atlantis and he knew I didn't. I think he figured once I got Kim and Arendiol to safety I would bail and leave them to handle things out on their own. I probably would have too if not for the Warlord's crazy plans for world domination.

I debated whether or not to tell him about Karakatos's planned offensive attack and decided if I was going to ask for his help in getting back into the capital, he should know what was going on.

So, I quickly told him about what the Warlord and Julake were up to and what I intended to do about them. I left out the part about Neal; I just felt the less who knew the better. Old habits die hard, I guess.

"Well, that would explain all the activity in the old machinery on the outskirts of the city. That was the ascension machine firing up, long ago built, never used equipment to bring us to the surface."

"Sounds like you're going to fulfill your destiny after all," he added, smiling at me like a cat with a mouth full of mice.

"I don't know about all of that. I just need a way to get to the roof. All the stairs are guarded, makes sense for the Warlord to have concentrated all his men in the capital, he doesn't want anyone stopping him. I only have a short amount of time left before we breach the surface and he fires the damn things, can you help me or what?" I asked, knowing the clock was ticking.

"Neal, I don't have my watch on me, how long until they are able to fire?" I sent.

We will breach in approximately fifteen minutes, the Warlord will need an extra five minutes to fire the weapon. He responded.

Another tremor shook the foundation of Atlantis and I had to grab the edge of a table to keep my footing. Dust and small pieces of the wall crumbled as we continued ever upwards.

"Of course I will help," he smiled, and something in his voice made me very apprehensive. "Follow me, I think I have just what you need," he added, with a dangerous gleam in his eye.

Chapter Eighteen

"There's no way in hell I'm putting that thing on my back," I said, looking at the "solution" Brigand had offered me.

"Those without, shouldn't be demanding when they are given that which they need," he held what looked like the first-ever jet pack.

I think what he was trying to say was beggars can't be choosers. They could if they wanted to live.

"I want to get to the roof, not get splattered on the wall," I said, knowing my feistiness was only because I knew I was going to fly through the air with this deathtrap on my back, but that didn't mean I had to be happy about the prospect.

He held the pack out stubbornly. I looked at the old flier again, seeing my death written all over the damn thing. The jet pack was old alright but was of Atlantean design, maybe there was one more good flight left in her, maybe.

I took the jet pack from his hands and put the straps on, holding my sword in one hand. He checked the straps, making sure they were secured.

"Good, it looks like you're all set. Here," he said, handing me the small control handle.

"Just squeeze this for lift and release the grip slowly to descend, you change direction by leaning," he gave me a quick tutorial, probably the fastest one in history.

"Just like riding a bike," I muttered to myself.

"Huh?"

"Nothing."

"I also thought you might need this," he reached out and handed me a pistol of Atlantean design, the firearm looked sleek and futuristic in appearance, but had a fierceness to it that gave me the impression it could shoot a hole through a bank vault.

"Sweet, but I didn't get you anything," I answered, taking the pistol and replacing the old antique with the newer model. The Atlantean weapon fit well enough, the holster held the pistol tight. I didn't have to worry about my new sidearm falling out during a compromising situation.

"Now I don't know how much fuel is in the tank, but there should be enough to get you to the roof," Brigand started when I interrupted him.

"If you don't know how much is in it, how do you know there's enough to get me up there, I mean that's pretty much the definition of not knowing, you kinda don't know," I was rambling, flying made me nervous.

"Once you're on the roof you will need to shed that thing quickly, the pack is bulky and will only slow you down," he said, ignoring me.

"Okay, fly up there, stop the Warlord and save the day, got it." I stepped to the edge, looking down.

The building we were on wasn't all that tall, but we sure looked higher than we should have, maybe that's because I was going to fly off of the roof and use a jet pack that was old by even Methuselah's standards to reach another roof four times as high as the one I was on.

Marcus Abshire   LOST SON

We were across the street from the capital, on the roof of the diner I had passed through to sneak over underground. I guess it was fitting this time I used the same building to sneak over, over-ground.

"No time like the present, I guess," I said, gathering my courage.

"How we doing Neal?" I sent.

We're doing great. I have the shield all set up and I am being amused at the programmer's attempts to gain access. I don't think you should come in here though, there are about fifty soldiers waiting for you.

That did not sound like the Neal I have known for all these years.

"Are you all right Neal?" I asked.

I think so, but I'm not sure what the extent of the rift's energies on my programming is having. I feel... funny. He answered.

Feel funny? Neal had never had a feeling for as long as I have known him.

"Okay, hang in there." I sent to him, unsure of what to say.

I gripped the throttle, my knuckles white from squeezing too tight and spread my legs, getting a wide base of support. I didn't know what to expect when I fired the engine up and wanted to prepare for anything.

I squeezed the trigger and felt the pack hum to life, only to be interrupted every few seconds as the old stubborn jet pack sputtered and coughed. I turned to Brigand, looking at him with a dwindling sense of confidence.

Marcus Abshire   LOST SON

"It will work, it will work," he said like a ritual, almost as if he was trying to convince himself.

I faced the capital, resigned to my fate. The flying machine strapped to my back would either get me where I needed to go or not, there was only one way to find out.

I squeezed tighter and the pack answered with a loud growl as I felt my feet lift off from the roof, I hung in the air for a few seconds, just hovering, then with a slight shift of weight, went forward, leaving the safety of the roof for the open air.

I increased the throttle and started ascending while also getting closer to the capitol building. I watched below, seeing as the fighting had intensified. The soldiers had far more firepower, but the fighters outnumbered them, making the struggle an almost even fight. From this high, though, I could see a couple of groups of soldiers coming from the back of the building, going to reinforce their comrades. I just hoped they didn't spot me; I wasn't sure how well this thing would hold up under fire.

The building grew as I got closer and closer, while at the same time getting higher, making everyone look smaller by contrast. I tried to keep my sights on the capital, not wanting to keep looking down for fear of what the view would do to me.

I was two levels from the roof and almost thirty feet away when the first rifle blast zipped past my head. I jerked and almost lost control of the pack as I veered forward and then stabilized. I looked down quickly, seeing one of the groups of soldiers looking up at me and drawing their rifles.

Marcus Abshire   LOST SON

Within a few seconds the air became filled with rifle blasts, the soldiers fired over and over, hoping to blow me out of the sky. I started to panic and leaned forward, increasing my speed.

I felt the dull impact of a rifle blast as my jet pack took a hit and the shock knocked me sideways. The thing started skipping and sputtering again and I began to lose altitude, I was only ten feet away but saw an open balcony I hoped to be able to crash land on. Smoke filled the air as the damage to the pack caused the engine to smolder and my eyes stung. I wasn't sure how much longer the pack was going to hold up, so I increased the throttle and angled towards my makeshift landing site.

With a slight kick, I rocketed forward, faster than I intended and a few feet from my destination the pack coughed one more time and died, leaving me to begin falling, taking me past the balcony and right into the hard marble surface of the building, knocking the wind out of me.

I reached out in desperation, hoping with everything I had that I could get a grip on something and stop myself from becoming a stain on the street. Somehow, my fingers found purchase and I held on for dear life, the view around me disappeared from the thick smoke being emitted from the dead jet pack.

I quickly wriggled free from the thing and sent the now useless jet pack unceremoniously down to a dramatic ending. I immediately began climbing, hoping to get to cover before the soldiers shot me full of holes. As I went, I noticed the air was strangely free of rifle blasts and thanked my lucky stars for whatever miracle was involved in that.

Reaching the balcony, I peered over. Just a few feet away stood three soldiers, each one looking towards Neal as he worked from inside his protective shield. Within the room stood dozens more, all standing with weapons at the ready, as if Neal was going to go berserk and start slaughtering them.

I dipped back down, realizing I had to climb to the roof while avoiding the balcony.

"*Neal, I'm on the outside of the building, making my way to the roof.*"

Sounds like fun. I'm having a little get together with thirty of my favorite people. Neal answered.

"*Ah, okay.*" I thought uncertainly, all the while climbing, hoping not to lose my grip and fall to my death.

I can tell from your response you think I'm being different. Neal sent.

"*Yeah, you aren't acting like yourself, and there's also...*" I stopped, not sure about how to proceed.

Also, what? Ohhh, you figured it out, didn't you?

"*Yeah, I did. There has to be another way.*"

I have run all the scenarios, figured my options; this is the only one that keeps the aftereffects of shutting the rift from killing thousands.

"*So, you're going to be the big hero, huh? Killing yourself in order to save all these innocents?*"

I suppose so. I really don't have any other choice.

"*I know, I know you wouldn't be doing this if there was another way, but it's just, I'm just....*" I paused, emotions I didn't even realize I had threatened to debilitate me.

Marcus Abshire — LOST SON

I'm going to miss you too.
My lord.

I had to stop, take a second to let my vision clear. For some damn reason they had gotten all cloudy, maybe something in the air made them tear up.

"*Any last advice you'd like to give me?*" For almost as long as I could remember Neal had been there to help, been there to guide, hell, he had just been there. I wasn't sure what I was going to do after all of this and he no longer could just be there.

Yeah, don't get killed.

"*Really? Now you're gonna get a personality? I mean you couldn't have been corrupted by an alien dimension's energy sooner, maybe made all those days hanging with you a little more fun?*"

Have you ever thought if I had been cooler, I wouldn't have hung around with you so much?

"*Unbelievable, where was this Neal all my life?*"

I finally reached the lip of the roof, getting ready to pull myself up and see what kind of hell I had climbed into. I stopped for a second, gathering myself for what was to come. I started breathing slowly and calmed my mind, opening myself to the dark energy, drawing that energy into myself.

Again, I felt as the muscle used to draw in power was weakened, my talent was still cramped, but I still felt as the juice I could draw in flowed into my body and filled me with a limited amount of power. I took one more breath.

"*Thanks for the advice, and one more thing, don't call me 'lord.'*" I said, hauling myself onto the roof.

Chapter Nineteen

I peeked over the ledge, getting a quick look at what I was dealing with. The roof was empty of the things you would normally see on a human-constructed building. There were no air conditioner units, no large pieces of equipment that kept the building comfortable; instead, the entire space was a well-organized and meticulously kept garden. Small, waist-high shrubs decorated the perimeter, leading into a beautifully manicured landscape, full of fragrant flowers, small decorative trees, and raised herb gardens. The surrounding area looked like something out of a gardening in the city magazine, an almost "how to" on urban rooftop landscaping.

Right in the middle of the small oasis, like some cancer of malicious growth, completely opposite of the healthy substance all around, arose a large cannon. The deadly gun's Atlantean design gave it a smooth and regal quality, but the weapon's very existence here amidst so much natural beauty marred the pristine landscape and made its presence hideous.

The barrel rose twenty feet into the air, pointing towards the sky. At the base stood Julake and the Warlord, each at their respective positions on either side of the weapon. They were focused on the cannon, completing whatever tasks needed to be done before firing the damnable thing.

Surrounding them stood a small squad of soldiers on high alert. Each one dressed in the blue battle armor that resembled the Warlords. They carried small, compact and dangerous-looking guns I thought best reminded me of Uzis. I didn't want to see what they did when fired, but I figured I wasn't really going to get the option of opting out of that choice.

I dropped back down and started shimmying to my right, towards a long section of bushes I could use as cover as I climbed onto the roof. Once in place I hauled myself up and kept low, not wanting to give my position up too soon.

I knew my time was running out, soon we would surface and then the Warlord would be able to fire his weapons, my shoulder was throbbing from the shot I had taken earlier, and I was incapable of drawing much energy into myself. I had my sword and the pistol Brigand had given me, but I was without my most powerful weapon. Neal. I felt alone and naked without his black silhouette nearby, knowing he had my back.

I looked around, trying to find something that might allow me to get a little closer, to let me shrink the distance between them and me. I reached over and picked up a small rock, tossing the large pebble once in my palm. The rock wasn't much, but hopefully, it would do.

I peeked around my cover and saw the soldiers in the same position, then tossed the rock, hoping the distraction would draw their attention. I heard the rock clatter to the ground and the soldiers all reacted, looking towards the sound. I kept low and dashed from cover, hurrying towards a small herb garden. The low wall was almost three feet tall and made from interlaced rocks; the fragrant aroma of the fresh herbs assaulted me as I closed the distance.

One of the soldiers whipped his head back and saw me scrambling towards my cover. He yelled something I couldn't quite catch. I didn't need to understand what he said to know what he meant when the air exploded in gunfire. I ducked low; cursing under my breath for my bad luck as my hiding spot slowly started dwindling as the soldiers began blasting chunks of the rock away.

I started panicking; I didn't know what to do. I had no real shield once my cover disappeared, I didn't have enough juice to get all of them with a dark energy attack and I was too far away to make sure I could take them out with my sword without getting shot full of holes.

Concentrating, I started slowing my breathing down, focused my mind and hoped I could gather more energy to allow me to send one large, energy-charged pistol blast towards the weapon, hoping to destroy the death machine and keep the Warlord from launching his attack, even if I was killed in the process.

My concentration shattered as I heard a loud noise, a sound very similar to what you hear on a rollercoaster, one-part fear, and one-part pure excitement. A moment later Brigand came flying over the lip of the roof, the same model of old and beaten up jet pack strapped to his back. The engine sputtered and stalled, then kicked back to life as he dropped and rose with each agonized malfunction, a large grin split his face as the smoke from the dying pack momentarily hid him from view.

He looked towards the soldiers and his smile turned devious as he tossed a small round ball towards them, a second later the pack finally died, and surprised fear shone from Brigand's face as he began to plummet from the sky.

"Uh oh," I heard him say as I jumped up and raced towards him, diving with my arms out.

Brigand's arms flailed wildly as he sank, I felt like I was watching *Wiley Coyote* as he runs off the edge of a cliff and just stands in mid-air, not falling until he looks down and realizes his predicament.

I hoped beyond hope that I could make it to him, moving with all I had, knowing the power within me would aid in my movements.

I reached out, and dove.

I grabbed onto his arm and slid to a halt, using my feet to try and anchor myself from falling off the edge myself.

We froze like that for a few seconds, afraid to do anything that might cause us to fall. I heard a loud pop behind me, followed by a few shouts of shocked pain only to refocus on my own situation as I slipped a few inches towards the edge.

Brigand squealed in fear and tried to scramble up my arms, inadvertently pulling me even closer.

"Stop!" I said, trying to get through to him.

He quit struggling, panicked eyes looking at me.

"Try and see if you can get your feet on the ledge," I said, far calmer than I was.

He nodded and swung his feet towards the building, finding purchase. The strain on my arms eased a little and I quickly readjusted, getting a better grip with my feet. I inched backward, slowly dragging him with me, the further back I went the more weight Brigand was able to take himself.

A few seconds later we were both on the roof, panting.

He wiggled out of the jet pack and smiled at me.

"Thought you might need some help," he said.

I peeked over the bush, seeing the soldiers still recovering.

"What was that?" I asked.

"It disrupts their weapons for a short time, it has a small range, but is good for disabling their firearms," he answered.

"Why the hell didn't you give me one earlier and where did you get that jet pack?" I asked, creeping forward again, getting back into my previous position, Brigand followed closely.

"I didn't have it earlier; my men have been raiding some of the Warlord's weapons caches. He's gathered all his soldiers to him, or to other places, leaving them open," he answered.

"Any other little surprises?" I asked.

"Not that I know of."

"Okay, they can't use their guns, right?"

"That's right."

"Alright," he had his crossbow in his hands, a bolt notched into place. "That thing wasn't affected by the stun grenade was it?" I asked.

"Nope," he answered with a mischievous air.

"Good," I said, standing up and walking towards the soldiers, acting as if I hadn't a care in the world.

They had all recovered and stood without their firearms; those had been dropped to the ground and replaced with very sharp and very strong looking swords.

They saw me coming and turned towards me, not surprised in the least. The Warlord had obviously briefed them on who I was, and they were expecting me.

One of them had three purple stripes on his shoulder, differentiating him from the rest. He stepped forward.

"You are far out-numbered; you are without your Sentinel and have no hope of stopping destiny," he said.

"We're just going to have to see about that, aren't we?" I asked, walking forward and drawing my sword, sending a small fraction of the energy within me into the blade, causing the metal to glow.

The commander walked forward to meet me, the rest of them keeping back. I guess he wanted me all to himself, that worked for me.

He got to within about ten feet and his hand flashed forward, sending two small knives straight towards my face. I spun and leaned away, easily dodging the flying metal, giving him his opening, or so he thought.

Thrusting for my heart, he closed the distance between us. The move was perfectly executed, using my distraction to strike, he had obviously used the tactic countless times, allowing him to easily take out his opponents, but not this time.

I moved faster than he anticipated and brought my own sword up, knocking his aside, I spun, lashing out with my blade and when I finished he stood there, his headless body unsure of what to do, until finally, he collapsed, his arms and legs twitching.

I looked around, meeting each soldier's eyes, before I focused on none of them, ready for anything.

"Next," I said.

A crossbow bolt thunked into the forehead of one of the soldiers to my left, who collapsed, instantly dead. The rest of them yelled in anger and defiance, rushing towards me.

I had used some of my pent-up energy on the commander in the hopes of making the rest of them hesitate, hopefully, to give me the slight edge I needed. Now I kept the rest to myself, not wanting to expend my reserves until I absolutely had to. I moved from soldier to soldier, using nothing more than my own skill and ability. The Warlord's men were good, they were disciplined and had the instincts of fighters, but they were fatally inexperienced. They had lived in relative peace and hadn't had the ability to hone their abilities like I had, giving me a far more important advantage, one that allowed me to cut through them like a boat through the water.

I took the first one out when he overextended a sideways slice, exposing his vitals to my sword. I thrust in deep, knowing the damage I did would put him out of the fight. The second one tried to take advantage of the chaos and attempted to stab me in the back. I kicked out with my foot, easily knocking his blade aside and then spun towards him, dipping low, chopping his leg off at the knee. A third soldier dropped dead from another one of Brigand's deadly bolts.

That left five more, three of which came at me at once, the other two, I couldn't see, most likely going after

Brigand. I worried about him, he had deadly accuracy, but I hoped he would be okay.

The soldiers came in fast and coordinated their attacks, obviously learning from their fellow's failures. I had to concentrate fully on their assault, ducking and diving as they each tried to stab, slice and chop me at the same time. The fight was fast, chaotic and brutal.

Wheeling from their first assault, I moved in a circle, always keeping one of them between the other two, cutting off their advantage in numbers. A sword sluiced towards my head and I dipped below the attack, spinning low and sweeping the feet out from my attacker. He went down with a solid thud and as I stepped over him, I kept his sword arm down with my foot and stabbed down, pushing my sword into his head, moving on.

The other two had spread out, not allowing me to play each one off of the other. They came in together, one going high, the other low. I blocked the high attack with my sword, the sounds of metal on metal clanging loud in the air. I tried to kick out and connect with the low attacker's wrist, but I missed, and pain erupted from my leg as he sliced a deep groove in my thigh. I felt warmth as blood flowed from the wound and more pain shot through me as I had to put weight on my leg.

I tried to ignore the hurt, turning, putting the wounded leg behind me, knowing they would try to bring more attacks on my injured side. I changed forms, fighting like a fencer, presenting only one side of my body, the side holding my sword.

I parried their attacks, adapting quickly and soon had both backpedaling as I pressed in. One of them tripped on a small ledge and I spun towards him slicing across my body and at a downward angle as he tried to rise, cutting a deep crimson line across his neck.

He gurgled wetly as he tried to breathe and cry out, grasping his throat and falling aside, his life's blood spilling out onto the rooftop.

That left just one more soldier to deal with.

My sword arm roared in pain as he took advantage of my death stroke to his buddy, taking the opportunity not to save his friend, but instead to land a blow on me.

I stepped back quickly, bringing my sword up in defense. My leg throbbed, and my arm screamed in pain every time I used my shoulder, which was always.

We eyed each other, each of us panting from our exertions, taking a second to get our breaths. Nothing was said, nothing needed to be. The next few seconds would decide our fates, one of us would walk away alive the other wouldn't.

I took a moment to focus, minimizing the pain for later. The discomfort didn't disappear, but it became a dull throb in the background, something that wouldn't distract me.

He narrowed his eyes at me, and I winked at him.

A snarl split his face and he moved first, rushing at me with his sword down low and behind him.

I waited.

He came closer and at the last second planted his foot and used his momentum to add strength to his attack, intent on ending our fight with one powerful blow.

He came at me with an upward sweeping stroke, one that would slice me from groin to neck. A second before his sword landed I moved, twisting sideways -- much like you would be scooting to your seat in a full theater -- and raised my sword, pointing the sharp tip towards his unshielded face, and as his sword swished through open air, mine sunk into his brain through his eye.

We stood like that for a second then I swept my sword back swinging downwards, flinging the blood off of the hard steel, leaving the blade clean.

Turning, I hurried towards Brigand, one soldier lay dead, a bolt lodged in his skull. The other one was nowhere to be found. Brigand was lying up against an herb planter, holding his crossbow tightly. His breathing came in ragged gasps, the front of his body covered in dark red blood.

I reached him and did a quick search for the second soldier.

"There is no reason to look for him, you won't find him," Brigand said through disjointed breaths.

"Why, what happened?" I asked, seeing a large open wound on his chest, steadily pumping his blood out.

"Because I sent his ass over the edge," he stopped, his body convulsed in bloody coughs.

I went to take off my shirt to press the soft fabric against his chest when he reached out with one hand, stopping me.

"It's okay; there is no need to pretend. He got me good before I sent him to his death." Another fit of coughing took him.

"I lived a good life. I have made a true difference," he said when he stopped.

"Thank you for helping me, I don't think I could have taken them all without your help," I said, I had only known Brigand for a short time, but I knew he was a good man, doing what he thought best for his people. A spike of loss shot through me, seeing him like this.

He waved me off, talking in quick gasps. "It was nothing. Listen, you have to help them."

"I am," I answered.

"No, I mean later, when they begin to awaken. They will be confused and lost. Many will leave when they realize the truth, some will become pregnant, they will need help on the land, they will need guidance," he pleaded.

"I don't know if I can help them." The burden of what he asked of me was enormous.

"You can, you must. There is no one else who knows the surface like you, no one they can rely on. You have to…," he paused for a minute, racked with coughs. His face paled and his eyes began to lose focus.

"You…are…their…king," he exhaled the last breath he would ever take.

I reached over and closed his eyes, giving him peace. I then turned to look at the cannon, seeing Julake and the Warlord behind a shiny shield, protecting them. This man died because of them, because of Karakatos's bat shit crazy schemes.

It really pissed me off.

The Warlord looked up from his work, to see the scene before him.

"You see, no matter what you do, no matter how many dies, it will never be enough, you cannot stop destiny, you cannot stop the inevitable," he said, a maniacal gleam in his eye.

I gripped my sword a little tighter, "That's not what your mom said," I said, walking towards him.

The building shook from another tremor as we continued to rise, the sky brightened as we began to reach the surface and into shallow waters where the sun managed to pierce. The Warlord noticed the change too and smiled again, turning back to his cannon.

"Neal, are you still with me?"

Ayup. He answered.

"You know I was thinking, why don't you just shut the rift once we are out of the water, taking out the cannon and the Warlord at once?" I asked.

That isn't a bad idea if it weren't for that shield they have. According to my calculations, their dome may have the ability to not only protect them from the rift's energy but just might allow them to funnel some of the energy for their own uses, basically giving them more than two shots. He explained.

"So, before you close the rift, I have to take out their shield and then get to safety?" I sent.

Ayup. He answered again, sounding like some old fisherman from the upper Northeast.

I don't think I can talk much more, I should concentrate on keeping the rift stable, things have gotten more, difficult, in here. Nothing for you to worry about, but before I go, I should warn you. There are three guests climbing the building, heading straight for you. I would advise caution. He said, then went silent.

Three guests, who could he be talking about? I hurried to the side of the building and looked down, seeing nothing. Maybe he was finally starting to lose his mind?

I felt something on the edge of my awareness, like a shadow flitting in my peripheral vision, there then gone, leaving me with an uneasy feeling, making me grip my sword tighter still.

Something strong grabbed my throat and wrenched me from the ground, my legs dangling in the air. I brought my sword up, intent on chopping the hell out of whatever was slowly cutting off my windpipe when my wrist was likewise encircled, leaving me defenseless.

I hung like that for a few seconds, panic began to grip me, and I thrashed wildly, not knowing where to strike. The sea witch turned me around so that I faced her, her tentacles holding me up and keeping me immobilized.

I saw behind her as another one climbed onto the roof. I heard soft popping sounds as her suckers helped pull her up as she scrambled away from the firepower being unleashed her way. I guess those on the ground had seen them and didn't like them climbing their capital any more than I.

A third sea witch began to gain access to the roof, but whoever was on the ground shooting had figured out how to zero in on their target as the thing let out a loud squeal and rocked from numerous impacts, the ugly creature's body ripped apart as the blasts hit home. The sea witch lost its balance, one side of the monster's head had been obliterated and the denizen of the deep slowly leaned back, then disappeared as she fell, her suckers reluctantly letting go with audible pops.

Three to two, I liked those odds better. My vision began to blur around the edges as the sea witch's tentacle tightened in anger at seeing her sister killed. She yanked me forward, only inches from my face.

"Whyyy do youuu call us heerrre?" her mouth hissed, large black eyes like pools of nothingness, small pockets of the abyss.

"What?" I managed to ground out, her grip made talking difficult.

"Theee power callsss to usss," it said.

I could see her other tentacles slithering around themselves, small charges of electricity arcing from one to the other.

I mentally let out a breath of relief. At first, I thought they may have been recruited by the Warlord. If he had been able to bring together not only vampires, yes they turned on him, but that's what they do, and sea witches he was more influential than I had imagined.

They were here because of the energies released from the rift. Somehow, they felt what was happening and the power drew them here, like a moth to a porch light. I wondered if they would fly into the heat and burn, or if something else would happen. I didn't really want to know the answer.

"What isss thisss that callsss to uss?" it said.

The sea witch was even uglier than I remembered, having gotten a much closer look. Her face was covered in small scales, so small as to look like smooth skin. She could breathe out of the water or else had the ability to hold her breath an amazingly long time. Seeing as how she was talking meant she was able to manipulate the air well enough to create sounds, which led me to the idea that she could breathe air. Scary.

I felt the hairs on my body tingle in response to the electrical charge she produced. I worried as if any movement may trigger a release, like when you walk across your carpet and grab something metal and are met with a small zap.

Her grip held me with relentless strength, both on my neck and my wrist. I wasn't going to manhandle my way out of this. Perhaps I could talk my way out.

"It's not me, it's him," I said, nodding towards the Warlord and Julake. "They are calling to you. Stop them and you stop the energy," my voice came out small and tight from the pressure.

The one holding me turned, looking towards the cannon, the other one did as well. They both turned their heads sideways, like a dog hearing a high-pitched sound and then they made a series of clacking sounds, like dolphins, before the one holding me turned back.

"You lie, theee power comesss from beneath usss." The pressure on my neck increased, my vision began to dwindle again, and I drew ragged breaths through a throat being forced shut.

"Dieeee nowwww," she hissed, her eyes never showed any difference, they sucked in all the light like a vast black hole.

I decided at this point all diplomacy had ceased and a more aggressive approach was in order.

I raised my other hand, the one she hadn't grabbed and placed the Atlantean pistol to the side of her head, the barrel pressed into her green skin, and I pulled the trigger.

Marcus Abshire   LOST SON

The blast was so close that the reverberating shockwave me hit me like a heavy right cross. I closed my eyes, feeling bits of brain and scales splatter my face. I was thrown aside as the sea witch undulated with chaotic spasms, losing the control center for all movement tended to make coordinating that movement a bit more difficult.

I landed hard, knocking the breath out of me, but I rolled anyway, instantly coming to a one kneeled shooter's stance, bringing the pistol up where I had last seen the second sea witch. I knew she would most likely be a little upset at me for murdering her friend, but I wasn't going to let her strangle me.

Sure enough, I saw her coming. She let out an ear-splitting squeal, the sound ripped through my head and made my nerves raw. The noise came from a place of primal need, deep and dark, something heard in the dead of night as creatures of the darkness hunt for food and find what they seek.

My vision was still dark around the edges and all I wanted was to take a huge breath, but I had to steady my aim and shoot before she was upon me. I fired twice, the first one missed, but the second one clipped her shoulder and drove her sideways and into the Warlord's protective shield.

When she impacted the shield, the whole thing lit up like the blaring light of a flash grenade, then flickered on and off for a second.

The sea witch recovered quickly but I managed to pick up my sword, then scramble backward, firing again, missing. I cursed under my breath and began to move, my leg buckled from my injury and I half stumbled, half rolled as the sea witch raked the air with her deadly claws, air I had been occupying a second ago.

I was still on my back, scrambling for purchase, when one of her tentacles whipped out for me, trying to get ahold of my leg. I saw the reaching limb was the same stump I had hacked off earlier. The tentacle was almost fully healed.

I swiped down, hitting the healing stump with my sword and opened a deep gash on the freshly mended limb. The witch spun towards me and leaped, leading with her poisoned claws. I blocked her sharp talons with my sword and brought me legs up only to push off and send her hurtling through the air, to once again connect with the shield.

The shield reacted like earlier, flickering off and on. She came to her tentacles and stood up straight, narrowing her eyes at me.

I managed to get to my feet and faced her, waiting for her next move; we stood like that for a few seconds, two gunfighters in the O.K. Corral at high noon, waiting for the other to draw.

The light increased all around us and I realized we had finally reached the surface and broke free from the waters of the ocean.

The Lost City of Atlantis, a city buried in history, known only as legend and conspiracy, finally, after thousands of years of being a ghost, being a whispered fantasy, was thrust from the bowels of ancient tales and into the reality of the modern world.

I reeled from the sudden stop, as we had reached our destination.

"Yes! A glorious day indeed! Julake prepare for launch!" the Warlord said with pride.

The sea witch never turned her eyes from me, and I never turned mine from her. Light, pure light began to stream in from above as the dome that had protected Atlantis for untold centuries began to part, like a large football stadium, the dome opened and slowly began to separate, allowing sunlight, for the first time in millennia, to touch the city.

The sea witch looked up at the sky and hissed, bringing her arm up to block her eyes from the light. I felt the air pressure change as the cool, crisp breeze above the Atlantic rush into the city, trying to establish equilibrium.

She looked at me, then at the sky and with a reluctant glare turned and started fleeing.

"Not so fast," I said, running after her.

She saw me moving for her and turned to confront me, thinking I was coming to attack, but I had something else in mind.

As I got closer, I feinted like I was going to bring my sword to bear, raising the blade above my head and yelling with everything I had. She brought her long claws up, just as I had hoped.

Five feet from her, I sheathed my sword and dipped my shoulder, connecting with her midsection with a satisfying thud. I hit her with everything I had, making even the most famous middle linebackers in the NFL proud. I lifted her up, hoping to keep her from using her tentacles to stop me and I angled her towards the shield, running straight for the barrier. I felt a stinging pain as she raked my back, but I ignored the slight numbness her poison caused, I only had a few feet left.

I never stopped my charge, using her body as a battering ram. If my theory was right, I would be able to stop the Warlord, if not I was going to have one hell of a headache.

I pushed the sea witch into the shield and was relieved to see my theory proved correct. The sea witches were like an electric eel, they had the ability to produce an electric current they could use when needed. It was this electric current that had disrupted the shield earlier and it was this electric current that allowed both her and I to pass through the barrier and run smack into the cannon, just a few feet from the Warlord and Julake.

Chapter Twenty

Karakatos looked up at us with stunned surprise, anger following quickly behind as the shield snapped back into place.

"How is this possible?" he snarled, reaching for his trident.

With the last of my stored energy, I lifted the sea witch and threw her at the Warlord, while at the same time raising my pistol and aiming the barrel at Julake.

I heard scuffling and saw as the Warlord grabbed the sea witch, wrapped an arm around her neck and with a mighty tug, snap it. "Enough, there is nothing you can do. Your efforts were valiant, but you are too late, the cannon is ready, the sequence has already been started," he said, unceremoniously dropping her dead corpse.

I swung the pistol around leveling the sights at the Warlord's head.

"Shut it down," I ordered.

He smiled at me, a large and knowing smile.

"I cannot, and furthermore, even if I could, I would not. The sequence has begun; the beginning of the age of Atlantis has started. You should be at my side; we will have much work to do when the new dawn awakens," he said, keeping still, showing he was no threat.

I turned my pistol on the cannon and fired. The blast didn't destroy the weapon as I had hoped; in fact, the shot was diverted by the shield's energy field and only seemed to give the cannon more life as it hummed a little stronger.

"You see, it cannot be stopped, destiny is at play here. Even you can see that." I swung my pistol back to Julake who had been inching closer to me.

He scowled at me, his scar making his visage deadly looking.

"Put the pistol down; let's settle this with our swords," he tried to tempt me.

I had to say the offer appealed to me. I looked around, trying to find some answer, some way to shut the shield off when my eyes settled on something that made me smile. I turned back to Julake and leveled that devious smile on him, slowly making my way towards him, keeping the pistol aimed for his chest.

"You guys have everything all figured out, don't you?" They looked at me skeptically as I inched closer.

"I mean your execution of the master plan has been almost flawless really, you only overlooked two things." Karakatos stared at me.

"And what was that?" he asked.

"One, the rift's energies would clean Neal of the virus you infected him with," I said, getting to the back of the cannon, five feet from Julake who had drawn his own sword, hoping I would give him the chance to attack.

"And two," I smiled even bigger, "You forgot to put a shield around your shield generator, a common rookie mistake," I finished and unsheathed my own sword, plunging the blue Atlantean steel downwards.

At the same time, Julake leaped from his position, flying at me with death in his eyes and his sword in his hands.

The Warlord yelled, something I couldn't understand, as I stabbed the odd-looking generator dead center, instantly causing the shield that surrounded the cannon to be disrupted, releasing the energy the generator was producing. A loud concussion rocked the air as the violent destruction of the generator resulted in a forceful explosion, one that knocked me back ten feet and disrupted Julake's attack, sending him away from the cannon and onto the rooftop.

"Idiot!" screamed the Warlord, who had managed to hide behind the cannon and protect himself from the blast.

I raised my pistol to fire at the cannon now that the weapon was unprotected only to have the sidearm knocked out of my hands by a projectile Julake expertly threw at me. My pistol skidded to a halt about ten feet away.

"The shield's down." I sent to Neal.

I had to refocus my thoughts as Julake tried to take my head from my shoulders. I brought up my sword and blocked his attack, kicking out and connecting with his thigh, making him stumble back, allowing me to gain my own footing.

Good, I cannot hold on much longer. Neal answered. *You have twenty seconds before I shut the rift.* He added.

Twenty seconds? That sure wasn't much time. Julake came in again, this time attacking with everything he had. I managed to block his sword, letting him drive me backward, all the while trying to count down from twenty.

Marcus Abshire   LOST SON

Out of the corner of my eye, I saw the cannon begin to glow a bright blue, the light streaming throughout the weapon, gathering at the base and slowly moving towards the barrel, getting ready to fire.

Julake pressed the attack as I ducked, dipped and parried his assault. Making sure he didn't land a hit took everything I had, but I managed to keep his sword from killing me.

Fifteen.

The light had gathered around the cannon's barrel.

Ten.

Julake knocked my blade aside as I was just too tired to keep up with his relentless offense.

Five.

I felt a stabbing pain as he landed a strike on my bicep, I kept moving backward until my feet came to the edge of the roof.

Four.

Julake saw my inability to muster a defense. He knew I was tapped out as my breathing came in desperate gasps. I held my sword up in defense, by sheer willpower alone.

Three.

The light from the cannon reached the tip and the glowing intensified as the cannon was a moment from launching an attack on a heavily populated city that would kill millions.

Two.

Julake's wolfish grin split his face as he lunged forward, his sword aimed straight for my heart.

One.

Marcus Abshire   LOST SON

The blast tore through the rooftop, the bright light blinding me. At the same time, the cannon fired, and a beam of pure energy blew through the roof, the shockwave from the energies released as the rift was shut hit me and I flew through the air, knocked from my feet.

I felt the power of the rift as a small fraction of the energies leaked out. They enveloped me and I reached out with my cramped muscle and tried to gather as much of the overflow as I could while I plummeted to the hard Atlantean street.

I knew I only had a few seconds as I rushed down to meet my death. Channeling the small amount of energy I was able to gather, I focused, creating a long cylinder in front of me. I had no idea if this would work and with the fear of my own imminent death before me, I was able to use the energy, bending the wild current to my will, from sheer desperation.

I pushed the power down until I felt the earth, as the unforgiving ground rushed towards me and focused on making a cushion, like a large spring that absorbed the momentum of my descent, hopefully slowing me down enough so I didn't make a large stain when I landed.

The strain of keeping the energy together beat at me. I felt like my skull was being ripped in half as the sheer force of my fall pressed against the energy I was controlling. The strain was like fighting against a huge rubber band, one already stretched tautly and wanting to be released. I saw the earth rushing towards me, which made my panic increase ten-fold, a panic I used to continue to push against the force of gravity and inertia.

Marcus Abshire   LOST SON

My body screamed in pain as I used every ounce of resolve to stop myself, to slow myself down.

I saw as the ground seemed to rush up at me a little less and less and I closed my eyes, keeping my focus on what I had to do. The pain in my head overwhelmed me as I fought for control, as though a sea witch was pulling my brain apart with her bare hands. I was a second from giving in and just letting the earth do its work, the quick release from this pain seemed welcome when the pressure evaporated, and the pain disappeared. I fell the last three feet to the earth and landed with an undignified thump.

I was on my back, looking up, watching the effects of Neal and my handiwork. A steady stream of pure energy still raced from the roof as Neal channeled the rift's power straight up, keeping the destructive force from killing us all. Light streamed from the windows of the floor Neal was on and the effect looked like spikes of pure gold, shooting out into the sky.

Then with one final explosion, the top third of the capital and my ancestral home exploded in an awesome display of power and destruction. I watched in awe before I realized all that rock had to go somewhere. I turned over, scrambling to my feet in order to get away from the debris that was surely heading down.

Instead of running away from the building I ran towards it, stumbling as my leg refused to support my weight. My whole body hurt, from the myriad of injuries I had sustained, but I kept moving, closing the short distance to the building.

I reached safety just in time as a few tons of rock, marble and building fell from the heavens and crushed anything in its way. I stood there, panting and waiting for the dust to clear. A few pebbles continued to fall, and small pieces of rubble still bounced off the ground, looking for their final resting place.

I just breathed in and out, trying to take a second to gather my wits as a strange sensation flowed over me, seeming to originate from the site of the blast. From somewhere far away I sensed something awakening, responding to the call of the rift. A vision flooded my mind, sweeping me up like a movie that came with feelings and smell-o-vision.

In an ancient tomb, deep under a huge church, I watched as a mummified corpse rose from a long-forgotten grave. Clawed hands grasped out with purpose as the oldest and most powerful vampire on the planet began to drag itself from the dirt. Eyes that thrummed with a silver radiance shone from a face that had lost the vibrancy of life during the time of the Pharaohs. A mummy moved, driven by the smell of blood, blood of the poor hapless souls who tended the church the vampire slumbered under in empty nothingness for millennia, ever searching, ever hungry.

Deep in a forest, high on a mountain a large boulder, the size of a small house, was pushed aside, the earth and rock keeping the passage sealed fell as the heavy boulder was removed. Air that had been trapped in the dark underworld blew out of the black hole as the rock unsealed the ancient passageway. A "thing" stepped out, shielding its eyes from the full moon's glare. The giant was almost twenty feet tall and had shoulders spanning a six-foot space. The great beast's face was hidden in shadow, but under deep brows, two eyes glowed a dark red as the powerful behemoth reached out and ripped a tree from the ground by the roots and stomped off into the forest.

In a landscape filled with ice and wind, deep in the bowels of an ancient glacier, a large figure stirred, finally moving, after having been curled in on itself for centuries. The white mound of fur stirred, and a werewolf larger and stronger than any I had ever seen rose from deep hibernation, shaking off the last vestiges of slumber. The monster stood on two feet and rose to its full height, turning its large canine-like snout towards the sky, towards a moon that shone down in full display. The werewolf's yellow eyes blazed as a loud howl split the night air, causing every dog on the face of the planet to take note, and every member of every pack to shiver in fear.

The mud stirred, in a long-forgotten swamp, filled with the nastiest animals, as a creature rose from the muck. The small compact body was only three feet tall but corded with muscle and wiry hair. Orange, beady eyes cut the dark night as the troll moved with a single-minded purpose, heading deeper into the unknown depths of the swamp.

Far under the ocean, where the light never reaches one more creature woke. The dweller of the deep abyss slithered from under a recess it had hidden in for countless years; six long tentacles pulled the vile thing forth into the dark black of the bare ocean floor. The risen fiend looked familiar as pitch-black eyes searched the surrounding area, for what I didn't know. This was the same creature I fought when I entered the city, the same creature I had battled on the rooftop, only this one was different, a broad chest and powerful arms and shoulders differentiated this one from his brethren, all of whom were female, yet this one was male.

They all seemed to turn and look at me, all at once, the effect caused nauseating discord to race through me as their ancient consciousness's made contact with mine, then as fast as it happened the connection ended and my mind cleared, coming back to the here and now.

I shook my head, trying to clear the last vestiges of the vision, what I saw had been as real as if I had stood there and witnessed their returns first hand, but the images already began to fade, like the whispers of a bad dream. Soon the revelation was nothing more than an uneasy feeling in my gut.

I came back fully to my situation, looking around. I felt a pain in my chest and looked down to see if I had been hit with something only to see my body in good shape. I wasn't sure what was wrong when my brain finally caught up to my heart and I knew why I was in pain.

Neal was gone.

I knew this; I couldn't feel him, not in my thoughts, not anywhere.

He was gone and I had no idea what I was going to do without him.

I tried to swallow my sorrow, knowing I still had Kim and Arendiol to care for. I looked around and saw the city had stopped fighting. The explosion had shocked everyone, and soldiers and fighters alike stood around, looking up at the blue sky and the strange fiery orb in that sky with wonder and awe.

I got my bearings and started walking, "Don't stare directly at it," I said to those I passed, they looked with their mouths hanging open, a few seagulls circled the air, looking at us with curiosity as well.

Chapter Twenty-One

I saw my pistol, lying amidst the rubble. The weapon smoked and looked a little dented and scratched, but other than a few nicks and bruises seemed fine. I went over and put the pistol in its holster.

There were groups of people everywhere, most were average citizens, wandering around, looking at the world from eyes full of wonder. The current break from organized structure left them in a daze, most took the new situation well.

Others were obviously lost, some mumbling to themselves as they moved, while a few here and there were more volatile, reacting with violence and anger. I saw a man attack a small group of soldiers, who subdued him and restrained him with some wire. They all treated him with respect, knowing why he was acting that way.

I made my way through the chaos, going towards the diner where I had met Brigand. As I walked, people saw me and moved aside. I don't know if they were standoffish because they recognized me or if their apprehension was because of something they saw in my face, but either way, they left me alone.

I entered the diner only to have five rifle barrels jammed in my face.

"Easy, easy," I said, holding up my hands.

"Stand down, he's okay," I heard a voice say.

I rose onto my tiptoes and was able to see a head full of scraggly hair that stood up everywhere.

"Hey, Jessif. What's up?" I asked, nonchalantly.

The men parted and I saw him standing behind the same table Brigand had earlier.

"Where's Brigand?" he asked, his eyes held a deep weariness in them, he looked like he was about to crack.

"He was up there," I said, pointing back to the capital.

He stared at me for a second; the implications of what I told him began to sink in. I saw his shoulders slump as the weight of the situation fell heavily on him.

Another fighter, one who looked more seasoned and almost cut from a mold made to build warriors stepped forward.

"It is as I have said. He is gone, we must move forward. The chaos must be brought under control, we are now exposed, and decisions need to be made," I saw a few others surrounding him, nodding in agreement.

Jessif sighed deeply; he also had a small group of supporters.

"Yes, I agree, but we cannot do it with force, we have to be compassionate." They were having an internal dispute for the future of Atlantis.

"Compassion only goes so far. We also have to deal with the remaining soldiers. They will not be dissuaded with nice words," he argued.

I saw Jessif sigh deeply, rubbing his nose.

"I hate to interrupt, but I need to speak with Jessif for a second," I said, as all eyes turned on me.

"Yes, of course. Please give me a moment," he said to the warrior who eyed me sharply then nodded once.

"What is it? I'm busy," he said.

"I can see that. I need to know where Kim and Arendiol are. Brigand said they would be kept safe. I have to see them," I said.

Jessif nodded. "They are about a block that way, with the rest of our families," he said, pointing behind him.

"Thanks," I said, turning to leave.

"Wait, where are you going, you are needed here," he said, grabbing my arm.

I slowly pulled away, looking at him sharply.

"You have this under control, you know more about what's best for your people than I do. I have a promise to keep. I'm going home and I'm taking Kim and Arendiol with me," I said.

"That cannot be allowed. No one is permitted to leave. Not until we can access our situation," Warrior said.

I turned to him, facing him squarely. "I'm leaving. No one will stop me. Do you understand?" I said to him.

"You will not leave," he said, motioning to his men, who began to take a step towards me.

"Stop!" Jessif's voice had lost all uncertainty.

"What are you doing? That is the same mentality that led us here. That is how the Warlord operated. That is not our way. Remember it was you who came to me, looking for a different course," he said, glaring at the warrior.

The large soldier looked at me for a few more seconds then turned his gaze on Jessif, seeing something there. He then visibly relaxed.

"Fine, let him go. We don't need him anyway," he said. His men too backed off.

I nodded my thanks to Jessif and then left, leaving him and his friends to decide the course of Atlantis.

"Jack!" Kim said as she saw me walking towards them.

She was outside with Arendiol and a large group of others, those who were old or injured.

She ran up to me and I knelt, hugging her tightly. As she reached me, something about the way she smelled staggered me.

Smell is a primitive sense, one that can convey tons of information and something that has been ignored for ages, especially since mankind moved into cities and no longer feared the large predators that hunted him. In the brain, smell is linked to memory so even a whiff of a familiar odor can bring back memories of childhood.

I held her at arm's length, studying her face, looking at the structure of her brows and nose, the way her mouth quirked up on one side and I realized this is what my mom would have looked like when she was a kid. Not my biological mom, the queen, but the one who raised me, the one who loved me and who I trusted.

It was then I realized why I loved Kim so much, why I had grown so fond of her so quickly, why she tugged at my heart. She was my mother, a clone who was made to worm her way into my soul.

I watched her smile, "What is it?" she asked.

I realized all that didn't matter.

"Nothing, let's get out of here," I said.

"About time," she answered.

A small trek through the city later and we finally reached the tunnel Neal and I had plunged through, fighting sea witches to reach Atlantis. I wasn't sure if the tunnels would still be intact after everything but knew if they were, we would be able to get to where we were going, now that everything was above water.

In an amazing act of stubbornness, the tunnel remained intact and I led Kim and Arendiol through, exiting on the newly formed beach that surrounded the city.

I had to squint for a few minutes while my eyes adjusted, the clear breeze blew my hair back. I hadn't realized how stale the air in the enclosed city had become, but now that I was outside the difference was obvious.

Even though we were on a large island, on which sat Atlantis, didn't mean we wanted to stay there. Since getting back to the mainland would require a trip of hundreds of miles, we needed a way to get home without swimming.

I wasn't sure how much of the surrounding seafloor had been lifted with the city but knew our transportation would be near. I saw the submarine sitting about fifty feet from the beach, the vessel sat in water that covered half of its surface, the waves lapped the hull rhythmically.

The water all around churned with mud as the violent and enormous feat of creating an island this size in such a small amount of time had stirred up the ocean for miles around. Thousands of birds circled overhead, diving into the water to pick off the myriad number of organisms that had been disturbed by Atlantis's ascension.

I held Kim's hand and just stood looking out over the water, taking a deep breath of the air, reveling in its cool purity, basking in the warmth of the sun.

My tranquility was destroyed by a voice, a voice that screamed one name, "RAAAIIPPHHHAAAIIIIIMMM!"

I leaned down to Kim, "I want you and Arendiol to get in the sub, if anything happens to me, I want you to take the sub and get to the mainland. Do you understand?" I asked, speaking with heavy intent, looking her right in the eye.

She looked at me and then over my shoulder. Arendiol was also looking that way, her face had gone pale and she hugged herself. I made eye contact with her, projecting the seriousness of my words.

She came over and took Kim's hand. Before they left Kim turned to me saying, "One more time."

I took a deep breath and stood up, turning around.

Warlord Karakatos had probably seen better days.

His armor had numerous cracks across his chest and on one leg. He stood, favoring the cracked one. His eyes were filled with hatred and his face was covered in a myriad of cuts and bruises. He stood with his trident fully extended, using the long shaft as a crutch. Dust and dirt covered his entire body, making him look like he had just walked out of an apocalyptic nightmare. He looked just like I felt.

On either side of him stood ten soldiers, twenty in all. Each one of them held a very powerful looking firearm, obviously of Atlantean design. They all stood at rapt attention; their weapons pointed at me.

"YOU!" He took a step forward, ignoring his leg and holding his trident with both hands.

"You will pay for what you've done. You have made quite a mess, but all is not lost. First, in order to establish order, the agent of chaos must be destroyed," he said, snarling the words.

"I take it that the agent of chaos is me?" I asked, focusing my mind and breathing, taking all my pain and fatigue and putting it in a box.

"I will kill you, and then I will bring your body back with me, to display it on the rubble of the capital. That way everyone will know what happens when they defy my will. All will see, all will understand," he recited, without a hint of doubt.

"Do you ever just shut up?" I asked.

"You are right," he said, focusing solely on me. "The time for talk is over."

He moved with the same confident quickness I had witnessed earlier. His leg seemed to not be as badly hurt as I had assumed, or maybe he just hid his discomfort, like I did.

His trident raced for my head and I blocked his attack, careful not to get my sword caught in the weapon's prongs. I thought about bringing my pistol out, but I wasn't sure if it had been damaged and feared the gun might blow up in my face when I pulled the trigger.

He swept the butt of his trident upwards, faster than I could counter. I spun and brought my elbow up, letting the brunt of his attack hit my forearm, instead of my chin. Pain swept through my arm and my shoulder tingled numbly from the impact, but I kept moving, swinging low, forcing him to move onto the defense.

He had lost a step somewhere, perhaps from his injuries, or from the psychological impact of me destroying his immediate plans of world war. Whatever the cause, he had lost some of his fire, his arrogance and speed. I was used to fighting through pain and injury, and his loss only fueled me.

I went after his injured side and watched him move, seeing how he defended against my attacks and how he shifted to offense when he could. Our fight was fast and nasty, but neither one of us gave an inch. After we had each landed a few minor, but painful hits we stepped back, taking a breather.

I watched him as he took a moment to get his wind back and for the first time, I examined his armor. The sturdy covering had blunted my sword more than a few times allowing him to shrug off an otherwise debilitating strike. I noticed what he wore looked like normal armor, with hard to see seams at the joints, places I assumed would be weak, places I could attack.

I almost slapped myself for being so dumb. This design flaw was something I should have noticed earlier, something I should have seen, no matter. I saw it now.

He leveled his trident at me, smiling mischievously, then without warning he did something on the shaft and the middle fork shot at me, giving me no time to react. The metal spike sunk into my shoulder, causing pain to race through me.

I yelled out as a new wave of sharp fire burned. I put my shoulder behind me as the Warlord came in with confidence and the look of someone who knows how everything's going to end splashed across his face.

He thrust the trident at me again, but this time instead of attacking his body, I went after the chinks in his armor, bringing my blade across the inside of his elbow and felt as my sword cut through skin and muscle.

This time it was his turn to scream out in pain and he spun the trident, keeping me from pressing. He switched hands as blood dripped from his elbow and from mine. We both stood there for a second, our blood hitting the ground, the only sounds that could be heard.

His face was now one of pain and uncertainty, he looked to his left and right, knowing his honor and reputation depended on the outcome of this fight.

He snarled and raced back at me, bringing everything he had, thrusting, stabbing, punching and kicking, forcing me back. I managed to hold him off and when he spun, trying to kick my head I dropped and stabbed his knee, sinking four inches of my blade into the delicate joint.

He dropped to one knee and I brought my sword overhead, swinging the blade down again, holding the handle with both hands as he held his trident up, in a desperate bid to block me. My sword slammed into his trident and the power of my swing shattered his weapon, sending small pieces of metal everywhere.

He cringed from my sheer aggression and began to scramble away, holding his hand up in surrender.

"Wait! Wait!" he said. His voice stopped my killing stroke.

"There is one more thing you have forgotten," he said.

"Please enlighten me," I said, knowing he was beaten.

"My men know what it takes to bring about order. FIRE!" he said, as all twenty soldiers raised their weapons, aiming for me.

From behind me, I heard what reminded me of Atlantean rifle blasts, only much louder and the ten men on the right flew as Arendiol, piloting the submarine, fired the vessel's assault cannon at them, providing me the protection I needed.

The scene erupted into chaos as everyone scrambled for protection from the sub's superior firepower. I raced towards the Warlord, who was limping away, his leg and arm streaming blood.

"Hey, asshole!" I yelled, stopping him.

"You forgot one thing," he looked at me like I was crazy.

"Don't fuck with my family," I answered, bringing my sword across in a clean stroke, separating his head from his shoulders.

I didn't wait to see how his men reacted as I spun towards the water and ran. Hoping one of them didn't shoot me in the back. As I ran, I reached up and yanked the metal spike from my shoulder, screaming in pain. I tossed it away and barreled forward. I managed to get all the way to the water's edge when a sharp pain erupted in my calf and I dove underwater, trying to hide from the soldiers firing at me. I swam in a few feet of water as Arendiol continued to pound the shore with the sub's weapons. My leg wasn't responding, and I feared what kind of damage had been done to it, but I kept going, quickly covering the distance to the back of the sub.

The rear door opened, and I hurried inside as it closed behind me. I slumped to the floor as all the pain and hurt of the last few days settled over me. My exhaustion finally took over and my vision dwindled as I let the pain, fear, and fatigue in.

"Jack, oh my God, your leg," I heard Kim say as she came near.

"It's fine," I said, before once again, passing out.

I awoke to pain, everywhere. I was lying on the floor of the sub; Kim lay next to me, her head resting on my shoulder. Her snoring filled the space with its soft noise and her chest moved up and down in a steady rhythm. The darkness inside the sub provided quiet tranquility. I tried not to wake her as I sat up, my shoulder screamed as I moved, but I managed to get up.

I looked down at my leg and saw my skinsuit was sealed, which was a good thing.

"You shouldn't try and move," Arendiol said from the pilot's console.

"You could reopen your wounds," she spoke softly, filling her words with care.

"How bad is it?" I asked, keeping my voice down.

"It looked worse than it was. A lot of bleeding, some muscle damage, nothing a little rest can't fix." I saw her staring at me, or at Kim and me and something in her eyes became soft.

"Thank you, for you know, saving us," she said, her eyes met mine and I felt the temperature rise about ten degrees.

I coughed and turned away. "Yeah, well, I wasn't doing anything anyway."

She smiled again, this time our eye contact lasted for a few long moments. Kim stirred and I went still, hoping not to wake her.

"So, where are we?" I asked.

"We're about ten miles off the coast of Texas. I wasn't sure about approaching, there seems to be a large military presence amassing offshore," she answered, looking at the sub's screen.

"Well, I guess that was inevitable," I knew it wouldn't take long for the world's nations to be interested in a new island surfacing, complete with a whole city and population.

"I wouldn't worry about it; Neal said this craft is undetectable by modern technology. We should be able to approach a river and travel upstream for a while," I said, laying back down, letting sleep take me.

My mind kept trying to wrap around the idea of Neal being a "said" and not a "says." I already felt an empty hole inside, the space Neal used to fill.

####

"Hey, put that down, you aren't ready to be carrying things that heavy yet," Kim said, hurrying over to take the box I was trying to unload from the van we had rented.

"Okay, okay," I said, feeling helpless.

Reaching over I grabbed my cane, the assistive device helped keep the weight off my leg while my wounds healed. The process was taking a little longer than usual, but Arendiol thought this might be because of the trauma my body had sustained. Even with my Atlantean healing, it still took time to regrow a portion of my calf.

I looked around my new place; the cool humid air coming in through the open windows brought a refreshing comfort. I could smell the ocean, which was only a few blocks away, living in Miami offered many things Oklahoma City did not, namely the ocean.

The sound of the nightly news came across the room, the anchor still talking about the most amazing story of the century. He was analyzing the military's latest reports about the strange city that just appeared off the coast a month ago. A city some were speculating to be the Lost City of Atlantis; other experts were claiming the appearance of a city on the gulf coast was the first wave of an alien invasion. Still, others said they were Russians, or even terrorists, plotting an attack.

Media helicopters were kept out of the airspace due to national security, so the reports about the island came only from the "official" government channels, and those few brave souls who flew planes or boats across the military's lockdown.

I went to shut off the television when I heard a knock at the door.

Arendiol was out getting some things for dinner and Kim was busy in her room, decorating and playing with her new puppy. I couldn't have separated them if I tried.

"I'll get it," I said out loud, to no one in particular.

I used my cane and hobbled over to the door, reaching over and checking the familiar weight of my pistol in the sheath under my arm, the cloaking pin keeping the weapon hidden from sight. I never went anywhere without either my pistol or my sword. Kim said I was too paranoid, but I called it insurance. I knew what Neal would say, he'd say I was being practical.

I opened the door and was greeted by a man in dirty clothes. My first instinct was that he was a panhandler, tired of asking for money on the street and was now going door to door. He had his head down, his dark hair hung over his face, his shoulders were slumped in defeat, but his frame was obviously robust, he presented an odd combination of strength and surrender.

"I hear you can find lost things," he spoke in a low voice, something about the way he talked tugged at me.

"I have found items people needed, but these days I'm mostly hired to find people, people that are missing," I answered. "Although I just opened shop here, how did you hear about me?"

"Are you good at it?" he asked, ignoring my question.

"Yeah, I'm pretty good," I answered. Something about him seemed familiar.

He stood up and looked at me, his eyes held a deep intelligence I immediately recognized. However, his face was covered in a month of unkempt beard and his hair was in dire need of a cut, yet it still held the rich black color I had grown used to.

"What about souls, have you ever been hired to find those?" The look in his eyes broke my heart.

He was different than the last time I had seen him, then he was still Neal, still a mix of machine and magic. Now he moved with an uncertainty that was unlike him. His face was an open book, showing fear, hope, and pain all at once. I knew without him telling me why he was in such dire need.

Neal had always been a machine at heart, he operated under strict programming and had an intelligence that was unnerving, but his potential for destruction had always been kept in check by his parameters, parameters that focused his power into a single drive, to help me.

Now I saw something else, Neal was alive. I don't know if he was human or Atlantean. He no longer moved with the easy fluidity of a well-oiled machine. He now moved as though he was just learning to walk, unsure of his footing or his direction. Emotions flooded through him, making their presence known as his face became a movie screen on which his innermost feelings played out.

He was lost, thrust into a world he was unprepared to deal with. He was alive, had feelings and knew fear, knew joy and excitement and he still had all his intelligence and most likely strength. I didn't know how much of his skills he had retained, but even if he had a fraction of what he used to have it would be scary to wield, especially with all the newfound issues being alive came with.

"I've never been asked to find someone's soul, but I have also never said no to a client," I opened my door wide, "Why don't you come in, get settled and we can talk?"

He looked in, optimistic hope sweeping through him. Kim came in and carried her puppy, a black lab, in her arms, the energetic puppy wiggled and wormed all over the place, trying to get free, wanting to run and pee and chew everything in sight.

"Hi. I'm Kim. Is he going to be staying with the others?" she asked, trying with everything she had to not lose her battle with her puppy, and failing mightily.

"Hi Kim, my name's Neal, and I don't know what I'll be doing," he said with trepidation.

She turned her head to the side, eyeballing him.

"I knew a Neal once, but he was shorter than you and hairier." The puppy finally won and escaped her grasp, only to go running down the hall and towards the back door, hoping for freedom.

"Hey, get back here!" Kim squealed and ran after him.

Neal watched her, a tear gathering in his eye.

"C'mon, let me show you your room, then we can sit down and eat, we have a lot to talk about," I said, turning, waiting for him to follow.

He nodded his head in agreement, stepping inside.

"Yes, we do," he said.

Chapter Twenty-Two

"It's been two weeks, how's he doing?" Arendiol asked, handing me a cold lemonade.

"It's hard to tell. When we are born we come into the world ignorant and innocent, learning how to deal with our humanity a little at a time, Neal was thrust into being human fully formed, with no way to handle all the feelings and uncertainty being human came with," I watched him as he and Kim ran in the lush grass of the small park near our home, the black lab hopping at their heels.

"But I think he'll be alright; I mean it *is* Neal after all."

He turned towards us as if he could hear us talking about him. He bowed his head slightly. His hair cut short and his beard was kept in a neat and trimmed fashion. Everywhere we went, women turned and stared at him.

"I hope so, there's so much at stake now," she said, watching them.

"I know," I answered.

"How many is it now? Ten?"

"That have come to us for help? Yeah, ten. I know there are more out there, afraid to come forward, afraid of me and of the humans," I said, thinking about the refugees that had come ashore since the Rise.

We had done what we could, buying the space above us and using the room to house Atlanteans that had come to us, looking for help, the ones that fled, leaving the cramped city for the freedom of the mainland. There were six women and four men, two of the women already showing signs of being pregnant. The Atlanteans had wasted no time in bringing about the next generation. I wasn't sure how I felt about that, but I knew I would help them. I felt like I had an obligation to, my way of keeping a promise to an old man, I suppose.

Neal came walking over, sitting on my other side.

"Arie, come play!" Kim pleaded.

Arendiol laughed, kissing me on the head, before getting up and going to join in the fun.

"Were you guys talking about me?" Neal asked.

"Yes," I said. I wasn't going to lie to him, ever.

"And?"

"And you are a pain in the ass, you eat more than Kim, your room is a mess and you still aren't paying me any rent," I said, looking at him sideways. "But you are good with the kid and I think have earned the right to not contribute, for now anyway."

I wasn't going to stop giving him hell, I mean c'mon.

"Actually, I was thinking about that last part, contributing I mean. I want to help you, I think I'm ready to get out there and start to make a difference again. I know we worked pretty well together before," he looked at himself, indicating his current form. "I think we can do so again if you are up for it?"

I don't think I'd ever get used to Neal having a sense of humor.

I thought about his proposal for a minute, wanting to be sure before I answered. Neal had come a long way in a short time. He seemed to be handling his new situation with Neal-like aplomb and had even been helping at the "refugee camp," even though I joked about him not contributing. I think it's important to have a purpose, I think Neal was desperately searching for his now, especially since he had a choice.

"Okay, I actually have a client coming at five tonight, we can work the case together, maybe pull your weight around here," I teased.

"Someone's got to do the heavy lifting, your lazy ass sure isn't," he answered.

I smiled, I liked the new Neal.

After a few moments, I said, "There's something I have been meaning to talk to you about, something that happened when you shut the rift."

I told him about the vision I had, about the creatures all awakening from some long sleep. I finished with the sea witch or seaman, or whatever, sea warlock maybe?

He went silent for a little while thinking. I let him contemplate my words.

"I think you know what the vision means; I just think you want to hear someone else say what you've been thinking," he said, still able to seemingly see my thoughts.

I smiled, "Am I that obvious?"

"You are to me," he answered.

"Okay, I think it was the Firsts, those who were first transformed by the energies released during the Fall, the most ancient and powerful troll, sea witch, giant, werewolf and vampire. When the sea witches came to the rooftop they were drawn there, drawn by the rift. I think the same energy woke the Firsts, who are now walking the earth somewhere, doing something, something most likely very bad," I finished.

"I think you are right. Now there is only one question that needs to be asked," he said, still counseling, still guiding.

I turned to him and smiled, knowing he was right, but needing him to help me face what was to come, help me realize what needed to be done.

"What am I going to do about it?" I said.

"What indeed," he answered.

End.

Continue reading for an exciting excerpt from HARD SKIP, the first novel in The Demon Hunter Series!

CHAPTER ONE

"C'mon James, you owe me one," Spencer said.

"How long are you going to hold that over me?" I argued. "It was *one* time. You saved my ass *one* time."

"Yeah, but I *did* save your ass."

Spencer would never be mistaken for tall, dark, and handsome. His bald head gleamed in the fluorescent light, but his smile was generous, and he had a good heart. It was hard to find, but it was there.

I turned away from him and walked over to the window. I pulled the string, drawing the blinds up, letting the early morning sun filter in to light up my cramped office.

"Listen, the skip's an easy one. I need her brought in fast though. It's a simple job, in and out, easy cash." He tried to keep his voice calm, but I could detect the underlying current of anxiety running through it.

I turned to him and just stared, not saying anything, letting him squirm.

"How many times, how many times have I heard that?"

"Just take a look for yourself, before you make up your mind."

He tossed a file onto my desk. On the cover was a black and white mug shot of a young woman, in her twenties maybe. Her face was full of pain and anguish. She looked like she hadn't eaten in a while, and her eyes had dark circles under them. Black hair hung limply, and she stared ahead in a drug-induced haze, but beyond all that, there was something about her that bled through. Deep within her dead gaze was strength, a thread of something better.

"You know I don't do low-level skips," I said as I flipped through the file.

Twenty-two years old with a few run-ins with the police, but nothing serious. A couple of previously known addresses and contact numbers, and then an arrest for possession. Most likely would have resulted in probation for a first-time offense. Skipping on bail, and failing to appear at her court date, just bumped it up a bit.

"I know, I know, but her bail was huge for a small offense. C'mon, man. I've got the insurance company breathing down my neck. I can't afford to not bring her in. Like I said, she's a young kid, probably ran home to her parents. You should be able to bring her in by dinner," Spencer tried.

"Unless you're getting soft. You're not getting soft on me, are you?"

I poured some water on my struggling herb garden by the window. It wasn't much, just a few things planted in a large planter. I never managed to keep any alive long enough to use, but I was determined to fix that.

"It's not her you need to worry about," I said, looking up at him. "It's her boyfriends or pimp. A girl like her is never alone."

"A big tough guy like you can handle some stoned-out kids."

I was still unconvinced.

"How about this; you get this one for me and I wipe our slate clean?" he offered.

I thought about it for a few seconds. I really didn't owe him that much, but I couldn't tell *him* that. He didn't know I wasn't just a normal bounty hunter. That I also picked up demons that happened to escape into our world as well. He had no idea that the guy he thought he had saved me from was as capable of hurting me as a kitten.

But if doing this made him think we were even then it might just be worth it.

"Clean? No more bringing it up for favors, or throwing it in my face?"

He shook his head, wiping his hands together.

"Yeah, yeah. Do this and we're good, even-steven."

I narrowed my eyes at him, making him wait a few seconds for my answer. "Alright, I'll do it. Now get out of here, I've got things to do."

"Woohoo! Thanks, James! And don't worry, this will be a piece of cake. By the way, you never asked how much her bail was."

I looked down, scanned her file, and saw the amount.

I turned my head back up at Spencer in shock.

"Damn right, buddy, damn right. Bring her back and we can all go on a nice vacation," he said, turning to leave my office.

I stared at the number again, knowing I had just agreed to do something I was going to regret. There had to be a very good reason a girl with no priors and one arrest had bail set at ten million dollars. A hard knot began to form in the pit of my stomach.

"Why is her bail so big?" I asked.

Spencer shook his head. "I'm not really sure, but I *do* know the insurance adjuster who put up the money for her bail put a big ole fat bonus to get her

brought in. They're freaking out about it."

Why do I allow myself to get into these situations?

I sighed deeply, knowing the sooner I started the better. Hopefully, my instincts were wrong, and this wouldn't turn out to be as bad as I thought.

Yeah, right.

A few hours later I had a place to start.

Rainah had a surprisingly small footprint on the world. She had no credit cards to track, no record of employment or phone number. All she had was one semester in the Phoenix Community College and an email account attributed to the college. Nothing in the emails but school-related stuff, campus police reports, and announcements for college activities, stuff like that.

She did have an account on a popular social media site that showed she was friends with three people, which for a person under fifty was almost unheard of. She was a member of a few groups; most were closed and dealt with matters of the occult and religious-based topics.

In a group called "Cthulhu, fact or fiction?" one of her three friends, Jasmine, posted about how she was worried about Rain and hoped when they got together tonight at Hell Below that she would be able to help her.

A quick Internet search showed Hell Below was a club catering to the Goth/punk crowd, heavy on noise and lights, and light on social interaction. Devil Spit was headlining tonight; sounded great.

My stomach grumbled, so I jotted down the club's address and then got up. I headed towards the door, intending on grabbing a bite to eat when I smelled brimstone a second before the demon opened my front door and walked across the threshold.

For a moment I saw her in her true form. Her glamour was thrown aside as she passed through the doorway's threshold, a threshold built up over years of living here. Places can hold power, power imbued to them by people that either visited or lived there. This creates a barrier around the place that makes it hard for demons to enter without being invited, giving a person a sanctuary from the evil in the world, at least the supernatural kind of evil. It does nothing against normal human evil.

She had to tuck her wings in tight to her body to pass through the doorway. They were membranous things stretched tight over a bat-like frame. Her red skin covered a lithe, yet powerful body, and shone with a metallic hue. Her dark black pits for eyes, not a bit of iris showing, devoured everything with a glance. Her sharp nose sat above a large mouth, full of murderous-looking teeth. She had to bend low to enter and her muscular frame moved with a fluidity of stealth. Her strong legs hinged backward and ended in cloven hooves and her tail swished back and forth.

There in a second, then gone. A woman took the demon's place.

"Leaving so soon?" she asked, her voice sensuous in its tenor, seductive in its quality.

The demon's glamour was of a beautiful woman, standing just an inch taller than me. She had blond hair that fell in waves just below her shoulders, skin that glowed with a healthy tan, and a body built like an athlete that exuded pure sexual desire. She wore a light blue sundress that flowed as she moved, swaying back and forth in time with her hips, drawing the eyes toward her perfectly sized breasts. Her entire outfit was designed to tempt, while at the same time presenting a sense of wholesomeness that was utterly confusing and enticing.

"What do you want?" I asked, keeping still. She wasn't here to attack, at least not physically. If she had been, it would have been much harder for her to pass through my door. My barrier would have pushed back at her, allowing me to prepare.

Marcus Abshire — LOST SON

"My, my, such hostility. Tsk, tsk, that is no way to treat a guest," she teased. She took a few more steps into my office.

She smelled of honey and lemons, sunshine and desire, but under the glamour, there was still the sharp acidic hint of brimstone, something only I could smell. She would have enraptured anyone else, her demonic aura hidden behind a façade.

"I don't have time to banter back and forth. I assume you are here for a reason Dalsheen. Your kind doesn't do social calls," I said, keeping my guard up.

Demons usually come in two different categories; those that are summoned and those that are inhabitants. A person who is skilled enough, strong enough, and knowledgeable enough can summon a demon. When a demon *is* summoned, they are usually called to accomplish a specific task, one of an undoubtedly nefarious nature. If their summoner is strong enough to control the demon, they will do what they were brought from Hell to do. If not, they turn on their summoner, destroying them while trying to gain a foothold in our realm. Most of the time they fail and are sucked back to Hell, leaving one hell of a mess behind.

Inhabitants are demons allowed to possess a person by an act of free will. If a human is dumb enough, or desperate enough, to allow such a thing then a demon can latch onto their soul, giving them immortality, but with tons of baggage. Depending on the strength of the demon, the human vessel is altered, forever living with the demon's curse, which can manifest in many ways. Vampires, werewolves, and ghouls are the most common demonic/human offshoots, but there are many others.

Some are far more dangerous; some are less so.

Dalsheen was unique, neither summoned nor an inhabitant. Most loose demons created tons of carnage before they were sent back, having been freed from their hellish prisons. Inhabitants lived much more civilized lives, at least civilized according to Hell's standards. I think Dalsheen wanted to keep loose demons from doing too much damage, so they didn't screw up her existence.

It was a theory, anyway. Her true motives were her own. I had worked with her a few other times, each time eliminating a very dangerous demon, something I was happy to do.

"Now what have I ever done to garner such scorn, such abject distrust?" she purred, as she took one step closer, her hips swaying slightly, allowing her ample bosom to accommodate the movement.

She walked over towards the window, looking at my herbs. The angelic power residing within me screamed at me to destroy this thing, to wipe the demon from existence and I wanted to, I really did, but I didn't like others telling me what to do, even angels.

"It's not what you've done, it's who you are. I might allow a rattlesnake to live, doesn't mean I'm gonna let one sit next to me while I watch TV," I said.

She turned from my 'garden' and smiled up at me, trying her best to hypnotize. "Are you saying you trust me? Not even you would be so foolish."

"Hardly," I answered, trying not to stare at her shapely figure.

Yes, she was a demon from Hell, smelled of brimstone and fire, but with a body like hers, most men would gladly give their soul to spend a night in her bed. I was a demon bounty hunter, able to track and kill the most dangerous beings, but it had been a while since I had anyone sleep beside me, and the effects of that were painfully obvious.

Her smile deepened, knowing the effect she was having on my libido. "We have gotten along fine in the past. There is no reason we can't come together again, for our mutual benefit, of course." The sexual desire in her voice was maddening.

I rubbed the bridge of my nose, using the opportunity to re-establish my resolve. I rubbed for a while.

"Let's get one thing straight. I don't like you. I will *never* like you. We have worked in the past to eradicate some very nasty demons, and that was only because you do not harm humans. You only feed off of demons. But make no mistake, the second you do, I will know. Then I will send you back to Hell where you belong." I glared at her, giving away nothing.

"Such anger, such fury!" she said in mock surprise. "And to think I was going to offer you a job."

I narrowed my eyes at her. "I will never work for you. Never," I said.

"No, not for me. I wish to hire you for a third party, someone who does not want to be known at this time," she walked over and sat down at my desk, reaching over to pick up Rainah's file. I took the manila folder before she could and kept it from her.

She just smiled at me.

I was a hair's breadth from sending her packing. I didn't have time to mess with her. Her jobs always led to a demon worthy of my wrath, but they were also always as dangerous as hell. I had already promised I would find Rainah. I wouldn't have time for another case, especially one requiring my full attention.

"What are you talking about?" I asked, knowing I would regret my words. But if working with Dalsheen could lead to sending an escaped denizen of Hell back home before it could kill innocent people, then the job might just be worth the extra workload.

Again, she smiled at me, enjoying setting me up. One day I would kill her, and wipe that smile from her face, but not today.

"I am prepared to offer you two million dollars to find a, what do you call them, skipper, who has escaped my client's possession," she proposed, her face was one of complete seriousness.

Two million dollars? That was big money. Wow, must be one badass demon.

"You know I do not take money to kill demons. I do it for the sheer fun of it," I said, also completely serious.

"I tried to explain this, but my client insisted on the offer. He believes every human has his price. I, however, believe they all just need their own special lure, the one thing that will entice them."

"And what is my lure?" I asked, curious.

"This," she said and handed me a piece of paper. It was old. Very, very old. On it was ancient demonic script, a language that could drive a human mad if they read too much. It was forged in the pits of Hell as the souls of the damned were driven mad with pain, and the language was only readable by a few.

I happened to be one of the unlucky few that could read it and I braced myself for the inevitable headache that would follow afterward.

I focused my eyes on the symbol and let the angelic power translate the script. One name appeared on the page before a mind-numbing pain ripped through my head.

"Agh!" I said, turning from the page.

Marcus Abshire   LOST SON

But it wasn't over. Demonic script was much more than a written language; it was like a movie, a music piece, an art exhibit, and a meal all in one. You didn't read the name: you lived through it.

An image flooded my mind along with the pungent and strong odor of wet fur, followed by urine, feces, and old blood. A beast's call ripped me apart as a huge bull appeared before me. It unfurled its large griffin wings and I saw deep and unbridled hate within its eyes, as well as an unfathomable depth of knowledge... dark, forbidden knowledge. I was unable to turn from this image as the bull stared at me and, with a voice that sent ripples down my spine, spoke one word. A word that reverberated in my brain.

"ZAGAN!" he bellowed.

The power of the name threw me from the vision and back into my office. I stumbled, grabbing onto the desk to keep from falling onto the floor. It took a few minutes to gather myself and put the pieces back together, but when I did, I saw Dalsheen standing nearby, watching me intently.

"Are you out of your damn mind? You put a bounty on Zagan, and you want me to cash it in?" I asked, astounded.

Zagan was an ancient and powerful demon. He was one of the first. He was pretty close with the head of all demons... yeah, that guy. For you to chum around with the Prince of Darkness had to mean you were in a weight class all your own. If Zagan was allowed to run free, he could cause all kinds of troubles--troubles of biblical proportions. He also commanded a troop of vicious demons himself, like his own small army of destruction.

"I did no such thing. My client did, and yes, he wants you to cash it in." She looked at me, unperturbed.

I'd put away tons of demons in the last few years. Working with Spencer helped pay the bills, but killing demons was my true calling. But none of them had been anywhere close to Zagan. Sure, I had taken out a few big-time monsters, but Zagan was different.

"I'm already stretching things by associating with you. You have no idea how much shit I go through because I haven't killed you. If you think I'm going to not only work with you, but with your 'client', without knowing who he is, you really are crazy," I said, hoping she would come clean. I didn't really think she would, but you can't blame me for trying.

"Does that really matter? Does not the fact you both want a very dangerous creature subdued satisfy you?"

"No, not really," I answered.

I'd been given my power to put demons away and to save innocents from their harm. I knew I was going to go after Zagan, even though he was a first-class badass, but Dalsheen didn't.

"I really am unable to tell you. Since I, myself, do not know who he is," she answered calmly.

"What? You want me to believe you have accepted the job of recruiting me, even though I might kill you where you stand, without knowing who you are working for?"

Beings like Dalsheen never worked without knowing everything they could.

"My reasons for my actions are my own. I am offering you a chance to rid this plane of one of the most dangerous demons in existence," she answered.

"I don't believe you for a second. But let's just say I *am* willing to go after Zagan, there is something I want in return," I said.

This time it was her turn to show surprise. I had never asked for anything before. She looked at me with a newfound wariness. I liked to keep 'em guessing.

"I'll do this, I'll go after Zagan and kill him, but when it's all over I want you to tell me. I want you to tell me who the third party is."

"I already told you, I don't know..."

I cut her off. "I know, but you have time to find out. Promise me this or there is no deal." I stood firm, not budging an inch.

I could see her mind racing, trying to figure out what I was trying to pull, what my angle was. Finally, she smiled again, her face erupting into beauty.

"Deal," she said, holding out her hand.

I reached over and took it, once again getting that horrible feeling in the pit of my stomach telling me I had just done something very stupid.

"Contact me when it's done," she said, leaving my office.

Will I ever learn?

Made in the USA
Coppell, TX
19 April 2024

31482331R00208